Sexy Beast II

Sexy Beast II

KATE DOUGLAS
NOELLE MACK
KATHLEEN DANTE

APHRODISIA

KENSINGTON PUBLISHING CORP.

http://www.kensingtonbooks.com

KENSINGTON BOOKS are published by

Kensington Publishing Corp.
850 Third Avenue
New York, NY 10022

All Kensington Titles, Imprints, and Distributed Lines are available at special quantity discounts for bulk purchases for sales promotions, premiums, fund-raising, and educational or institutional use.

Special book excerpts or customized printings can also be created to fit specific needs. For details, write or phone the office of the Kensington special sales manager: Kensington Publishing Corp., 850 Third Avenue, New York, NY 10022. attn: Special Sales Department, Phone: 1-800-221-2647.

ISBN-13: 978-0-7582-1490-4
ISBN-10: 0-7582-1490-1

First Trade Paperback Printing: April 2007

10 9 8 7 6 5 4 3 2 1

Printed in the United States of America

CONTENTS

Chanku Fallen

Kate Douglas

1

"If he hits her again, I'm going to kill the bastard."

"Why? So she can testify against you and send you back to Folsom? Been there, done that. Look at her. She's not crying—she's glaring at him. The guy's probably her pimp, just making a point. Don't interfere with business. Finish your beer and let's get out of here." AJ Temple threw a couple of five-dollar bills on the scarred surface of the bar and stood up.

Miguel Fuentes rose slowly to his feet, his attention still on the couple at the other end of the bar. The beer can he left on the counter resembled a small chunk of crushed and mangled aluminum. AJ seemed to recognize Mik was just about ready to blow, and grabbed his arm to steer him toward the door.

Unfortunately, they had to walk right by the muscle-bound jerk hanging on to the fragile-looking waif with the big, sad eyes. The lighting inside the tavern was dim, but it wasn't dark enough to hide the distinct marks on the girl's arm where square, meaty fingers kept a tight grip.

Mik planted his feet and refused to move beyond the mismatched pair.

"Let go of the lady."

When AJ tugged at his arm, Mik jerked loose. "I said, let her go. Now."

The stranger at the bar turned slowly and glared at both AJ and Mik through narrow, bloodshot eyes. Then he lumbered to his feet. As tall as he was, and as broad, he still had to look up at Mik, but that didn't appear to bother him a bit. He curled his lip in a soundless snarl. "Who the fuck are you?"

Mik almost laughed. If only he could tell him. Even better, show him. He could shift, right here in this seedy little bar. Change into a ferocious, snarling wolf and rip the guy's throat out, just for effect. Damn. Times like these, Mik wished the Chanku weren't such a deeply guarded secret. Wished he could follow his true nature as a shapeshifter.

He'd go for the bastard's throat and settle the problem, once and for all. It might make a mess of the place, but it would certainly shut the jerk up. Unfortunately, Mik knew he had to control himself no matter how badly the beast in him wanted a bite of this idiot.

That didn't mean he couldn't go for a little alpha-male posturing. Mik straightened his spine and puffed out his chest. His open hands hung deceptively loose at his sides.

Of course, now the die was cast, AJ seemed to think it prudent to add his bulk for emphasis. He stepped up beside Mik, not quite as big, but every bit as powerful. "My buddy asked you to let go of her arm. It's obvious you're hurting the lady."

Before the jerk could answer, the woman slipped off the barstool and moved to one side. The big guy released his grip slowly, reluctantly, almost as if he caressed her bruised skin. She glanced nervously toward the back of the tavern, then wrapped her arms tightly around her narrow waist. Her long dark hair floated over her shoulders and down her slim back, almost to her butt. Thick bangs obscured her forehead and eyes. "It's okay. We were having an argument. I . . ." She stepped away, a small step, but it took her farther from the man who'd hurt her and closer to Mik. "I was wrong. Jimmy here, well, he had a right to get upset."

I told you so. She'll side with the bastard. AJ's silent comment, *mindtalking* in the way of their kind, echoed in Mik's head.

She's scared out of her fucking skull. What else is she gonna say? C'mon, Mik. Out of here. Now. This guy's not alone. For emphasis, AJ nodded to his left, in the direction the woman had glanced. Mik turned slightly, but it was enough to see the half dozen rednecks lounging near the pool table, just waiting for a fight.

He felt his hackles rise in response. Natural in a wolf but damned uncomfortable in a human. The bully was a local. AJ and Mik were fair game. Cursing under his breath, Mik turned away from the hopeless expression on the woman's face and followed AJ out of the bar. He couldn't help taking one final glance back at her, though. She looked frightened but still defiant next to the muscular bully. Her gaze lingered on Mik and AJ. Then her face twisted with pain as the man wrapped his fist in her long dark hair.

Mik's gut twisted, as if the bastard had reached inside and grabbed him as well. It almost killed him to turn away, but he followed AJ. He had no choice. Years of experience had taught Mik to trust his partner.

It didn't mean he always had to like it.

Once outside the tavern, Mik took a deep breath of hot, dry air before he turned on AJ. "We could have taken them. There were only seven of 'em counting that sonofabitch."

AJ laughed and headed down the dusty street. His shadow stretched straight out in front of him, long and thin as the setting sun dropped lower in the sky. "That's almost word for word what you said when you beat that last guy half to death.

She is not worth seven to ten years in prison. Didn't your first incarceration teach you anything?"

Mik shook his head, trying unsuccessfully to erase the waif's lost look from his mind. "Same thing your five years in Folsom taught you—not to get caught. Poor kid. She looks like she's used to getting beat up."

AJ stopped and stared at Mik for a long, uncomfortable minute. "She probably is. Get over it. You cannot right every wrong. You can't rescue every stray. Face it, you can't save the world. You can only do what you're able to do, then move on to the next job."

Mik stared into the eyes of the man he loved more than anyone else in the world and realized he'd never yet won an argument with AJ. He felt the anger flow out of him, leaving only disappointment, and he sighed. "I know you're right. Unfortunately, being right doesn't make it any easier to walk away." Mik shoved his hands in his pockets, took another deep breath and let it out. "Let's get dinner and get moving. I can't stay here in this dump, not knowing that little girl is hurting."

AJ slapped Mik's shoulder. "She's not a little girl and she's not hurting. She's probably just getting ready to go to work. Like I said, that guy's most likely her pimp. She's a whore, Mik. She's probably a lot tougher than she looks, but if she's broken, it's too damned late for you to fix her, okay? C'mon. I'm with you . . . let's find a bite to eat and get out of this dump."

Mik looked around the squalid town square, at the scattered papers and trash blown into filthy piles in corners and up against fences, at the broken benches and dry grass in what might, at some point, have been a park. Now the area reeked of decay and misuse, and the few men standing on the corner opposite them were obviously there for reasons that would get them arrested in any other town.

This place was ugly clear through, but they hadn't come here for the scenery. Mik stared at AJ, looking into eyes so much like his own it would have been eerie if the similarity weren't so comforting. "I really thought we'd find her. Baylor was so certain she'd still be hanging around here."

AJ shrugged. "Not if she's smart. She's probably long gone." He stopped at their car, an oversized SUV parked under a gnarled, leafless tree, and tossed his jacket inside. Then he and Mik walked across the street toward the only restaurant in sight. "Bay said he hadn't heard from his sister in years, and as good as Luc is at finding folks on the Internet, he's not had any luck. No one around here even blinked when we asked about Mary Ellen Quinn. Without a picture or any real identification other than short, round, and blonde, I think finding her is a lost cause."

Mik felt a lump in his throat and swallowed it back. *Lost cause.* Just like the girl they'd abandoned back there in that seedy bar. He didn't want to abandon Mary Ellen, either. Not with Chanku females so few and far between.

Not that he and AJ needed a woman. They had each other. The two of them had realized their love was special shortly after they met, both of them serving time in Folsom on assault charges. They'd bonded years ago as fellow prisoners. Then, once released from prison by Ulrich Mason, the head of Pack Dynamics, they'd mated as wolves beneath a harvest moon and discovered an even more powerful love. The profound link that occurred during that mating had bound them with the sharing of every secret, every dream they'd ever held.

Mik glanced at AJ as they stepped up on the curb in front of the restaurant and felt the familiar clench in his gut, the hot flow of blood to his damned cock. AJ Temple embodied every sexual fantasy Mik had ever had. Even better, Mik knew AJ felt the same about him. It was impossible to keep secrets from a bonded mate.

Still, even knowing he didn't want a woman for himself, the fact that they might be leaving one of their kind in this desolate town sickened Mik. The mere thought of a Chanku female, un-aware of her heritage, unawakened, out there in the world with a mind filled with questions . . .

"You coming?"

AJ held the door open to the diner. A rush of cool air spilled out into the dry heat of the desert evening. Mik tabled his worries and followed his lover inside.

AJ dug into his rare steak with obvious pleasure. Though their meal was surprisingly good, Mik spent more time shoving his food around the plate than actually eating.

He couldn't get the girl off his mind. Neither one of them. Not Mary Ellen. Not the whore.

"It's still early," AJ said between bites. "We can probably make Phoenix by midnight if we leave now."

Mik nodded. Maybe distance would make him feel better. Right now he felt as if he wore his sense of gloom like a shroud.

When the waiter came to clear their table, more than half of Mik's huge slab of blood-rare prime rib was still sitting on his plate. He had the waiter pack it in a Styrofoam container, tucked the leftovers under his arm, and followed AJ out the door.

The sky had turned from blue to black and the few working streetlights gave the town an even more ominous appearance than it had in daylight. It was time to go. Mik tossed the keys to AJ. The two of them had become a running joke within the pack, the fact that Mik carried the keys but AJ almost always drove. Mik wasn't sure where the habit had formed, but for whatever reason, he felt perfectly comfortable with AJ behind the wheel.

Maybe because it was so much fun to heckle him.

Mik tossed the bag with the leftovers in the back of the SUV and hoped it wouldn't get lost amidst the piles of gear they were hauling. They'd pulled the back seats out for this trip and thrown in a foam mattress in case they got caught out in bad weather without a hotel room available. Messy, but it worked. As part of Pack Dynamics, Mik had learned long ago to be prepared for the unexpected.

This trip had been no different, following up on an international smuggling operation along the hurricane-ravaged Gulf Coast. The side trip through this southern part of New Mexico in search of Baylor Quinn's missing sister had been an added bonus, if he could call it that. Not finding her didn't sit well with Mik, or AJ either, for that matter.

Mik climbed into the front passenger seat, buckled his seatbelt, and leaned back as AJ pulled out into the main street and headed for Phoenix. There was no rush to get home to San Francisco. Most of the pack was off on one assignment or another. Baylor Quinn had gone back to Maine to settle in with Shannon and Jake. Tinker, Luc, and Tia had something going on with the Montana pack. Ulrich Mason, head of Pack Dynamics, was off on one of his solitary hunts for more Chanku.

Mik wished he had Ulrich's uncanny ability to spot others of their ilk. Wished he'd been able to find at least one of Baylor Quinn's missing sisters. The ex-secret agent hadn't seen his two siblings for almost ten years, but if Bay was Chanku, so were they.

Two women carrying the genes of the wolf. Unaware of their potential, their wolven heritage alive merely as unsatisfied longings and unfulfilled dreams.

Mik settled back into the soft leather seat and closed his eyes. AJ turned on a country western station, all they'd been able to pick up in English out here in the desert, and headed west. They'd sleep in Phoenix tonight, maybe make it home tomorrow.

Home. Nothing more than a room shared with AJ. One job after another. Mik thought of Luc and Tia, and of course,

Tinker. Would Tinker ever find someone of his own, or was the relationship with Luc and Tia enough? The big guy seemed happy and Tia obviously had more than enough love to share.

Still, Tinker always looked so lost, as if he were searching for something or someone. Pondering on Tinker and other questions of note, Mik drifted off to sleep to the glorious sound of Patsy Cline telling him to stand by his man.

Tala never expected to sleep, not with every bone in her body aching and her eyes almost swollen shut from the beating Jimmy had given her, but she realized she was awake and her hiding place was moving. More importantly, she smelled food. Something warm and delicious and not too far out of reach.

Tala stretched her hand over the piles of camping gear and miscellaneous duffle bags and bit back a groan. Every move was agony. Damn Jimmy and his drunken pack of fools. After those two gorgeous men bailed out on her, back at the bar, Jimmy'd just turned her over to the guys. For punishment, he said. To teach her a lesson she deserved.

She could still hear the click when he'd turned the lock on the front door. At the time, Tala hadn't been sure if she was going to come out of that damned bar alive, but she should have known Jimmy wouldn't let anyone do anything to injure her permanently.

Tala wanted to think it was because he cared, but the truth of it was she was worth too much to Jimmy alive. She'd always known he didn't mind seeing her hurt. She knew he liked to watch, too. Jimmy'd been laughing when he shoved her into the waiting arms of his buddies.

Not that Tala didn't like sex, but taking six stinking idiots in just under an hour had almost pushed her over the top. Her ass hurt, her throat burned, and she didn't even want to consider what kinds of STDs they'd exposed her to. As bad as it was, though, Jimmy's beating had hurt more. Somehow, somewhere along the way, she'd convinced herself he actually loved her.

Now how pathetic was that?

Tala felt an unfamiliar burning at the back of her eyes. It took a minute to realize she was crying. No! Tala did not cry. Never. With an act of supreme will, she stopped the moisture and gritted her teeth against the pain.

She'd wanted to leave Jimmy Cole for a long time now. Maybe this time she'd make it. At least the road was smooth and she'd found a good spot behind the driver's seat, tucked down on some kind of soft mattress on the floor and wrapped in an even softer blanket with a couple of unrolled sleeping bags to hide beneath.

If only she couldn't smell food. Mouth watering, Tala steeled herself against the ache in her belly and hoped like hell the two men just on the other side of the seat wouldn't hear her moving around.

They'd wanted to help. At least the big one had, the one with the flowing black hair and the gorgeous cheekbones. He reminded her of an ancient warrior, almost like he'd ended up in the wrong century. She'd felt his concern. It had been the strangest sensation, almost like a voice in her head. He'd looked at her with compassion, not pity, and for some reason she'd felt as if they had something in common, as if they both under-stood suffering.

Well, after tonight, Tala was through suffering. Jimmy might have taken care of her in his own rough way for the past three years, but tonight was the last straw. He'd called her a whore, which she was, of course, but then he'd gone and thrown her to that pack of sex-starved lunatics like she was nothing more than a piece of meat.

They'd fallen on her, dogs after a bitch in heat. Three at a time, stabbing into her like she was just a convenient hole.

And isn't that all you are? Damn. Tala wished the voices in her head would go away, or at least shut the fuck up. It was bad enough she couldn't remember anything before Jimmy found her in that stinking alley, but between the voices and the dreams, sometimes Tala felt as if she were losing what little mind she had left.

Well, maybe she was. Wouldn't that be a lot better than the real stuff she lived? There might be something pleasant about a nice, calm psycho ward and one of those tight, white hug-me coats.

No. That was giving in. That was being a loser of the first degree, something Tala refused. She might have no memories of her life before Jimmy, but damn it all, she was not nuts. She was just searching.

Always searching. Somehow she'd gotten caught in that backwater town with a bastard like Jimmy Cole, but he'd made sure she ate, kept her in clothes, helped her with her constant craving for sex.

If he hadn't been such a rat bastard, it might even have worked. Might have been the perfect relationship. Jimmy might have been a pimp, but some of the time he'd been kind to her. He was a surprisingly good businessman and it was more than obvious Tala was a whore. Born and bred to be a whore.

She had no memories of her mother, none of her father. None of any life before three years ago, but it was obvious she wasn't a virgin when Jimmy found her, and from the way she craved sex, playing whore to his pimp hadn't been a bad setup.

If only he hadn't gotten so damned mean. Tala shifted quietly within her soft, warm haven, thankful for the foam rubber pad beneath her butt. She wriggled her hips and tried to find a more comfortable position for her aching body.

Tried to figure out how to snag that delicious-smelling package lying just out of reach.

Clint Black was singing now. She'd really enjoyed Patsy Cline, and there'd even been some Willie Nelson and a couple of old dudes she didn't recognize. Whichever one of the guys was driving sort of hummed to himself, and she'd heard soft snoring from the passenger seat.

She couldn't stand it another minute. Tala reached out from under her blanket and stretched her fingers across the lumpy piles of gear. Finally, after a few minutes' quiet search in the darkness, she found a warm Styrofoam box next to a pair of big hiking boots. *Eureka!*

Tala brought the box close to her nose. It smelled absolutely delicious and her mouth watered. She'd learned not to be picky, living with Jimmy, but this smelled better than anything she could remember. Carefully she lifted a corner of the lid. It squeaked so loudly she was sure the sound echoed over the SUV's engine noise. Tala held perfectly still while the wonderful aromas teased her nostrils.

No one seemed to notice how much noise she'd just made.

She finally managed to pop the lid and sighed with barely restrained ecstasy. Mashed potatoes, a huge piece of meat, even horseradish. Sliced carrots, perfectly steamed and seasoned to perfection. Tala practically moaned aloud. It tasted even better than it smelled. Slowly but thoroughly, she devoured every bite, running her finger around the inside of the container to make sure she didn't miss a single scrap.

Then, tummy full and mind totally relaxed for the first time in months, Tala pulled the blankets and sleeping bags back over her head and snuggled down against the back of the seat.

Running. The night wind blowing hot against his thick coat, rough sand burning his paws. Sounds of night creatures and the usual stew of scent, of rodent and bird, deer and predator.

The scent of his packmate just ahead. Another, not familiar.

Chanku? Stopping in his tracks, he raised his nose to sniff the air. Felt his body quicken, the thick ruff of fur between his shoulder blades rise up.

Female. Most definitely female. He cast ahead, searching for AJ, finding another. A new mind, open, welcoming. AJ? Where the hell was AJ?

"Hey, bro. Wake up. You're having one hell of a nightmare."

AJ's soft grip on his shoulder brought Mik out of whatever dream held him. He shook his head to clear his thoughts; then inhaled deeply.

Scented the female. Slowly, Mik turned and stared at AJ. "I was dreaming I smelled a woman."

AJ laughed. "I've never known that to get you all hot and bothered. Now, a good-looking guy, maybe . . ."

Mik shook his head. "No, Chanku. In my dream I scented a Chanku female. I'm awake, now. I still smell her."

This time AJ grinned, then nodded toward the back of the vehicle. "Don't know about Chanku, but we've got ourselves a female whether we want her or not."

"What?" Mik spun around and looked over the seat. There was so much crap thrown back there it was hard to tell what AJ was talking about. The sleeping bags and a couple of old blankets were right where he'd left them.

The scent tickled Mik's nostrils and his Chanku senses stirred again. With his night vision, much clearer than that of a normal human, Mik studied the pile of blankets for a moment. They moved, ever so slightly.

Grinning, he turned back around in his seat, this time choosing silent conversation. *You're right. Sleeping, I imagine. The little girl from the bar?*

You tell me. AJ concentrated on the road ahead. *I didn't get close enough to smell her.*

Mik inhaled again. *Neither did I. I just smell female, and . . .*

He took another deep breath. *The stink of at least three or four other guys on her. Maybe more.*

You don't think that bastard turned her over to those butt-uglies in the bar, do you? AJ's eyes flashed at Mik before he turned his attention back to the long stretch of highway.

Yeah, I do. Imagine that's why she finally decided to get out. Sometimes it takes something over the top to motivate a person to stop acting out the victim's role. Mik studied AJ's profile while he thought about the problem. The odds of this woman being Chanku were about a million to one, but they couldn't just leave her out here in the middle of nowhere. He didn't want to even think about the fact he felt attracted to her. Mik imagined that might be a tough one for AJ to handle.

I don't want to leave her along the road. I'd like to take her with us, at least for a while. You okay with that?

AJ nodded. *Yeah, of course, it depends on what she wants. She might have a particular destination in mind. We'll have to leave her somewhere at some point. She can't come all the way with us. It's too risky.*

Yeah, I know. Just far enough that old Jimmy can't find her, okay?

AJ nodded again and glanced briefly in Mik's direction. His expression, usually so open, was guarded. *Just far enough. That's all. We can't let her know what we are.*

2

She'd had the most amazing dreams. Her mind had spun with confused images of wolves and dark, damp forests and the sense Tala ran on four legs instead of two. A sense of two huge, black wolves chasing her, of the wind blowing through her own thick pelt. Dreams so real she wanted to check her hands to reassure herself they truly were her hands and not broad, nail-tipped paws.

Tala knew she should have been frightened, but instead she woke up horny as hell in spite of her aching body. Needy in a way that consumed her. She felt sore vaginal muscles tighten involuntarily and knew there'd be no stemming the rush of fluid, no controlling her swollen labia and needy clit.

Damn. What was wrong with her? Women didn't lust like this, weren't consumed by carnal needs that drove them like . . . like exactly what she was. A whore. Nothing but a whore.

Suddenly the thick blanket lifted away from her. Straight teeth glinted in the pale glow of street lamps and she cowered back into her nest of sleeping bags and pillows.

"Did you sleep well?"

It was the tall one, the guy with the long sweep of black hair and cheekbones a model would kill for.

"Uh, yeah. I guess I did."

Tala rolled out of the pile of bags and reached for the door handle. "Thanks for the ride. I'll just . . ."

The hand that grabbed her shoulder was gentle enough, but Tala knew there'd be no breaking his grip. He leaned over the back of the seat. Up this close, all she saw was the shimmer of light over the muscles in his forearm.

"Wait. Don't go. Don't be afraid. It's damned cold out there and AJ and I were going to get a room. Stay with us tonight."

A startled laugh burst out of her. Men. They were all alike. She flipped her hair back over her shoulder. "You expect me to do both of you?"

The one holding her glanced toward his buddy and then back at Tala. Light glinted off white teeth and she had a feeling he was quietly laughing at her. "Actually, I was planning on doing AJ later, but you're welcome to watch."

She almost choked. What a waste! "You guys are gay? You're like . . ."

The one called AJ turned around in the seat and grinned at Tala. "I'm not sure what you think we're like, but I'd like to think we just want to help you. It's your call. We'll get a room with two beds and you're welcome to have one all by yourself."

She hadn't really looked that closely at him in the bar, as scared as she'd been of Jimmy. Hadn't realized quite how gorgeous he was. Amazing eyes, thick, dark brown hair, lips that made her mouth water and her pussy weep.

To be honest, she'd love nothing better than a chance to fuck both of them. How contrary was that! Just a minute ago she'd mouthed off about . . . "I'd like that. Thank you. And I apologize."

"No need." The fingers grasping her shoulder dropped away,

freeing her. The man turned his hand, palm up. Tala placed her much smaller hand in his.

"I'm Miguel Fuentes. Mik to my friends." He nodded toward AJ. "This reprobate is Andrew Jackson Temple. We call him AJ." Then, in an aside, he whispered, "It was easier for him to learn to spell it that way."

Tala laughed. She felt the tension in her shoulders fall away. "My name's Tala and I would love to stay with you, if you don't mind. In fact, I'd like to travel with you for a while if it's okay. I won't feel safe until I'm farther away from Jimmy." She felt an involuntary shudder race down her spine. "He thinks he owns me."

"I got that feeling." Mik unlatched his seat belt and got out of the SUV. AJ did the same and held the door open for Tala. She stepped out into the glow of an overhead light.

"Shit."

AJ's quiet gasp reminded Tala how she must look. She didn't even want to think how she must stink. Her cotton T-shirt was stretched out at the neck and covered in stains. Her short skirt was ripped along one side and stained as well. The bastards hadn't even taken her clothes off of her, just shoved them out of the way.

Tala figured her panties were probably still somewhere on or under the pool table, not that she'd ever want them back. She took a deep breath and answered AJ's unasked question. "I'm okay. Really. I just need a shower something awful."

"She needs a doctor." Mik had come around the front of the car and was shoving her tangled hair back out of her eyes. The left one was hard to see out of, so it must be swollen almost shut by now.

Tala shook her head. "No. No doctor. They'd call the police and I'd end up right back with Jimmy."

AJ stared at her for a moment. "No way would any cop send you back to a bastard who did this to you."

Shrugging her shoulders, Tala refused to meet either man's eyes. "They would if the bastard's brother was the county sheriff. Believe me, I found that out the hard way. It's the reason I haven't been able to get away from Jimmy. His brother always helps him find me."

Mik nodded toward AJ. "You go get us a room. One with a big tub, preferably, so this little gal can soak for a while." AJ headed across the parking lot to the hotel office. Mik turned back to Tala.

"Did Jimmy turn you over to that bunch of idiots at the bar? Did they do this to you?"

Tala hung her head. Heat swept across her face. Strong arms came around her and pulled her filthy body up against a hard, warm chest. Mik's kindness was her undoing.

She felt the stinging behind her eyes again and a shudder raced throughout her as she struggled for control. Mik's big hand swept slowly along her spine. Surprisingly, the need for tears slowly ebbed. There was something so comforting about him. Something that made her feel safe.

They were still standing like that, arms around each other, when AJ returned. He didn't say a word, but Tala thought she heard him chuckle. He handed a keycard to Mik.

"We're number twelve, just around the back. I'll bring the car and meet you over there."

Tala's legs felt like rubber. Mik seemed to understand without her saying a word, because he picked her up like she was a little kid and held her against his chest. Once again she felt like crying, but she managed to wrap her arms around his neck without making a fool of herself.

His hair felt like silk. It was longer than hers, falling board-straight down his back. It should have felt coarse but it wasn't. Not at all. Tala concentrated on Mik's hair as he walked quickly across the parking lot.

Concentrated on the feel of it, the glossy shimmer and the

silky texture, and not the broad expanse of his chest or the muscles in his powerful arms or the fact he smelled so good.

Gay! What a waste, especially since her body certainly hadn't figured it out. Mik's touch made her cunt throb and her nipples pucker against her soft T-shirt. He had to know she was turned on.

Then again, maybe he didn't. If he liked just guys . . .

Mik set Tala down in front of the door, slipped the plastic keycard into the slot, and held the door open for her. AJ pulled the car into a space just outside.

Tala forgot about both men the minute Mik turned on the lights. The room was gorgeous. Big and luxurious and a far cry from the cheesy rent-by-the-hour dives Tala used when she worked. Two huge, king-sized beds piled high with pillows took up most of the space at the far end, but there was a separate sitting room and a bathroom that was bigger than her bedroom at Jimmy's.

"Good. It's got a tub." Mik leaned over Tala's shoulder to inspect the bathroom and she fought a powerful compulsion to lean back against him.

"Looks more like a swimming pool to me." She wasn't exaggerating. It was round, at least six feet across and three feet deep.

Mik laughed. "Hey, we're big guys. We need a big tub." He stepped around beside Tala to take a closer look. "It's got jets. Should help your sore muscles." He flipped the lever to plug the drain and turned the water on high. "I expect you to stay in here until you're all pruny. Turn the jets on with that control." He showed her a switch and then turned to leave. At the doorway, Mik paused for a minute. "Are you hungry? Should we order something for you to eat?"

Tala blushed. "Umm . . . I ate somebody's leftovers in the back of the car. I'm sorry, I . . ."

Mik just laughed. "Well, at least I know they went to a good cause. You could use a few pounds. The bathroom is all yours. I'm going to see if I've got something else in there you can wear. Your clothes have about had it."

AJ met him just outside the bathroom door with a hug. "Shit, man. You could get an Oscar for that performance. You sound totally calm and together."

"I'd like to kill the bastards." Mik soaked up some of AJ's warmth, then pulled away. "We need to burn her clothes. They stink of half a dozen dead men."

"They're not dead, and you, my friend, are not going to kill them." AJ headed for the door. "There's a gift shop in the hotel lobby. I'm going to see if I can find her something to wear."

Mik nodded, but his attention was on the bathroom door. He'd left it partially open.

Tala hadn't closed it.

The sound of running water finally stopped.

"Mik?"

He practically swallowed his tongue. "Yeah? You need something?" Mik realized he was standing just outside the bathroom door. He didn't even remember walking across the room.

"My back. It hurts really bad and I can't tell what . . ."

He didn't need an engraved invitation. The bathroom was steamy. Warm and intimate. Tala sat in the middle of the big tub with water frothing and bubbling about from the underwater jets. She had her knees drawn up under her chin and her back was turned to him.

She looked about twelve years old, sitting there in the bubbles with her shoulders rolled forward and prominent vertebrae marching down her narrow spine. She was covered with bruises, but her back was a raw and angry red. Mik noticed flecks of green caught in her injured flesh. When he realized what he was seeing, he bit back a litany of curses.

He grabbed a soft washcloth and, kneeling next to the tub, dipped it in the warm water. "This may sting. In fact, I know it will." Without pausing, he asked, "Did they rape you on the pool table?"

Tala jerked. She didn't answer aloud. Mik barely caught the small nod of her head.

"You've got really bad friction burns. There's some felt caught in them. I need to wash this whole area so there's no infection, but it's going to hurt like hell. Are you okay with that?"

She nodded again. Her body stiffened when he touched her with the soft cloth, but she didn't make a sound. Mik wondered how many times in her life she'd been hurt. How often she'd just taken the pain without complaint.

He heard the door open, the sound of bags hitting the table. AJ's light tap on the door.

Tala's shoulders rose and fell as she sighed. "You might as well come in. It's not like I've got any modesty left."

"What the fuck?"

"AJ, you are not a subtle man." Mik glared at AJ, but he had to admit he'd wanted to say the same thing. *Bastards screwed her so hard on the pool table they drove felt into her back.*

I've got some antibiotic in my overnight kit. AJ flashed one of his killer smiles at Tala. "Be right back."

He returned with three surprisingly nice wineglasses and a bottle of very good wine . . . and the antibiotics. Mik handed Tala a glass filled to the brim with cold Chardonnay. She giggled when she took it and then took a big gulp that made her choke and sputter. Her next sip was much smaller.

"You realize this is way beyond every woman's fantasy. Soaking in a hot tub with two gorgeous men attending me, and a glass of wine to sip. All I need now is for you both to be willing to fulfill my every desire."

AJ parked his butt on the broad tile edge of the tub. "We'll check on those desires later, after Mik finishes your back. I brought the wine because I thought it might dull the pain while Mik works on you."

Tala smiled at him and took another swallow. "I sure hope so, because whatever he's doing hurts a lot."

Mik jerked his hand back. "Why didn't you say anything?"

Tala turned and looked over her shoulder at him through her water-soaked bangs. "You told me it was going to hurt. What would be the point of complaining?" She shoved the wet hair back from her face.

Mik almost fell into the tub. Without saying a word, he turned to see AJ's reaction.

AJ stared at Tala. He was shaking his head slowly back and forth with a look of total disbelief on his face. *Her eyes. She has Tia's eyes.*

I know. I was sure I scented Chanku. Do you think . . . ?

I don't . . .

"Well? What are you staring at?" Tala frowned. Her brilliant amber eyes darted back and forth as she looked from AJ to Mik and back again at AJ.

Mik had to shake himself just to answer her. "You remind us of someone we both know. A really good friend of ours. Her name's Tia Mason."

Tala turned back around so that Mik could finish cleaning off her back. "I don't know any Tia, but then I don't know very much at all."

"What do you mean, you don't know much?" Mik rinsed Tala's back and draped the washcloth over the edge of the tub. Without really thinking about it, he grabbed the small vial of complimentary shampoo and squirted some into his hand, then proceeded to wash Tala's hair.

She moaned beneath his gentle touch and scooted closer to the edge of the tub. Water from one of the jets was pounding against her lower back, just below the skinned area, but Tala didn't seem to notice. "I mean I don't know anything before three years ago. Jimmy found me passed out in an alley, naked. No jewelry, no ID. He figured it was a drug overdose and took me to his house to sleep it off. When I woke up, I didn't have any memory."

"None?" AJ handed the bottle of conditioner to Mik. Tala took another swallow of her wine and held out her glass. AJ filled it, then added more to his own.

"No. Nothing. I didn't even know what foods I liked. It was so weird. I could talk and find my way around town, but no one recognized me. You probably guessed Jimmy was my pimp. I figure I must have been a prostitute before because it all seemed so natural to me, getting paid for sex."

There really wasn't a response to a bald statement like that. Mik gently kneaded her scalp, then ran his fingers through her hair until it flowed like a dark, silken curtain across the water. "Lean back. I want to rinse the soap out." Once Tala's hair was free of shampoo, Mik worked the conditioner into her scalp. He wished he knew what to say, what questions to ask. She was too matter-of-fact about too many things. She hadn't complained about anything, even when he'd been rubbing too hard on her tortured back. Hell, she'd been gang-raped just a couple of hours earlier but she acted like it was no big deal.

Maybe things were different in her world. Maybe sex had lost meaning for Tala. Maybe she'd reached a point where she was beaten so far down she couldn't see up, but Mik doubted that. Tala still seemed to have some spark, though right now, with the warm, relaxing bath and her third glass of wine, she was obviously beginning to fade.

She was such a beautiful little thing. Her eyes really were more catlike than any Chanku he'd seen. Tilted slightly at the corners, they gave her a mysterious, seductive look. She was fine-boned and petite, but Mik sensed strength beneath that fragile exterior.

Even as bruised and battered as she was, Tala still managed to sparkle. She'd managed something else, too. She'd not done a thing on purpose to arouse either Mik or AJ, but Mik knew he had a damned big hard-on shoved into jeans that were now way too tight. He glanced at AJ. His lover was studying Tala with an expression caught halfway between compassion and desire. Mik bit back a grin and wondered about the state of AJ's pants.

3

She hadn't wanted to get out of the tub, but since she'd far surpassed Mik's directions to *get pruny*, Tala figured it was about time. AJ had bought her a toothbrush and some really cheesy clothing at the hotel gift shop. Mik had brought her one of his clean white T-shirts to sleep in, then told her to soak as long as she wanted because he and AJ were going to bed.

Tala managed to rub antibiotic on her back and slipped the shirt over her head. She lifted the hem and sniffed the soft fabric. She'd hoped to smell Mik's wonderful scent, but all she caught was a faint whiff of detergent and bleach. It felt so good to be clean, almost as if she'd washed the past three years out of her life, but Tala knew there was too much filth in her to go away after a single long soak.

She carried her wineglass out with her. It appeared AJ had filled it once again, but he was right about it making her feel better. She didn't hurt nearly as much and instead of feeling scared of Jimmy, she was sleepy and relaxed. Just in case, though, Tala took a couple more swallows.

The lights were out in the bedroom, but she left one small

one burning in the bathroom so she could find her way around. AJ and Mik had taken the bed closest to the door.

Gay. Just her luck, to be rescued by two of the sexiest, most gorgeous—and honestly nice—men she'd ever met, and they had absolutely no interest in her. Both men practically oozed sex appeal, but their love for one another was too obvious to ignore.

Tala stood between the two king-sized beds, sipped her wine, and studied her saviors. Mik's back was to her, and what a beautiful back it was. His naked shoulders glistened in the faint swath of light and he held AJ close against his chest, spoon fashion. Tala had the strangest urge to join them in their bed, to squeeze herself in between the two of them like jelly in a sandwich and soak up all that wonderful male warmth, but that certainly wouldn't do. Not after they'd been so kind to her, and so upfront about their sexuality.

Feeling oddly bereft, Tala finished her wine and crawled into the big empty bed all by herself. She was warm. She was clean, and for the first time in forever, she felt safe.

If only she didn't feel so terribly alone.

Tala wasn't quite certain what woke her. It was either the dream, the same one she'd had for years about racing through the forest on four powerful legs, or the sounds coming from the next bed.

Generally Tala slept through her dreams, so it had to be the sounds. She came gradually awake and lay still, listening to the rhythmic rustle of sheets, the soft moans, the lush, wet sounds of sex. After a moment, Tala opened her eyes and watched the men in the bed beside hers.

For all her sexual experience, she'd never watched men making love before. She'd witnessed the rape of a man one time, something so foul and disgusting she'd felt sickened by it, but this was totally different. AJ knelt with his face pressed against his forearms, his hips raised to meet Mik's slow, smooth thrusts.

Mik knelt behind AJ, his powerful thighs pressed close against his mate's. Light spilling from the partially open bathroom door illuminated the two men, bathed them in a soft, golden glow.

Tala couldn't recall watching anything that moved her more than this. Nothing in her short memory of the past three years had even come close to the eroticism, the pure sensuality of Mik and AJ making love.

All Tala had ever known was sex. This was something else altogether. Sweat glistened on Mik's chest. His head was thrown back, his eyes closed and the sharp lines of his face stood out in stark relief. The heavy mass of his shiny black hair spilled down his back, all the way to his perfectly rounded ass.

The strands parted over his muscular cheeks with each thrust, following the hollows and curves of Mik's butt with his deliberate in-and-out dance as he slowly but thoroughly fucked his mate.

Tala swallowed back a moan when Mik rubbed his big hands along AJ's sides, stroked his thighs, reached around AJ's waist and captured his swollen cock. Tala wondered if their balls touched, if each forward thrust of Mik's pressed his sac against his mate's, but she couldn't see.

She wanted to see. Wanted to be part of this beautiful sharing.

Her fingers seemed to find her wet and ready pussy all on their own. She caught Mik's rhythm, stroking herself as he stroked AJ, penetrating her swollen labia, dipping into her warm pussy with her fingers, pretending it was AJ's cock, or Mik's.

Either man would do.

She couldn't imagine being with one man without the other. They were such a perfectly beautiful, exquisitely matched pair, their love and respect for one another obvious in every word they said, everything they did. Especially this. An act so intimate, so filled with trust, yet rife with potential for pain.

Tala sensed their heightened passion as Mik increased his rhythm, thrusting harder and faster inside AJ. It killed her, being so far from them, apart from their loving. She wanted to be there, wanted AJ's mouth on her, Mik's cock inside her. Wanted . . . desired . . .

Tala's fingers flew. Stroking her needy clit, arching her back, alone in her bed, her body reaching for her own fingers, imagining they were part of the two men mere feet away. She felt herself grow closer to climax, felt the love between AJ and Mik . . . then, without warning, Tala felt Mik's cock, only now it was *her* cock thrusting deep inside AJ's heat. At the same time, she was AJ, awash in pleasure as Mik speared her.

Startled, Tala's first reaction was to back away, but the sensations were too powerful, her need too great. She opened her mind to the images, opened to the potential of being a part of their loving.

Almost as if her brain were divided, she experienced what both of them felt. The burning impact of Mik's cock through each downward thrust, the gentle caress of his fingers over her/AJ's testicles. Impossible, but much too real to ignore.

AJ reached back, his hand slipping between his thighs to clutch Mik's balls. Not rough, no, not at all. He caressed the wrinkled sac, finding each testicle with his fingers, rolling the orbs carefully and encircling the entire sac with his hand.

Tala's fingers curled in response to the image. The muscles between her legs clenched tightly.

Mik stiffened, his cock jerked inside AJ's ass, and he bit back a moan as his climax overtook him. Tala felt his pleasure more than she heard it, experienced his climax as if it were her own. Moaned aloud through the climax Mik shared with her.

Mik's hands tightened around AJ's cock and suddenly Tala

was in AJ's head, so much a part of his experience that it was *her* cock trapped in Mik's powerful grasp, exploding with spurt after spurt of hot seed, her body shivering in response to Mik's gasping cry of completion. Then she was Mik, back straining, hips thrust forward. Again the sensation was of *her* cock clenched tightly, deep within the wet heat of AJ's body.

A kaleidoscope of images, of lush and arousing sensations, of pain and pleasure, heat and overwhelming ecstasy, bombarded Tala from the hearts and minds of both men. She was only peripherally aware of her own orgasm, the clenching of her vaginal muscles, the hot rush of fluids, the tightness in her womb. So much a part of AJ and Mik's shared experience, Tala lost all sense of self, all sense of where and who she was.

A union unlike anything Tala had known, a communion of souls, of minds and hearts. She was all of them. AJ, Mik and Tala, all of them in the throes of one immense orgasm that rocked her world, changed her entire sense of herself and suddenly, without any warning, opened a door into an entirely new existence.

Mik lay across AJ's back, his cock still buried deep inside his mate, and wondered how his entire reality could have shifted so totally between one moment and another. AJ's muscles still clenched and released around him and Mik felt the rise and fall of his lover's body with each deep breath he took. Never, not once in his life had he experienced anything as profound—not their first mating, not their bonding. Nothing like the climax he and AJ had just shared.

But they hadn't shared it alone. Not this time.

AJ was going through the same emotions, his thoughts as convoluted as Mik's. Both men, their bodies sated after an amazing climax, felt their worlds tilting on an axis neither had ever experienced and definitely didn't expect.

Mik stroked AJ's back and opened his mind to AJ's tumbled

thoughts. But it was Tala he watched. Tala, lying in the bed just three feet away, who held both men in thrall. Lips parted, fingers still thrust between her legs, she stared directly back at both of them.

She'd been there, a part of their loving, part of their climax. A new dynamic neither man had expected. Watching Tala watch him had an amazing effect on Mik. His cock, totally flaccid only moments ago was suddenly hard again, filling AJ as if they'd just begun their lovemaking.

Mik tilted his hips forward, just enough to alert AJ to his reawakened state. AJ watched Tala, his focus entirely on her even as Mik felt himself drawn to the woman. The link that joined them was a tangible thing, a solid line from Mik to AJ to Tala and back to Mik.

But she was just too far away. Without thinking of the consequences, Mik held his hand out to her. The distance was too great, their fingers too far apart, but only for a moment. As if tugged by an invisible thread, Tala slid her legs over the side of the bed, reached out and grabbed Mik's hand.

Her grasp was strong, her fingers warm. Mik pulled her close, conscious of the bruises covering her waiflike body, the injuries none of them could see. Conscious of her inner strength, her spirit. Mik tugged lightly, but it was enough.

Tala crossed the gap between the beds, crossed between two worlds. Entered Mik and AJ's world as if she were the third half of their whole. She crawled up on the big bed and lay on her side next to AJ, kissed the smooth skin along his ribs, touched the flat nipple over his heart.

She reached up and kissed Mik, her mouth a sweet benediction, an unspoken request. Touching, kissing, she added a dimension of sensation neither man had expected. Her small fingers sliding over the curve of Mik's balls as he slowly moved in and out of AJ. Her mouth kissing AJ, moving lower until she'd fit her tiny self beneath him, found his cock and taken it between her lips.

AJ groaned, his pleasure spilling over onto both Mik and Tala. Her mouth suckled him, one hand wrapped gently around his sac, the other holding on to Mik's. Linking both men through a mere wisp of a woman. Small fingers stroking, fondling, touching.

Mik linked with AJ when his lover cupped his hand around Tala's bottom and tugged her beneath him. Shoved the loose T-shirt aside and found her swollen labia with his lips and tongue and feasted on her cream. Mik felt as if he were floating in a fantasy beyond reality, beyond anything he'd ever experienced.

His cock filling AJ, Tala's fingers stroking his balls, the taste of her cunt when AJ licked and suckled her hot and ready folds. Their minds had found perfect synchronization, a link so profound Mik wanted to weep with the power of his pleasure, the amazing emotions that took all this sensation to an even higher level.

He sensed Tala's impending orgasm, knew his own was close. Felt the pressure growing in AJ and knew when Tala's lips clamped tightly around his lover's cock. Heat and pleasure and pain surrounded them, building one upon the other.

AJ was the first, and though Mik knew he tried to pull his cock free of Tala's grasp, she held him tightly in her mouth, sucking even harder as he climaxed, her tongue pressing against the base of his cock, her lips compressed and holding on, the muscles in her throat working as she swallowed his seed. AJ brought her with him, his mouth between her legs matching the push and pull of each stroke of Mik's.

All of them gasping, shouting, bodies clenching, muscles contracting, all together. Three. Together.

AJ fell to one side with Mik draped bonelessly over his back. Tala continued sucking gently on his cock and kept her fingers wrapped around both AJ's and Mik's balls as if she would never turn them loose.

Maybe she couldn't. Mik knew his own muscles felt frozen, as if the orgasm he'd just experienced had burned itself into his body for all time.

They lay there, unmoving, each lost in thoughts shared, one with the other. Tala's mind spun in amazement, AJ's with pure satisfaction at having a secret fantasy brought to life.

Mik wasn't sure exactly what he was thinking. He only knew what he felt, that for the first time since he and AJ had joined there was an even greater sense of completion to their union. As if a piece long missing had suddenly been found.

Had his hunch been right? Was Tala Chanku? He couldn't imagine any normal woman able to link as she had, but he couldn't be sure. Not until she had the supplement, and not until she shifted. If Tala proved to be one of their kind, could they figure out a way to add a third person to what had been a dynamic pair bond between him and AJ?

Mind roiling with questions, Mik carefully pulled out of AJ and headed for the bathroom. Tala turned around and snuggled close to AJ's chest. Mik glanced back as his lover wrapped strong arms around the waif, the only woman they'd ever known with the power to tear them apart. Tear them apart, or make them stronger.

Mik paused at the open doorway and watched the two together in the bed. Tala looked perfect, wrapped snugly in AJ's strong embrace, as if she belonged. A wave of dizziness passed over Mik and he grabbed the doorframe for support.

As if she belonged . . .

Maybe a shower would clear his head. He definitely needed something. Mik closed the door behind him and turned on the spray, but when he finally stepped out of the shower, Mik was no closer to answers than he'd been when he started.

Tala stared at the big, brown capsule Mik set in front of her and wondered why he seemed so intent she swallow it. *Nutrients*, he'd said. *Vitamins to help your body heal.* Then he'd popped one into his mouth, as had AJ, before they tackled breakfast.

She didn't take pills. Especially not pills she couldn't identify. With memories barely three years old and an implied history of drug abuse, Tala wasn't too crazy about popping any unknown substance into her mouth.

She gazed from AJ to Mik and back at the pill. There was certainly no sign of drug use in either one of them. No, they were as healthy and sane as anyone she'd ever met, though after her experience last night she'd been almost afraid to delve too deeply into their motives.

Never in her entire life had Tala experienced anything remotely like sex with these two gorgeous hunks. Not just physical sex, but mental as well. She'd been in their heads, one at a time and both together, felt what they felt, even tasted her own flavors through AJ's senses.

Shit. If she thought about it too much it would make her nuts. With that point as her guide, Tala picked up the pill and swallowed it with a big gulp of orange juice. She had to trust someone, and if she couldn't trust these two, well . . . there was no one else. No one.

She'd ordered a bowl of oatmeal. Without a penny to her name, it seemed the prudent thing to do, but the amount of food AJ and Mik consumed was absolutely mind-boggling. Fried potatoes and sausage, bacon, eggs, bagels, and fruit— huge servings that seemed to disappear as if by magic.

Of course, they were big men, and if they had sex the way they had last night on a regular basis, she figured they must burn off a ton of calories.

Tala felt a coil of heat deep in her womb followed by a hot rush of moisture between her legs. She practically moaned aloud with the sudden arousal slicing through her body.

Both AJ and Mik raised their heads, nostrils flared. Almost as if they scented her! Tala felt her skin heat with embarrassment. She'd showered this morning, used deodorant. They couldn't possibly smell the fact she was horny, could they?

She squirmed uncomfortably in her seat. "How far are you planning to go today?" An honest question, since she really wouldn't relax entirely until she was a lot farther from Jimmy Cole. Neither AJ nor Mik had mentioned their plans for the day. In fact, no one had done much talking, though she'd awakened to warm kisses from both of them.

"Depends on how far you'll let us." AJ winked with his double entendre and Mik just shook his head.

"C'mon, AJ. It's too early for that." Mik smiled at Tala when he said it and sipped at his coffee. AJ just laughed.

"We're based in San Francisco. You're welcome to come with us as far as you want." Mik put his fork down and glanced toward AJ. "I know you're concerned abut Jimmy, but I can't see him following you all that way."

Tala shook her head. "He might. I've made a lot of money for Jimmy Cole. He's never had anyone quite like . . ." Her voice trailed off as Tala realized what she'd almost said. That Jimmy had never had a slut willing to do anything with anyone before. That he'd struck gold with Tala because she never got tired of sex, never wanted to walk away from the business.

Until now.

These two amazing men had to know what she was like. The fact she'd joined them last night, that she'd been able to move beyond the beating and gang rape she'd been through just hours earlier as if it were all part of a day's work.

Well, wasn't it?

Tala stared into her bowl of congealing oatmeal and wondered if there was ever a chance of redemption for a hooker who loved her work?

Except it wasn't necessarily the work she loved, just the sex. Maybe she'd gone from one addiction straight into another when she'd exchanged sex for drugs.

Tala raised her head and realized two sets of amber eyes were staring at her. *Odd,* she thought, how she'd not noticed before. Both AJ and Mik had eyes the same strange shade of green and gold as her own. "What?"

Mik's smile was so tender it almost made her cry. "You just sort of faded out in mid-comment. Is something wrong?"

Something wrong? He had to be kidding! All of a sudden, everything in Tala's life seemed to burst. She took a deep breath, then another as she felt her tightly held control slipping away, farther and farther away until she snapped.

"Oh, no, nothing's wrong. Nothing at all." She threw her napkin on the table and glared at Mik. *Damn him! Damn both of them for being so nice.* "I'm a whore. My pimp's probably after me and I've hooked up with two really wonderful men who, unfortunately, happen to be gay . . . yeah, gay guys who all of a sudden decide they want a woman to share their bed."

Tala took a deep breath and lowered her voice. Shit. It wasn't necessary to tell everyone in the hotel restaurant how fucked up her life was. She put both hands on the table, leaned forward and dropped her voice to a whisper. "Only they don't just share their bed. No, they suck me right into their heads like something out of a weird sci-fi movie. Neither one of you has said a word about that. Not one fucking word. It's not normal, what happened last night. People don't do that kind of shit in real life. What happened to me?"

AJ and Mik shared a glance with one another, AJ signaled for the tab, and Mik stood up and took Tala's hand. "Not here. Let's go back to the room where we can talk. You're through eating, aren't you?"

Tala nodded. It didn't make sense, the way Mik and AJ

seemed to know what the other was thinking, the way they could look at each other and then each man seemed to do exactly the right thing. Did they communicate all the time the way they had last night?

Who the hell were these guys?

We have to tell her something. AJ glanced at Mik, trying really hard not to be too obvious. *The poor kid thinks she's losing it . . . or maybe that we're aliens.*

Mik chuckled. *Who's to say we're not? No one knows quite where our species originally came from. The Chanku had to start somewhere.*

That's not our problem right now. We're almost to the room and Tala's suspicious as hell.

Mik shrugged his shoulders and reached for the keycard. *We tell her it's the pills. They help us communicate telepathically but they only work when someone's already got talent. That's not a lie.*

AJ's smile lit up his whole face. *I knew there was a reason I stuck with you.*

Mik opened the door for Tala. She stared at him for a long, solemn moment, then walked into the room. *You stick with me because the sex is so damned good.*

Well . . . yeah. That too. Laughing, AJ followed Mik and Tala into the room.

"We work for a company called Pack Dynamics, based in San Francisco. It's a detective agency. All of us can communicate telepathically. The pills just enhance an ability we already have. You're a natural. You slipped right into our heads last night." Mik set the bottle of pills in front of Tala for emphasis.

She reached out and picked up the plain, unmarked bottle. "Where do you get them?"

AJ answered Tala this time. "They're produced specially for our pack. They're herbs, nutrients from certain grasses. It's a combination that merely enhances our natural ability to communicate."

"I can't hear you now, and I know you've been talking to each other. Why could I hear you so clearly last night?"

Mik laughed. "Sexual arousal heightens the mind's ability to link with another. We were all pretty aroused."

"That we were." AJ picked up the pill bottle and stuck it back in his overnight kit. "But if you don't believe me, we could always see if it works again in the bright light of day . . ."

Tala laughed. "You wish. I thought we were going to San Francisco."

Mik stood up and grabbed her hand. "That we are, m'dear. First, though, I need a kiss." He hadn't planned it, but Mik pulled Tala close and kissed her. She stiffened at first, as if surprised by his bold move, but she didn't pull away.

He slipped his tongue between her lips, ran the tip along the roof of her mouth. She whimpered, a needy sound that seemed to originate deep in her throat, and it brought his unruly cock to attention in a mere heartbeat.

Tala broke away from his kiss, panting. "I thought you guys preferred each other."

Mik laughed. "We do. Most of the time." He captured her mouth once again, drew her body close against his and cupped her bottom with his palm. She wore nothing but a cotton tank top and the light cotton shorts AJ had bought for her.

Mik knew she also wore a tiny thong bikini beneath the shorts. Pale blue with the words PHOENIX, ARIZONA printed in pink script across the front, just over her pussy. It was the best AJ had been able to do, shopping in the hotel gift shop.

The thought of her wearing the tacky satin panties had kept Mik hard all morning long. He'd never craved a woman's love, never needed the feminine touch of lips and hands, the warmth of a welcoming pussy for his needy cock. No, he'd needed only AJ, his mate . . . his one true love.

Shattered, Mik raised his head and looked directly into AJ's eyes. There was no condemnation, no sense of outrage. Only desire. AJ's desire for both the woman and the man.

Tala clung to him. Her feet no longer touched the ground, her arms were wrapped around Mik's neck, her lips pressed against his mouth. He felt heat where her mons pressed against his belly, felt the pressure of her taut nipples touching his chest, the sharp little poke of her heels digging into the backs of his thighs.

Groaning with need, almost incoherent with desire, Mik carried Tala to the rumpled sheets of their unmade bed and lay her in the middle, being careful of her injured back.

AJ was already slipping his pants down over his legs. His shirt lay on the floor; his shoes were still at the doorway. Mik stripped out of his clothes with almost frantic haste. Tala waited for him, still fully dressed, lying in the middle of the bed with a look of pure desire on her face, lips parted, amber eyes wide and waiting.

This time Tala, not AJ, ruled Mik's thoughts. Mik held his cock in his hand, fingers wrapped around his solid length and thought of the woman, not of AJ, his bonded mate. Thought only of the sensation of his cock buried in her wet heat, of her small hands stroking his back, her lips pursed tightly over his sensitive nipple.

Mik looked up, just once, into AJ's eyes. He saw the same lust there, the same need for Tala, and he understood. With a shrug, Mik acknowledged his desire for another. With a matching shrug, AJ accepted and agreed. It was all so simple, so basic, and done without any input at all from the woman in question.

Mik crawled onto the bed and knelt between Tala's thighs. She was so tiny, so fragile looking, truly nothing more than a waif. Her body was still marked with bruises, her eyes wide and accepting. Did she really need, really desire? Or was she so used to the role of victim that it was the only way she knew to respond?

Then, as if answering his unspoken question, Tala's slim arms rose into the air. Her fingers beckoned. Mik stroked his cock, felt it grow in width and length, rolled his thumb over the sensitive crown and felt the slick wash of pre-cum that gathered there.

Slowly, almost reverently, Mik tugged Tala's shirt over her head. Her breasts fascinated him—surprisingly full and round, sprouting out from her slender frame, the nipples a dark rose against pale skin. He swallowed, then leaned forward and licked one dusky tip. It puckered beneath his tongue, so he licked it again.

AJ joined him, kneeling next to Tala and drawing her right breast between his lips. She arched her back and moaned and her hands came up to hold both men close against her breasts.

Mik felt a huge weight lift from his chest, knew that whatever he did with the woman was accepted, even welcomed by the man he loved. Together they suckled at her taut nipples, each of them sharing the sensation with the other.

Tala hadn't joined them. Not yet. Her arousal was growing, but she wasn't at a level that would free her thoughts and open her mind. Mik communicated that thought with AJ and almost laughed when his mate silently took Tala's need for arousal as a challenge.

Mik backed away and slowly pulled the cotton shorts over Tala's slim hips and down her legs. Those tacky satin panties called to him. Wth his fingertip, Mik traced the cursive letters stitched across the small triangle of fabric, then leaned close and nuzzled the satin. He nipped it with his teeth, tugged and pulled and managed to thoroughly excite Tala with even more teasing licks and nips, sucking her clit through the satin, swirling his tongue over the narrow strip of wet fabric between her thighs. Finally Mik tugged the panties down her legs and tossed them on the floor.

He sat back on his heels and watched while AJ shifted position. Mik's lover leaned against the headboard with his legs spread wide enough for Tala to fit between his thighs. AJ pulled her into his lap, covered her breasts with both hands, and squeezed her nipples between his thumbs and forefingers.

I'm holding her still for you. I do hope you appreciate it.

It certainly looks as if Tala appreciates it. Tala had thrown her head back against AJ's chest and her fingers were already between her own legs.

Mik watched her pleasure herself for just a moment. Then he touched Tala's swollen labia with his tongue, delved inside to taste the lubricating juices that gathered and spilled for him, for his cock.

She moved her fingers out of the way. Thrust her hips forward, silently begging for more.

Mik leaned back, grasped his erection in his hand and swept the sensitive crown over her clit. Tala jumped as if he'd hit her with a charge of electricity. Mik laughed, but this time he aimed his cock directly toward her hot sex, right at the point where creamy liquid pooled, waiting for his penetration.

AJ lifted Tala higher into his lap and spread her legs wide, an open invitation to Mik. She sat on AJ's cock and the swollen crown poked out between the cleft in her cheeks. Mik held his own cock in his fist, stroking himself slowly as he stared at Tala's swollen sex, at AJ's cock.

Mik's breath caught. As if a leash pulled him down, he knelt lower and first touched his tongue to Tala's hot folds, then licked the moist tip of AJ's cock. Again, sweeping his tongue from AJ to Tala, circling the smooth crown, delving deep inside Tala's wet heat. Tasting AJ, tasting Tala.

If he didn't stop, Mik knew he'd be shooting all over Tala's belly. The flavors, the sensations against his tongue of smooth, hard cock and moist, soft labia, all combined with AJ's mental link, then AJ's strangled whimper as Tala clenched her buttocks around his cock.

Too much. Heart pounding, Mik backed away with a final lick of Tala's cream. She whimpered now, the strangled sound barely escaping.

Mik took a moment to regain control; then he slipped his cock inside her waiting folds, barely entering Tala's heat. Her muscles clenched tightly, holding him. Mik pressed harder, made entrance, buried himself all the way to his balls and touched the hard mouth of her womb, the very center of her sex.

AJ shifted, lifting both his own hips and Tala's. Mik felt the velvety crown of AJ's cock press tightly against his sac. Felt the first drops of moisture as his mate struggled for control.

Tala groaned and arched her hips forward, sliding along AJ's cock, forcing Mik's even deeper. AJ still played with her nipples, his fingers tugging and pulling at the sensitive peaks, but his movements weren't as smooth, and the grimace on his face told Mik he was close to coming.

Mik concentrated on the slow in-and-out thrust of his cock sliding deep inside Tala's warm pussy, of the hot pressure of AJ's cock against his balls. The slow, satisfying release as he pulled almost all the way out.

Again, and then again. The slow friction building, Tala's arousal growing. Mik felt it then, the slightest touch of her mind on his. AJ was there as well, stronger, easier to read, but Tala was close and growing more powerful.

Sighing with the pleasure, the pure sensation of lust and love surrounding him, Mik sank back into Tala's wet heat, then slowly withdrew. On the next stroke, he leaned over Tala's shoulder and kissed AJ. Their mouths met, tongues twisted together, but his cock was buried deep inside a woman even as his balls felt the pressure from his lover's erection.

Mik held the position, hips pressed tight against Tala's groin, and concentrated on the myriad sensations of sex with both AJ and Tala, of the sweet rippling of her powerful muscles, the way her pussy held so tightly to his cock even as AJ's cock pressed perfectly against his sac.

Muscles quivering with effort, Mik moved once again. Now his lips were on Tala's, his tongue invading the hot recesses of her mouth while his cock filled her sex.

Mik felt the hard mouth of her womb, pressed against her cervix, and she lifted her hips and cried out. Tala's body shuddered, her mouth opened as she took great gasps of air. AJ's fingers pinched and tugged at both her breasts. Fascinated, Mik watched the way the flesh quivered with the force of her orgasm, saw the flush spread from Tala's belly to her breasts, across her cheeks.

Mik rolled slowly to his back and dragged Tala astride. She rode his cock, still moving through her first climax, searching shamelessly for another.

AJ slipped between Mik's widespread legs, kneeling directly behind Tala's perfectly rounded ass. His face held a glazed expression. Curious, Mik opened his mind to AJ's and found sexual fantasies so explicit, so arousing, they took him to the very edge.

Images Mik fully intended to help AJ turn into reality.

4

She'd never dreamed they'd end up having sex this morning, but Mik's kiss had removed thoughts of anything else from her mind. Tala rode astride Mik's narrow hips and felt his enormous cock all the way to her womb on each downward stroke. His hands cradled her hips, guiding her up and down his full length, and the expression on his face was one of almost mindless arousal. He was absolutely beautiful, his profound desire breathtakingly exquisite.

Tala moaned when AJ kissed her shoulder, just above the area that still hurt so badly. For some reason, his tender kiss was a surprise. These men knew what she was, yet they'd treated her with nothing but respect. Tala knew that if she'd asked Mik to stop kissing her, he would have. If she asked him to stop now, he would.

There was no way in hell she wanted Mik to stop. Or AJ either, for that matter!

She couldn't remember sex this fulfilling. Hadn't known tenderness from any man she could recall. Not before these two amazing men. Tala bit her lips and held tightly to her emotions.

It would be so easy to fall in love. So easy to believe they actually wanted her beyond the few short days they still had to travel.

She leaned forward and kissed Mik, raising her hips in blatant invitation to the man behind her. She felt the soft caress of AJ's fingers along her buttocks, the slight pressure as he paused over her anus. Would he go there? Would it be like fucking Mik, or would he care he dipped inside a woman?

Obviously Mik didn't have a problem. His big hands cupped her face now and he kissed her like a man possessed. She wondered if his thoughts would be in her head again, but for now there was nothing beyond sensation. Sensation and desperate need.

Would she always be so damned needy?

Not if Mik and AJ continued with what they were doing. Tala's world narrowed to pure sensation, to the heat from Mik's cock sliding in and out of her greedy sex, the taste of his tongue matching the rhythm of each thrust as he slowly and carefully made love to her mouth.

Something cool and wet touched her backside and Tala smiled into Mik's kiss. AJ appeared to have found something for lubricant. She'd been a little apprehensive about that. She was still a little tender from yesterday's episode, but not nearly as sore as she'd expected.

Certainly not sore enough to interfere with the amazing waves of pleasure washing over her entire body. AJ's touch was magic. Pure, gentle magic.

His fingers stroked the moisture up and down the cleft between her cheeks, teasing at first, then pressing more firmly on each pass over her anus. One finger rimmed the tight muscle, pressed harder and then passed through. He added another finger, stretching softened tissues, slowly easing deeper inside her.

Tala moaned, totally caught up in the multiple sensations between AJ's intimate play and Mik's tongue against hers, Mik's cock filling her, his hands holding her face as he kissed her senseless.

It was AJ's mind that linked to Tala's first, his arousal almost beyond conscious thought as he prepared her for greater penetration. Tala saw through AJ's eyes, and with AJ's perception realized how turned on he felt to know he was going to enter a woman this way.

A first for him, though he'd had vaginal sex with a woman before, and she sensed his fears along with his desire. Felt the solid grip of AJ's hand around his own cock, the odd sensation as he pressed the hard, smooth crown against her tight opening, and she experienced it from her own perspective as well as from his.

As if aware of his mate's hesitation, Mik slowed his thrusts and tilted his hips, lifting Tala just a bit higher. She stilled all movement for AJ and concentrated on relaxing her muscles to make his entry easier.

When he first breached her opening, Tala gasped with the sharp, burning pain. She took short, shallow breaths and pushed back against the head of AJ's cock as her tight passage stretched to allow him entrance. She wanted to fight him. He was big and it hurt. Then the pain slipped away, replaced by a dark, delicious sense of fullness. Slowly, as AJ pressed deeper, Tala realized her trembles of fear had given way to shivers of pure ecstasy.

The moment AJ's groin pressed against her rounded bottom, when he buried his cock alongside Mik's, all three of them sighed in unison.

Tala giggled. Nervous giggles, but once she started, she couldn't stop. She felt Mik's chest bounce beneath her, heard AJ snort.

"That's not the reaction I was expecting." AJ tried to sound offended, but Tala wiggled her butt against his groin and laughed.

"Well, it's a first for me, too, and I was nervous, okay? I've never had two men as big as you inside me at once and I wasn't sure you'd both fit. It's not like you're normal sized, or anything like that."

AJ laughed and slapped her butt lightly. The small sting sent a shiver up Tala's spine. She turned and looked over her shoulder, intending to glare at him, but damn! AJ Temple was so gorgeous he just about took her breath away.

His jaw was clenched. Sweat bathed his muscular chest and the veins in his arms stood out. For all his teasing, AJ looked like a man on the edge of losing control.

He wrapped his long, narrow hands around Tala's hips and slowly withdrew, then once more filled her. Mik matched AJ's stroke, going deep in counterpoint. Moving slowly and carefully, teasing strokes that aroused Tala, that took her slowly but surely to a place she'd not reached before.

This time when their thoughts invaded hers, she was ready. AJ was the clearer. His quiet vulnerability as he worried about hurting her, about coming too soon, was more of a turn-on than Tala would have expected.

Mik's arousal was so powerful, his fight for control so strong, it carried her along. She felt powerless, yet filled with power, her body as much a vessel as a shrine in the minds of these beautiful men who loved her so thoroughly.

It was all that and more, here in this rumpled bed in a hotel somewhere east of Phoenix, her past a mystery, her future just as unknown. Here, sandwiched between two amazing men who loved one another, who included Tala in that same overwhelming love.

She'd not known love before. Wouldn't believe it now, but dreamed it was hers, took their shared feelings for each other, the love Mik and AJ accepted as their due, and made it her own.

It was only a little fantasy, but it had power. More power

than Tala had ever experienced. Riding the wave of Mik and AJ's love, she arched her back and screamed, felt her body clenching, holding tight to the men who filled her.

The link persisted, took her through AJ's powerful climax, carried her along with Mik when he finally gave in to sensation, cried out and arched his hips, thrusting deep inside Tala, filling her body with his seed, and her mind and heart with love.

Shit. Mik still pulsed deep inside Tala, his cock separated from AJ's by nothing more than a thin wall of moist tissues. Tala's muscles clenched and released, so tight and hot, so damned good he wondered why he'd always preferred men.

And that was the problem. Before he was Chanku, Mik always used protection. After he'd turned, there'd only been AJ and the Chanku immunity to most human disease including everything sexually transmitted.

That didn't mean he couldn't get a woman pregnant. Every pulse of his cock reminded him how stupid he'd just been. Even now, one of his busy little spermatozoa might be wending its merry way deep inside Tala's womb. Finding an egg to fertilize.

A baby to make. *Shit, shit, shit.*

Tala raised her head off Mik's chest and smiled at him. AJ peered over her shoulder, but he wasn't smiling. *If she's Chanku, she'll be able to control fertilization.*

What if it's too late? What if she doesn't change in time and ends up pregnant?

Tala frowned. "What are you two talking about?"

Mik blinked, startled by her comment. "Could you hear us?"

She shook her head. "No, but you're obviously staring over my shoulder at your buddy, here, and leaving me out of something. Kind of rude when you're both still stuffed inside me, don't you think? What's going on?"

Mik kissed her. Thought about lying. Couldn't. "I didn't use protection. I'm sorry. It's always just AJ and me, and we're both clean."

"And neither one of us has to worry about pregnancy." AJ kissed her shoulder and winked at Mik.

"I'm sorry." Tala turned her gaze away from Mik and her body stiffened. "I've got an IUD, so I won't get pregnant, but I never thought about STDs. Those guys yesterday could have given me anything. They're all a bunch of losers, and they sure as hell didn't use protection . . ." Her voice drifted off and she tried to shift away from Mik. Impossible with AJ still sprawled over her, his penis deep inside her body.

Mik wrapped his arms around Tala, including AJ in his embrace. "Hush. Everything will be fine. We'll be more careful from now on." He kissed Tala and nuzzled the tender skin behind her ear. "I've discovered I like the feel of your body holding mine."

"Me too." AJ wriggled his hips just a bit, then slowly withdrew. He lifted himself away from Tala, kissed her shoulder, and headed into the bathroom.

Slowly, regretfully, Mik pulled out as well, but he cuddled Tala close against his chest and kissed the top of her head. "You have nothing to be sorry about. What happened to you was wrong and it was horrible, but it was not your fault. Jimmy Cole has a lot to answer for. I almost hope he finds us."

"I don't. I don't trust him. Sometimes he carries a gun." Tala shivered and pressed close against Mik. He wrapped his arms around her and held her tightly. Protected her.

A few minutes later, AJ came back into the room with a warm, damp washcloth. When he bathed Tala, washing gently between her legs, she knew the feelings she'd had during sex weren't make-believe. They weren't a fantasy.

Whether Miguel Fuentes and Andrew Jackson Temple loved her or not didn't matter.

Tala realized she loved them both. Loved each man equally with every cell in her body. Loved them both and would never, ever let them go.

Sun streamed in through the window and the day was growing late, but Tala slept in the midst of the rumpled sheets and neither AJ nor Mik had any desire to wake her. Instead they leaned back against the headboard, one on each side of her, watching her sleep.

AJ glanced at Mik and shook his head. *What if she's not Chanku? You know what the boss says . . .*

Mik shrugged. *I'm not killing her, that's for sure. We haven't said anything at all about what we are.*

We told her we're telepathic.

Mik turned and stared at him. AJ almost laughed. It wasn't often his mate got so intense. Right now Mik was definitely intense. Even his words in AJ's head sounded intense.

That's not the same as telling her we can turn into wolves.

AJ shrugged. *We need to be really careful until we know for sure, that's all I'm saying.*

I'm going to call Shannon.

AJ thought about that for a moment. It made sense. Shannon Murphy had only recently become Chanku, helped along by their packmate Jacob Trent. Jake had given Shannon the same dietary supplement AJ and Mik were giving to Tala, going on blind faith she carried the Chanku genes. He'd been lucky. Hopefully Shannon could shed some light on the situation with Tala.

Mik quietly rolled off the bed and reached for his cell phone. *I'll go outside, but I need to talk to her. She can tell us what to look for, how to recognize the signs of Chanku in a female.*

AJ nodded. *Good idea. And while you're talking to Shannon, ask what we should do if there aren't signs. Are you willing to walk away from her?*

Mik looked down at Tala sleeping so soundly, looking so innocent and young, and shook his head. *No. I think it's too late for that.*

AJ sat beside Tala while Mik went out to make his call. If anyone could help, it would be Shannon. Even though she was clear across the country, living in Maine now with one of their packmates, she'd always have a place in AJ's heart.

Jacob Trent had given Shannon the pills without telling her why, and in so doing, had almost lost her. AJ wondered if they faced the same risk with Tala if she turned out to be Chanku, but he didn't think so. At least he hoped she wouldn't hate them.

How could anyone hate a person for giving them such a gift? The ability to shift from human to wolf in a heartbeat. AJ thought about that first meeting with Ulrich Mason so long ago. Thought about the sense of disbelief he'd felt when the prison warden said he was free to leave, that his sentence had been reduced to time served.

The only caveat being he had to go with Ulrich Mason, an imposing ex-cop with a most improbable story. A tale of creatures who were half human, half wolf, who could shift at a moment's notice, once their bodies had received the right combination of nutrients.

It all had sounded so absurd, but he'd eaten those delicious grasses, realized they were tastes his body had always craved. And then, just a couple of weeks later, he'd done it. Shifted from human to wolf, run through the forest on four legs for the first time in his life. Made his first kill, an aging buck that went down with a broken neck when AJ caught it by the throat.

Would Tala hunt? Would she find the same pleasure in the kill that the rest of them did? AJ found it hard to believe Tala could kill anything. He watched her sleep and wondered at her hidden past. Wondered why and how she'd ended up with Jimmy Cole.

It had to be the sex. That was one thing they all had in common . . . an almost insatiable sex drive. Suddenly it all made sense, the reason Jimmy might actually follow Tala until he brought her back. Her sex drive made her the perfect whore. A woman always in search of sexual gratification, driven by an overwhelming need, constantly aroused, always ready.

Chanku. Finding satisfaction only when they were mated, only when they finally found and connected with the other half to their whole.

AJ thought of the amazing relationship he and Mik had. How the hell were they going to add another half? AJ ran his fingers through the long, dark strands of Tala's hair and couldn't help but grin at his convoluted thinking. No one had ever heard of a three-way bond among the Chanku. Of course, the history of their kind had been lost for hundreds of generations. Maybe it was time to create an entirely new culture, a new set of rules.

Rules that joined three as one. Wrapping the silken strands of hair in his fingers, AJ hoped Mik might find the answers they needed.

Mik returned just a few moments later and sat on the bed beside Tala. *Shannon told me what to look for. She'll start rubbing her arms, especially if she's upset about anything. Her dreams will become truly vivid . . . not nightmares, but unsettling because they'll feel so real.*

AJ ran his fingers along his forearm, remembering. *I'd forgotten about that damned irritation, the feeling my bones wanted to crawl out through my skin. I remember scratching bloody furrows in my arms and legs before my first change.*

Then it ended, right? I was the same way. The dreams scared the shit out of me at first. What about you?

Shaking his head, AJ smiled. *Not really. I'd had dreams about being a wolf since I was a kid. Didn't you? They got more vivid, but they were still much the same.*

Of course I dreamed of wolves, but my grandfather was Sioux. He raised me for many years after my mother died. Mik shoved his hair out of his eyes and looked over Tala's sleeping form, directly at AJ. *I was supposed to dream of wolves. If I'd dreamed of rabbits or mice or frogs, he would have disowned me.*

AJ reached over Tala and pretended to punch him.

Mik just grinned, eyes twinkling. *Shannon said to watch for the dreams, for her to start rubbing her arms and acting nervous. Her human senses will become more acute, so she might react to loud noises or bright lights differently. If she starts craving blood-rare meat . . . well, that's a definite sign, too. Shannon said she was practically a vegetarian before the first pills.*

Mik tilted his head and his long hair mingled with Tala's, flowing over his shoulder to her pillow. AJ's first thought was how similar the shade yet how different the texture. Tala's was every bit as dark as Mik's but the strands looked like fine silk next to his mate's.

The two of them would make a beautiful pair. A perfect match. Both of them his. *How long will it take?*

That's the interesting part. Mik wrapped Tala's hair around his fingers and seemed to compare it to his own before he looked up at AJ. *I don't know about you, but it took me almost two weeks. Shannon made her first shift just three days after her first pill and said it seems to happen faster with women. She suggested we not go back to San Francisco right away. I'm thinking we get on 395 and head up to the cabin. It's quiet and isolated and we can be there in a day if we push it.*

AJ had to agree. The pack's cabin, located in the northeastern part of California in the Sierra Nevada mountains, would be the perfect place for Tala to make her first shift.

That was assuming, of course, she was Chanku.

Tala sat up in bed and rubbed her eyes, then studied her arms and hands for a moment. Normal hands, regular fingers.

She shuddered, then looked around. The room was fairly dark, but then the shades were drawn so it was hard to tell if it was day or night. The TV was on with the volume turned low. Both AJ and Mik seemed absorbed in a baseball game.

"What time is it?"

"About three. So, you decided to wake up after all, eh?" AJ turned around grinning.

Laughing, Mik spoke to AJ, not Tala. "I told you she was avoiding us. Probably hoped we'd give up and be gone by the time she woke up."

Tala shook her head. "No. I can't understand why I'm so tired, though."

Mik winked at AJ. "Well, I could offer an explanation . . ."

Tala felt the blush creep across her cheeks.

"Did you sleep okay?" AJ stood up and stretched. He was bare chested, his jeans unbuttoned and riding low on his slim hips. Tala's fingers practically itched, she wanted so badly to pull those jeans just a little lower, to follow that trail of dark, curling hair to its source. She had to swallow back a groan before she could form a coherent answer.

"Fine, actually. In spite of some of the strangest dreams."

AJ stopped in midstretch. "What kind of dreams?"

Tala shrugged as if they were nothing, but she couldn't get the sense of something deeper, something amazing, out of her mind. "Weird shit. I've always had them, at least as long as I can remember, but these were much more vivid than usual. Dreams about running, only I'm not really me. I'm some kind of an animal." She crawled out of bed and headed for the bathroom. "I think I'm a wolf, but these dreams were so real, I was afraid to wake up. Afraid I'd still be a wolf."

She closed the bathroom door behind her and leaned against it. Her hands were shaking. In fact, her entire body shook and her skin crawled like she had ants running over it. Rubbing at her forearms, Tala squinted against the bright bathroom light and stared at herself in the mirror. She hoped she wasn't sick. Hoped like hell she hadn't contracted some deadly disease from the bastards in the bar.

That all seemed like nothing more than a bad dream, hazy in the way of incomplete memories. The dream she'd just had, of racing through damp forests and across a wide-open grassy plain, hearing night sounds and feeling cold air blowing across her back . . . now that was so damned real it was creepy.

Tala peed quickly and washed her hands. She smoothed the T-shirt over her hips, then used Mik's brush to work the tangles out of her hair. She knew it was his by the long strands of black hair caught in the bristles.

She stood there a moment, staring into the mirror but seeing Mik. Feeling him making love to her. Remembering the hard length of his cock buried all the way to the hilt.

Buried deep inside, right along AJ's equally massive erection. Good lord! Two men hung like bull elephants and she'd managed to take them together. Both of them gorgeous and built and sexy as hell, and so damned nice to her.

She couldn't figure out which one turned her on the most.

Mik was the first man she'd ever had sex with who had hair longer than hers. Imagining those long, silky strands trailing across her breasts and between her legs made Tala's pussy clench. Then she thought of AJ. Damn! He'd been so gentle, such a thoughtful lover, but he'd taken her places she'd never gone, filled her so completely she wondered if she'd ever again be satisfied with just one man. They'd had sex all morning and here she was, wanting them both all over again.

AJ and Mik didn't seem like they were in any hurry at all to leave. Tala had thought they were going to San Francisco today, but then they'd ended up in bed together and the last thing Tala remembered was the warm, soothing sweep of a soft, damp cloth between her legs. AJ bathing her after sex.

She felt her eyes tear up. No one did things like that for her.

No one. At least they hadn't until now. Tala glanced toward the door, knowing AJ and Mik were there, just on the other side. They didn't seem the least bit impatient that she'd held them up by sleeping the day away.

Damn but her skin itched. Tala rubbed at her forearms, then splashed cold water on her face. The water felt icy, as if her skin were ultra-sensitive.

Must be this dry desert air. She dried her face and hands, took one last look in the mirror, and reached for the doorknob.

A loud, angry knock on the front door rattled the entire room. Tala turned out the light and opened the bathroom door just a crack. There was only one person she could think of who might be looking for them.

Jimmy Cole wasn't a man who gave up easily.

5

"I told you, she's not here." Mik had one hand hooked over the top of the door and leaned insolently against the frame, essentially blocking the view of the interior of the room with his body. His bare back rippled with muscles. The long fall of black hair brushed his butt.

He was absolutely beautiful. Powerful, a warrior standing at guard. Protecting Tala. Though his stance appeared totally relaxed and at ease, there was an intimidating sense of menace about him.

Tala couldn't see to whom Mik spoke, but whoever it was hadn't come alone. She glanced around the edge of the door, realized she couldn't see AJ, and wondered where the hell he was hiding.

"I don't think that's a very good idea."

There was a definite edge of steel in Mik's voice. Tala saw the muscles in his shoulders bunch, as if he was prepared to attack. There was an ominous sense of foreboding about the scene barely glimpsed through the crack in the partially open bathroom door.

The hair along the nape of Tala's neck felt as if it suddenly stood on end. She felt the sound before she heard it, a long, low growl. Menacing. Feral, coming from outside, beyond the door to the room.

Voices clamoring in sudden panic, a loud snarling, the sound of many feet running. Mik leaned around as if he peered along the corridor in front of their room, then stepped back inside.

He left the door unlocked. Moments after Tala slipped out of the bathroom, AJ sauntered into the room. He wore only jogging shorts and a big grin on his face.

His feet were bare. Now why would he be outside in bare feet and running shorts?

Mik glanced in Tala's direction and tossed a can of cold beer to AJ. "They're gone for now, but they'll be back. I'd planned on another night here . . ."

"Like last night?" AJ leaned close to Tala and kissed her. He smelled different, like the night wind. Like the scents in her dreams.

"Only if Tala wanted it." Mik smiled in her direction. "Anyway, before the jerks regroup, I think we need to hit the road. I hate like hell scattering dead bodies around. It gets messy. Leaving their territory is just easier. That okay with you?"

He looked at Tala when he said it. She blinked, taken aback by his light comment about killing, even more so to think he would even consult her. "You're still willing to take me along?"

Mik shrugged. His chest rippled with the subtle movement and Tala realized she'd focused on his nipple, the left one, just near his heart. Focused on that flat, copper disk and wanted nothing more than to lean close and lick it.

To taste him.

She blinked, aware he hadn't answered her question. Instead, Mik looked quizzically in her direction. "Why wouldn't we want to take you?"

"I could bring you lots of trouble. You don't want that."

AJ grinned. "Says who?" He leaned over and gave her a noogie on the top of her head and Tala thought of her brother, how he used to . . .

"I just remembered something!" She sat down on the edge of the bed and closed her eyes, but the brother in her memory didn't miraculously spring forth into her thoughts. She shook her head. "Nothing. I thought I remembered something about my past."

"Relax. It'll come." AJ was still smiling at her, but Tala knew he wondered where her thoughts had gone. What had caused them. Why they'd disappeared in the first place.

Tala had expected a quick getaway under cover of darkness, but Mik and AJ showered before dinner, waited patiently for Tala to clean up, and then took her back to the restaurant at the hotel, where they ordered dinner. She'd slept through lunch and didn't hesitate when Mik ordered a rare steak, green salad, and baked potato for her.

She was wearing another of the outfits AJ'd found for her at the gift shop. The bright yellow halter-top dress clung to her breasts and fanny and barely brushed her knees. The name of the hotel was discreetly stitched over her left breast, not so noticeable or gaudy as some of the things AJ had picked out.

For some reason, Tala thought of the thong panties she wore. They were just like the blue ones, with PHOENIX, ARIZONA stitched across the crotch. AJ had bought her three pairs, all the same slinky satin, tasteless to the extreme.

The ones she wore tonight were lemon yellow, the same bright shade as her dress. They even matched the yellow rubber flip-flop sandals she wore—but why did she have to think now of Mik sucking her clit through the satin? She knew the panties were already drenched, but once the thought of his talented tongue probing between her legs had taken root in her mind,

Tala was unable to move past the image. She squirmed in her seat, much too aware of the insistent throbbing between her legs, the slick moisture soaking the thin satin.

"You okay?"

Tala blinked, bit back an audible gulp and smiled at Mik. "Yeah. Just daydreaming, I guess." *More like fantasizing.* Imagining Mik's mouth on her, his tongue working wonders on her needy flesh.

She cut another bite of the succulent steak and forced her mind back to the dinner table and her delicious meal. Generally she preferred her meat cooked a little more, but for some reason the blood-rare filet mignon tasted like ambrosia. Tala popped the piece into her mouth and chewed, savoring every bit.

Their waiter stopped at the table and refilled Tala's wineglass. Mik took more as well, but AJ passed. "I'm driving," he said, smiling at Tala. "You don't want me falling asleep."

They laughed and teased Tala as if there weren't three men following them. Three men with every intention of returning her to Jimmy Cole. They teased her as if they knew her, as if they'd been friends for years. Tala felt herself relaxing and found a sense of humor she'd forgotten existed.

AJ finished his meal first and stood up. "I'm going back to the room. I'll load the car. You two finish up and meet me." He leaned over and kissed Tala on the lips before he left. Then he did the same to Mik, kissing him in full view of the other diners, definitely putting more of himself into the kiss with Mik than he had with Tala. When AJ stepped back, he brushed his palm lovingly over Mik's hair and rested it on his shoulder with obvious affection. Then he turned away.

Mik grinned at Tala as AJ sauntered out of the crowded restaurant. Every patron in the room watched AJ leave, though as handsome as he was, Tala figured the women, at least would have noticed him anyway.

"They'll remember the two gay guys but will totally forget you."

Tala's mouth fell open in disbelief. "What? You mean that was planned?"

Mik nodded as the waiter brought their check. "People like to think they're open-minded, but they're still a bit shocked when they see two masculine men kissing in public. That's all they'll remember. Not the fact we were with an absolute knockout of a woman. Merely that one man kissed another in a public place. Anyone asks where we went, who we were with, they'll only remember AJ and me."

Knockout of a woman. Did he really think that? Tala couldn't wipe the grin off her face as she followed Mik out of the restaurant, staying a few steps behind. He was right about one thing, though. People watched Mik. Tala might as well not have existed.

It was dark when they left Phoenix. Tala sat between the two men in the front seat for the first couple of hours as AJ followed a meandering route to Kingman. Then, yawning and unaccountably sleepy, she crawled into the back and made herself a bed on the mattress. She wrapped herself in warm blankets with a sleeping bag for a pillow and dozed to the hum of the tires and soft strains of country western music. When she woke up, Mik told her they'd crossed the state line into California and were stopped for gas.

"I don't know why I'm so tired." Tala sat up and rubbed her eyes, then scratched at her arms. "I slept almost all day, too."

Mik just shook his head. "You're fine. You've had a lot going on in your life. It's your body's way of telling you to take a break. If you need a pit stop, you might want to go now. We're going to see how far north we can make it tonight."

Still groggy, Tala headed for the restroom. The bright lights practically blinded her. She squinted at herself in the cracked mirror. Her black eye had faded to green, but luckily her long hair hid most of the bruises. She splashed some water on her face, washed her hands and got back to the car just as AJ finished washing the windshield. Determined to stay awake, Tala climbed into the front seat. It was tight for the three of them, but neither AJ nor Mik seemed to mind a bit.

Tala certainly didn't. Being gently compressed between two absolutely gorgeous men wasn't a bad way at all to travel. They talked a little, napped a bit. AJ finally turned the driving over to Mik at Bridgeport and slept beside Tala for a couple of hours. They followed 395 north through high desert washed in moonlight, saw the sun rising near the little town of Minden, and stopped there for breakfast.

Tala hadn't realized they'd crossed into Nevada until she saw slot machines in the women's restroom. All she knew was that they'd continued heading north after eating a huge breakfast, following the highway back into California somewhere north of Lake Tahoe. She'd taken her second pill, swallowing the big capsule down with a glass of orange juice. AJ and Mik took theirs as well. Somehow, sharing a simple thing like a vitamin supplement made Tala feel even closer to both the men. She still found it hard to believe the capsules might help her communicate telepathically, even though she couldn't deny the link she'd shared with both men.

It really was too much to take in all at once.

Once they were back in California, they stopped at a grocery store in the town of Susanville and loaded up on supplies, enough food and other products to keep an army fed for at least a month as far as Tala could tell. Of course, she was used to feeding one rather slight female body. Mik and AJ obviously needed a lot more to keep them going.

She helped load the groceries into the back of the SUV, struggling with a thirty-pack of beer. Mik grabbed it out of

Tala's hands as if it weighed nothing at all and set it next to a sack of potatoes. He grinned at her, then tapped her on top of the head. "I bet this beer weighs almost as much as you do. What are you, about eighty pounds, dripping wet?"

Tala stuck her tongue out at Mik and grabbed another sack off the bottom of the grocery cart.

AJ socked Mik in the shoulder. "I give her ninety pounds and about five foot nuthin'."

Tala straightened up, shoved the sack into Mik's hands and put her fists on her narrow hips. "I happen to be five feet, two inches tall and I weigh almost a hundred pounds."

Mik leaned over her head, put his mouth close to AJ's ear and whispered, "She's lying."

Tala leaned close to AJ on the opposite side, though as short as she was, she couldn't get anywhere close to his ear. "Tell him to watch it or I'll kick him in the ankle."

It got worse when AJ suggested they stop at a small clothing store and buy Tala some warm outfits before heading to the cabin. The guys insisted she pick out a couple of sweatsuits, warm socks, and a pair of shoes so she wouldn't freeze. Nothing Tala looked at fit until Mik wandered into the children's section and found things just her size.

Acting indignant as possible, Tala stood to one side while Mik paid for the small pile of clothing. She bit her cheek to keep from laughing. Unfortunately, Mik and AJ thought it was absolutely hysterical, which got Tala started as well. She was still giggling when they finally climbed into the SUV and headed northwest this time, with Mount Lassen's snow-capped peak rising off to their left.

After the dry New Mexico desert, the rugged landscape of the eastern Sierra Nevadas seemed like a veritable Eden to Tala. She'd never seen such gorgeous mountains, never smelled air so fresh, seen trees so tall nor creeks running so high. Snow, even

in April, still covered the high peaks and even some of the shadowed areas in the forest along the highway.

She should have been tired of riding after so long a trip, but
Tala wished she could stay like this forever. Mik to her left, driving
casually with one arm out the window, the other looped over
the steering wheel. AJ sound asleep beside her, his head resting
on her shoulder, his lips mere inches from her right breast. She
felt the heat of Mik's thigh along her left side, AJ's relaxed
weight a comfortable pressure along her right.

She couldn't remember feeling so safe, so completely at peace.

So unbelievably turned on. Tala tried to concentrate on the
road but the subtle pressure of both men surrounding her, their
heat and their clean male scent had her fighting the urge to
squirm in her seat. She felt the muscles between her legs clenching and releasing in a rhythm over which she had no control.
Her nipples puckered beneath her cotton top.

The strange crawling sensation was back as well, the feeling
that her bones were too big for her skin. It felt almost as if her
flesh rippled along her arms and legs and she realized she was
gritting her teeth in an effort not to scratch deep furrows into
her skin.

Concentrating so hard on not scratching, not squirming, not
turning herself inside out, Tala missed the point where Mik
turned off the main highway. Belatedly, she realized they were
driving through thick forest, stands of cedar, fir, and pine, and
other trees she didn't recognize.

Mik took another turn onto a narrower road, then turned
again to one even less traveled. They appeared to be dropping
elevation as well, and Tala noticed there was less snow and more
green grass, more new growth on shrubs and bushes along the
way. Eventually they followed nothing more than a muddy dirt
road meandering through thick forest before popping out into
a sun-drenched meadow surrounded by tall trees.

A large cabin nestled in a thick stand of mixed fir and pine at the far edge of the meadow. Wildflowers of every hue and shade vied with the brilliant green grasses for attention, and a narrow creek meandered through the middle of it all. Huge, barren mountain peaks towered over the small clearing, their tops covered with snow.

The cabin was made all of logs with a huge deck wrapped around the outside. Neatly stacked firewood framed the front door, but there was no sign anyone had been near the place in ages. Mik slowly drove across the meadow. The long dirt drive-way was barely visible beneath the spring growth, but the deep tracks left by the SUV looked as if they'd been etched with silver.

"This is absolutely gorgeous!" Tala got out and stretched, then shivered in the cool air. "Good thing you guys thought to get me some warm clothes! It's colder than it looks."

"It's the elevation. We're still around three thousand feet here." Mik tossed the bag of clothes to Tala, then grabbed up half a dozen plastic bags of groceries. AJ opened the front door and came back for more of their stuff.

By the time Tala changed into a warm set of bright pink sweats, Mik had a fire going and AJ was carrying the last of the bags inside. Working together, the men quickly had the propane fired up for hot water and the gas range, and recharged the solar system for backup power. They ate lunch on the deck, thick deli sandwiches from their last stop in Susanville. Tala wiped her mouth with a paper napkin and yawned. "I can't believe I need a nap already."

AJ stood up and grabbed her hand. "C'mon. I'll show you where you can sleep."

He led Tala up the flight of stairs leading out of the great room to a large open loft. She stopped on the top step and slapped her hand over her mouth, but it wasn't fast enough to stop the snort of laughter.

Instead of the expected beds, there were four huge mattresses shoved close together, covering a large portion of the loft. The blankets were scattered and rumpled, pillows piled here and there as if an orgy had recently occurred.

AJ raised one dark eyebrow. "You had something you wanted to say?"

Tala shook her head, still giggling behind her hand. "No. Nothing. Nothing at all . . ."

"Actually, if you don't mind helping me, we can get some clean sheets on a couple of these mattresses. Looks like no one has been back here since we all came up last fall." AJ leaned over and began pulling sheets and blankets off the mattresses. "Usually we don't leave things in quite such a mess, but we had to take off in a hurry."

Tala grabbed clean sheets out of the closet AJ directed her to and helped AJ remake all four of the mattresses. "What happened?"

"Business emergency. Some work for Pack Dynamics, the agency Mik and I work for."

Tala nodded. "Ah, the telepaths."

AJ's head jerked around in surprise, then he smiled. "Yeah. That's us. Telepaths."

Later, Tala awoke to absolute quiet. AJ had said something about going out for a run, but dark shadows filled the loft and Tala knew she must have slept for hours. Could they still be gone? The cabin certainly felt empty.

She lay there, warm and comfortable, unwilling to get out of the soft bed and thinking of the odd conversation with AJ. When she'd called them telepaths, he'd acted surprised, though he'd quickly covered his expression and looked away.

Something obviously was not as it seemed. She wondered about Pack Dynamics and the way AJ and Mik talked about their coworkers as if they were lovers.

All of them.

Here? In the cabin together? It would certainly explain the need for a room with what was essentially one large bed, but the image of four or five men making love, all of them touching and tasting, their huge bodies straining, thrusting . . .

The sound of water running downstairs startled Tala out of her daydreams. She quickly pulled her hand from between her legs, frowning. She'd been totally unaware she'd been touching herself, so caught up in the images of Mik and AJ and their equally well-built though faceless companions. For that matter, she hadn't heard the front door, either, but obviously someone was in the shower.

Maybe two someones? She crawled out of bed and finger-combed her tangled hair out of her eyes, then followed the sound of running water to a bathroom on the ground floor.

Steam billowed out of a partially open door. Tala quietly peeked through the narrow opening and saw the shadowed images of AJ and Mik in the huge shower together. Partially obscured by both the frosted glass on the shower door and the thick steam filling the room, their bodies took on a sensual, artistic flair. Mik, identifiable by his long black hair, had his back to the spray. He appeared to be washing AJ's back.

AJ bent forward with his forearms pressed against the wall, the edges of his lean body softened and distorted, but the lack of clarity made the scene in front of Tala all the more sensual.

As if in a fog, she slowly pulled her sweatshirt over her head and stepped out of the pants. Without a word, she quietly slipped the shower door open and stepped beneath the spray.

AJ had sensed Tala's presence mere seconds before she joined them in the shower. Thank goodness he'd warned Mik or there might have been a problem. Trained to react on instinct alone, both men were killers. Just back from their first good run as Chanku, they were also primed for either sex or violence.

Or both.

It didn't really matter when they were this wired and aroused.

Nothing mattered but sensation, reaction . . . instinct. Tala was the last person either one of them ever wanted to harm.

Mik closed the glass door behind her as she slipped into the steaming shower between the two of them. AJ turned around and sat on the small molded bench in the corner of the shower. His cock rose straight up, giving Mik a good idea of his mate's intentions.

Instead of settling herself onto his lap, Tala surprised both men when she knelt in front of AJ and took him into her mouth. Hot water streamed around her shoulders and swept her hair down her back like a curtain of dark silk. AJ threw his head back against the tile wall of the shower and gasped as Tala's lips tightened around his cock.

Watching them, the way Tala's cheeks hollowed with each strong pull, the look of absolute rapture on AJ's face, was too much. Holding his cock in his hand, Mik stepped over Tala and, with his feet planted firmly on either side of her kneeling form, fed his straining erection to AJ.

AJ wrapped his lips around the purple crown and swallowed him deep. He wrapped one fist around the thick base of Mik's cock; the other tangled in Tala's wet hair. Water cascaded off their bodies, steam filled the air, and Mik braced himself against the dark blue tile walls of the shower.

Mik opened his mind to AJ and found Tala instead. Tala, her thoughts unguarded and honest, as clear as if she spoke them in his head. He experienced her arousal, the sense of power she felt with two beautiful men at her beck and call. The love she had for both him and AJ, the fear they wouldn't want her when this journey ended.

Tala's vulnerability was Mik's undoing. The knowledge that, should he and AJ be wrong and discover Tala was not Chanku, this relationship would somehow have to end. It couldn't. She was too much like them, had too many of the signs of the beast within to even consider she might not be one of them. Arching his back, Mik thrust against AJ's hot mouth, welcomed the scrape of teeth, the tight grasp of his lover's fist around the base.

AJ, obviously aware of Mik's tortured thoughts, sent his own message of love, of desire and hope. Filled Mik's heart with the passion each man carried for the other, shared the heat of Tala's mouth, the warm caress of her fingers as she held his testicles in her small hands.

So close, each man hovering on the brink of climax, but it wasn't enough. Wasn't completely shared. Mik pulled free of AJ's sucking mouth, lifted Tala away from AJ and turned off the water. Practically shaking with need, with emotion and fear, Mik wrapped her in a large towel and carried her out of the bathroom and up the stairs.

AJ followed close behind, leaving a damp trail in his wake.

6

Tala had been lost in sensation, in a wet world of heat and taste and texture. The thick cock filling her mouth and the salty taste of AJ's pre-cum, the harsh rasp of Mik's hairy legs against her sides and shoulders as she knelt in the shower with him standing over her.

There'd been the hard porcelain beneath her knees, softened only by a thin rubber mat and the hot needles of water cascading off her back and buttocks. Lost in sensation and loving the feel of AJ's testicles in the palm of her hand, the wrinkled sac that held them, the smooth, satiny skin over his unbelievably hard cock, the sense of power to think she had two gorgeous men all to herself, two men who wanted her, who cared for her.

Then suddenly Mik was sweeping her up, wrapping her into a warm, fluffy towel and carrying her away. It took Tala a moment, so caught up had she been in the act of suckling AJ, to realize all three of them were now ascending the stairs into the sleeping loft.

She stared at Mik, at the look of pure determination on his face and wondered if he was jealous of her attention to his mate, if for some horrible reason he'd decided what they all did together was wrong.

"No. Never wrong." His voice was harsh, the words sounding gruff, almost angry.

"How did you know . . . ?"

Mik gently set her down on the mattress closest to the door and slowly pulled the towel from around her body. He sat nearby but not touching her, as did AJ. "I know because your thoughts are an open book to me . . . to AJ as well. I couldn't stand it, watching you make love to AJ, knowing my cock was getting attention just as powerful, while you were left there doing all the touching. All alone, untouched and unaroused."

Tala laughed. "Unaroused? You weren't reading me all that well, were you?" Mik and AJ sat next to one another, Indian-fashion, legs folded in front. Mik braced himself with palms planted firmly on the mattress. Tala rolled to her knees and leaned close enough to kiss Mik on the mouth. Thoroughly, using her tongue, rubbing her peaked nipples over his chest, trailing her fingers down his belly almost to the root of his cock, until she broke away and left him breathing as if he'd just run a mile. Then she turned and kissed AJ in exactly the same fashion.

When she was through, Tala sat back on her heels, out of reach of both Mik and AJ. Their lungs bellowed in and out with each harsh breath, their cocks stood straight and powerful against their hard bellies, each with a trail of white flowing from the swollen crown. Two gorgeous men, obviously hanging by a thread, right on the precipice. On the edge of orgasm, barely under control.

Tala felt ten feet tall. Not only sexually aroused but powerful, omnipotent. They wanted her. Wanted her so badly they ached with the need, yet they waited. Waited for Tala.

Slowly, she palmed her own nipple, rubbing lightly at the taut peak, and took a deep breath. Both men watched, their gazes locked on the slow rolling motion of her hand. Fascinated by their extreme arousal, aware on some level of their deeply carnal thoughts, Tala slipped her other hand between her thighs.

When she penetrated herself with two fingers and arched her hips forward to meet her own thrusts, she felt the tension in the room go up another notch and knew she had both AJ and Mik exactly where she wanted them. "Okay," she said, slowly stroking herself. "Let's get this straight. I love sex. I especially love sex with you two. Tasting you, feeling you close, both of you, turns me on as much as when you're both inside me. Maybe it's the power, the control I have when I'm sucking you deep in my mouth, when I've got your balls in my hands."

She almost laughed aloud at the expressions of pure lust on each man's face. She'd never seen any male this aroused yet still under control. Barely, of that she was certain. Tonight, something was different about them. Something even they might not recognize.

It should have frightened her. It didn't. Instead, Tala felt her own arousal grow, felt the fluids streaming from between her legs and the slow, steady clench of muscles desperate for something more than her slim fingers inside.

"Point being, don't ever think I'm not enjoying what we're doing. It was my choice to go down on AJ. I'd planned to bring him off and then it was going to be your turn, Mik." She shrugged her shoulders and grinned at both of them. "Don't get me wrong, though. I would have come, too. At least twice, if not more. Sucking cock does that to me. It makes me very hot." She dragged the words out, slowly, seductively.

AJ's eyes glittered. He reached for his own cock, hesitated, then put his hands back at his sides. Tala grinned in approval. "I loved what we did yesterday, when both of you were inside me. Would that make you happy, Mik? I hate to think of you feeling badly on my account."

Mik managed a strangled noise that might have been a yes. Tala grinned and rose up on her knees, still pleasuring herself.

"Only this time, I want AJ inside my pussy, and you, Mik—I want you in my ass. What do you think?"

Mik bent forward and crawled close, leaned down in what Tala thought of as a terribly submissive posture, and licked her between her legs. His tongue was hot and the pointed tip curled delightfully around her clit on the upward sweep. She moaned, but kept her fingers in place.

He raised his head and stared intently at her. "I think I like your idea. You okay with that, AJ?"

"Oh, yeah . . . definitely all right." AJ cupped the back of her head in his broad palm and kissed Tala. This time, he controlled the kiss, using his tongue like a mobile cock, making love to her mouth until she felt as if her entire being were caught there, in the space between lips and tongue and teeth. When he pulled away and ended the kiss, Tala was the one breathing like a runner at the end of a sprint.

AJ rolled to his back and brought Tala with him. His cock was swollen and thick, but so nicely lubricated with his own pre-cum that Tala slipped easily over him, eased herself down on his full length until the hard crown of his cock met with the equally hard muscle at the mouth of her womb.

She paused then to settle herself and both of them sighed. AJ's face was a picture of absolute bliss and she wondered if he'd ever had sex with a woman before.

Yes, but not often . . . obviously not often enough. Damn, this feels good!

Tala giggled. Would she ever get used to voices in her head? The pills must be working, because the sensation was growing stronger, more vivid. She leaned forward and slowly raised and lowered herself over AJ's full length, at the same time kissing and nibbling his lips and chin.

She felt Mik then, stroking her smooth buttocks, trailing one thick finger along the tight cleft between her cheeks. He'd coated his finger with something slick and wet, and the pressure against her sphincter lasted barely a heartbeat before he slipped beyond the tight muscle.

She wiggled her hips, as much in invitation as to let him know how good it felt, this subtle penetration while AJ filled her so nicely.

Another finger joined the first and Tala concentrated on relaxing, on giving Mik total access to her body. She heard his voice in her mind, the gentle words of praise and encouragement, then felt the pressure of his cock against her anus.

Maybe it was the fact she'd just accepted AJ in this manner, maybe she was merely more relaxed with both men, but this time there was very little pain. She felt pressure, heard AJ's sensual murmuring and soft whispers in her mind, and then the slick fullness of Mik's cock sliding deep inside.

He sighed and his breath was a soft whisper along her spine. Then he began to move, finding his rhythm with AJ, each of them filling and retreating in turn. AJ leaned forward and suckled her right breast. Mik's fingers found the left while his other hand clasped the smooth contour of her belly.

A moment came, a shared moment, when all of them escaped the mere logistics of three people fucking and concentrated solely on sensation. Concentrated and shared, so that Tala felt the slick heat of her pussy grasping AJ's cock on each thrust, felt the slide of Mik's cock against his mate's with nothing more than a thin wall of tissue separating the two.

Even more than the physical sensation was the mental. A sharing unlike anything Tala could recall, a sense of belonging, as if they were some sort of feral pack and she was the central part, the alpha bitch to their alpha males.

She felt the cool forest and the darkness of a starry night, caught the scents of wild things and heard the scatter of creatures running through thick grass. Bits and pieces of images that were all too familiar, all a part of the dream world she inhabited night after night.

Now, though, encountering them while wide awake, the images seemed to make some weird sort of sense, as if they were experiences she should know, should already be familiar with. Caught in the beauty of the dreamlike state, Tala gave herself over to both men, gave her body, her soul, and most of all, her heart. As her body tightened and readied itself for orgasm, her heart and mind spilled forth as well.

When it came, when the light burst behind her eyes and her body convulsed in perfect synchronization with her two lovers, Tala saw a world, an existence, she'd always known but never touched.

At the height of her climax, when her body twisted and writhed between both men, Tala suddenly saw the world of Chanku.

Gasping, his mind reeling, Mik slowly rolled to one side, taking Tala with him. He felt AJ turn as well so as not to pull free of her welcoming heat. As tightly as Tala's inner muscles hugged them both, it wasn't nearly as difficult to readjust positions without losing contact as it might have been.

He'd glimpsed something in Tala he couldn't explain, had sensed an awakening that shuttered itself just as quickly as it breached whatever barriers held it. Brushing her long hair out of her eyes, Mik kissed her unresponsive lips.

He felt her breath, knew from the tight contractions around his cock that she lived, but had no idea where she'd gone. AJ's concern rolled through his mind.

Is she okay? What happened?

I don't know. Try projecting calm, loving thoughts. Something weird was in her head, but I'm not sure what. Remember, this is a woman who only recalls the past three years of her life, and she's got to be close to thirty.

She looks about sixteen.

Mik snorted. *She's not. Trust me. Tala? Sweetie? Are you there? Do you hear me?*

There was no response. "Tala? Can you hear me? Are you okay?"

Slowly she raised her head, blinked owlishly, then smiled. "Oh, my. That was truly amazing."

"You okay?" Mik leaned close and kissed her cheek. AJ found her lips.

"Hmm, I think so." She clenched the muscles between her legs, squeezing both men. "Oh, yeah. I'm definitely fine."

Mik ran his hand along her hip. "Do you remember anything? Did something happen when you climaxed?"

Tala opened her mouth as if to make some wisecrack, then stopped and frowned. "Yeah. Now that you mention it, I do. It was like I was in one of my weird dreams, a wolf running in the forest. Only there were two wolves with me and I was sure they were the two of you. It's definitely odd." She grinned then and laughed. "Shit, sex with you guys really is a mind-blowing experience, isn't it?"

AJ chuckled. "Definitely that." He slowly pulled his cock out of her pussy. "I think it's time for dinner. I'll meet you guys in the kitchen. We can draw straws for who cooks."

He sauntered toward the steps, but Tala's giggles stopped him.

"What?" he said, standing at the top step with one hand on his hip.

Mik couldn't help but grin. Damn but the man looked good. Every bit as good as the woman still holding a big part of his body inside hers.

"I can't cook." Tala giggled again, then burst into laughter. "I forgot my past and forgot how to cook. How's that for a memory lapse?"

AJ just grinned. "We'll teach you. Anyone who sticks with

me and Mik better know how to put a meal on the table." With that he turned and disappeared down the stairs.

Mik wrapped his arms around Tala and felt her sigh.

"I really can't cook, you know? I can't remember a lot of things, and cooking is one of them. Mik, do you think I'll ever get my memory back?"

He kissed her. Slowly and with feeling. "Yes. You'll get your memory back. I promise. I also promise you won't have to cook until you do. I doubt my stomach could handle it."

Reluctantly, Mik pulled himself free of her tight hold and headed into the bathroom for a warm washcloth. Tala was still lying in the same position when he returned, so he washed her carefully, aware of the emotions swirling in her mind.

"Mik?"

"Hmm?"

"I don't know if I want my memories back." She rolled over and faced him. Her eyes were dark and troubled. "Maybe there's a reason I can't remember. Maybe I shouldn't know what happened."

He kissed her, even though his heart was breaking. If only they could be sure. If only he knew he wasn't promising a lie. He was so sure, almost positive. Almost.

"It's okay, sweetie. Whatever it is, you know AJ and I will be here for you. You don't have to go through anything alone. Not anymore. Never alone." He shook his head for emphasis. "Never."

Never alone, he'd said. Then why the hell was she alone now? They'd all spent a wonderful night together in that big mass of mattresses, making sweet love without the violent undertones she'd noticed earlier. They'd slept, eaten a wonderful breakfast, hiked in the woods, then returned to the cabin for a nap.

Only Tala awakened alone. The SUV was still out in front, but the fire had died down in the big fireplace and the cabin felt cold and lonely in the dying rays of the late afternoon sun. Tala wandered downstairs, searched the yard and deck all around the cabin, but all she found was a pile of clothing and two pairs of shoes. Unless AJ and Mik were running naked in the woods, she couldn't explain their absence.

She poured herself a glass of wine and went out on the porch to wait, but the air was cold and the sweatshirt and pants she wore were not quite warm enough. Her arms and legs kept twitching and the sensation was driving her absolutely nuts. The wine didn't help, so Tala went back inside the cabin and added a couple of logs to the smoldering coals.

The fire eventually roared to life. Satisfied she wouldn't freeze, Tala decided to check and see what was in the refrigerator. After all the teasing she'd gotten about not being able to cook, it might be a good idea to see if she actually did have some culinary skills. If the meal turned out absolutely inedible, they'd at least quit bugging her.

There was a lot of food, but she didn't have a clue what to do with any of it. After digging through one of the bookshelves, Tala found an old cookbook and settled into a comfortable corner of the sofa to read. The fire was warm and cozy and the sky outside grew darker, shifting from brilliant blue to lavender, then purple. There was still no sign of AJ or Mik.

A thump on the deck brought Tala alert and glancing toward the door. "AJ? Mik? Is that you?" She set the book down, stood up, and headed to the front door. It was almost entirely dark outside, so Tala flipped on the battery-powered porch light and opened the door.

"Jimmy! What are you doing here?"

Jimmy Cole and three of the men who had raped her stood just outside the door. Tala tried to slam it shut, but they muscled their way inside and shoved her against the wall.

"Bitch. You don't really think you're going to get away from me, do you? You owe me."

Tala saw his fist coming but didn't have time to duck. The blow caught her just below the left eye. She might have fought him, but crumpled to the ground instead. Instinctively, she sent out a silent plea to AJ and Mik.

Jimmy smiled then, as if satisfied he'd taught her a lesson. He nodded to the men with him as he reached down and grabbed her left shoulder. "Tie her up and let's get out of here before her boyfriends get back. I'd hate to have to mess up those two pretty boys."

Panic welled up, almost choking Tala so that she struggled to breathe. Her heart pounded in her chest. She twisted out of Jimmy's grasp and scrabbled on all fours across the wooden floor. Jimmy's foot caught her in the ribs with an audible crack. Tala rolled to one side, writhing in pain.

AJ? Mik? Help me!

Two of the men came for her. The third held a roll of duct tape and slowly peeled off a long strip. Sobbing, her stomach heaving and breath tearing her lungs, Tala felt everything around her go dark.

Felt the tearing, stretching sense of bones moving under skin, only multiplied tenfold. Saw her world shift and shimmer from one reality to another. A reality she remembered with unrelenting fear. With dread and terror.

She heard AJ and Mik over a cacophony of screams as they burst through the front door, only they weren't men. They were huge, slavering wolves, their ivory teeth bared and ears laid flat. Wolves just like Tala, standing here over Jimmy, her broad paws planted firmly on his chest while his life's blood poured out of a gaping hole in his throat.

She snarled but didn't interfere when AJ and Mik attacked the other three men. It was hardly a fair fight, two against three. The three didn't stand a chance against two ferocious wolves.

Tala lost track of time, lost all sense of reality. She wandered over to the hearth and curled up in front of the warm fire like a big dog, her body shivering uncontrollably. Mik and AJ suddenly reappeared as men, though she didn't recall watching them shift. They dragged the bodies outside and were gone for quite a while. When they returned, Tala was still wolf. Still waiting by the fire.

AJ sat with her, silently stroking her back and smiling while Mik showered. Mik did the same while AJ cleaned up. Their presence was comforting, but still Tala wondered where they had gone. Then she wondered if she had blood on her muzzle. She didn't want to lick it to find out. Somehow, the thought of Jimmy Cole's blood on her was both abhorrent and disgusting.

She also wasn't ready to wonder why she lay here in front of the fire in the shape of a wolf. Her mind was still Tala, but the body was something else. There was a subtle sense of knowledge, a sense that she had more control of this form than she ever had as human. Lying here with Mik's human fingers stroking the thick fur around her neck, Tala realized she knew how her reproductive organs worked, understood the process of breeding and how to control its timing.

She also realized her IUD had fallen out during the shift, but since she could no longer get pregnant unless she wanted to, it didn't really matter, did it?

Still, the image of that little coil lying in the middle of the living room floor stayed in her mind. It was such a simple thing, a safe thing to think about. Or was it? There was a reason it had fallen out. A reason she didn't want to think about right now.

She felt Mik's thoughts pressing against hers, knew she should open to him, but she wasn't quite ready. So much had happened, yet she didn't know if she really wanted answers. Not yet.

AJ returned, hair wet and slicked back from his forehead, the thick mat of hair on his chest glistening with droplets of water. He sat down next to Tala, opposite Mik. She was surprised at the tears in his eyes.

She couldn't speak, obviously. Wasn't ready to open her thoughts. Her only recourse was a low whine, more a whimper than anything.

Without warning, AJ leaned over, buried his face in her thick fur, and wept. Even more confused, Tala looked to Mik. There were tears in his eyes as well, but he held himself together. He cleared his throat and held her wolven head in his hands, forcing her to look into his sparkling amber eyes.

"We were so worried you weren't one of us. Tala, we are Chanku. You, me, AJ . . . part of a race of shapeshifters that goes back for thousands of years. The pills we gave you wouldn't have done a thing if you were merely human. Because you carry the Chanku genetics, you were able to change. To become a wolf. We knew women could do it faster than men . . . but damn! I took about two weeks and so did AJ, but you shocked the hell out of us. It's only been three days for you. Are you okay?"

Tala nodded her head, but the human gesture felt strange . . . foreign in this wolven shape, so she forced the walls in her mind to go, pushed through the barriers to make herself heard.

I'm okay. I had no idea, yet it feels right. The dreams . . . for so many years there have been dreams.

"I know, sweetheart. AJ and I had them too, long before we knew what we were. Can you shift back? Can you become Tala again?"

Tala dipped her broad head until her muzzle rested on Mik's thigh. *I don't know if I want to be Tala again.*

AJ's voice whispered in her mind. *Then run with us. Let Mik and me show you the wonders of the forest . . . as wolves.* AJ sat back and scrubbed his hand over his eyes and looked almost desperately at Mik. "The forest is such a place of healing. She needs to run."

Mik nodded. Then he stood up and suddenly Tala saw the wolf again. He'd shifted so quickly she missed the moment of transformation. She looked toward AJ, but he'd shifted as well. He whimpered, standing beside her, his ears laid back along his broad skull. Tala stood up and shook herself. Maybe they were right. Maybe some quality time in this strange form was what she really needed. Maybe something would finally make sense.

It was truly magical, running through the forest as a wolf, finally understanding a lifetime of dreams and images, sensing the creatures of the night, the small sounds and large scents of wild places she'd never ventured to before.

Tala ran behind Mik and AJ at first, following their lead, learning the parameters and abilities of this strange form. Then it finally dawned on her that it wasn't strange at all, that she'd lived the life of the wolf in her dreams since she was just a child.

Those memories refused to surface completely, though. Everything clear stopped just three years ago. She hated to think her life would forever begin with Jimmy Cole.

What did you do with the bodies? She'd broadcast the thought without really thinking about it. Realized she wasn't really certain she wanted to know.

They're deep in the woods, in a cave often visited by coyotes and other scavengers. Their car went into a canyon with all identification removed. They were here to hurt you and they deserved to die. Mik's mental voice left no room for argument. Tala felt AJ's silent agreement.

She ran on, taking the lead now. Leaping over small creeks and fallen logs, chasing a rabbit until it disappeared within an impenetrable tangle of blackberry vines. As they ran, Tala felt her arousal grow, her need to mate becoming an essential part of her existence.

She looked first to Mik, only because he was closest. Then to

AJ, and knew she could never take one without the other. Accepted the bond between the two of them but knew there was room for Tala as well.

But not tonight. This form was all too new, this body untried. Tonight Tala would run as a wolf and make love as a woman.

Who knew what the morning would bring?

"Has anyone ever done it before? Bonded with two at the same time, instead of a single mate?" Tala's question was purely conversational, but the tension in the room was enough to make her stomach ache.

Mik took a sip of his coffee and shook his head. "Not that I know of. When AJ and I bonded, it was like nothing I'd ever experienced. A complete merging of our lives, all our thoughts, our feelings. I can't imagine what it's going to be like when the three of us do it."

AJ laughed. "With Mik and me, when it was over, I had this crazy thought run through my mind, that I was really glad we agreed on politics and religion or we could have had a problem."

Mik snorted, but Tala just sighed. "I don't have a past. Maybe I can't bond with anyone."

Mik swept her hair back from her face and kissed her forehead. "Don't worry. When you're ready, everything will happen the way it should."

Damn him! Every time he did that, every time he got all sensitive and understanding, Tala's eyes filled with tears. Grumbling silently, she wondered if he did it on purpose.

"The logistics alone are mind-boggling." Tala tried to laugh, but the noise she made was too strangled for humor. She'd tried to imagine three wolves tied together in sex and realized it could prove fatal if not done right. When they'd made love last night, the three of them in the big bed a tangle of arms and legs, mouths and sex, it had all worked just fine.

Sandwiched between two gorgeous men, she'd had one massive orgasm after another. They'd linked and the bond alone would have made her come, but that was last night and this was the light of day.

That was human. This was wolf.

She took another sip of coffee and wondered about her past. Wondered if two men like AJ and Mik really wanted to bond with a woman who was, for all intents and purposes, incomplete?

"You worry too much." This time it was AJ whose eyes were filled with compassion. Tala's throat convulsed with the effort to control her own swirling thoughts. She shook her head.

"When you bonded, you and Mik shared everything. Every little thing you'd ever done. What if, somehow, I end up sharing things I don't remember? What if you find out I'm someone totally awful but it's too late and you're both bound to me for life? What if . . . ?"

Mik's laughter cut her off. "What he said. You worry too much. Finish your breakfast. You need to learn to be a wolf, first. We'll worry about bonding later."

The sun had slipped lower over the western horizon before they actually shifted and ran. Tala's mind spun with the knowledge she'd gained today. AJ and Mik had told her what little they knew of their race. No one had figured out exactly where the Chanku originated, whether as an anomaly of nature, an alien lifeform, or something altogether different. Records describing the first of their species were few and far between. What little they knew pointed to the first Chanku existing somewhere along the Himalayan steppes, where easy access to the grasses that kept their nature alive insured generation after generation of shapeshifters.

As time passed and the population grew, the Chanku spread out, leaving their birthplace for other parts of the world. Leaving the nutrients, the combination of grasses that gave them the ability to shift, behind.

Tala found it hard to believe this amazing birthright had been hers all along. Her mother's as well, and her grandmother's before them. However, since they'd never consumed the right combination of nutrients, the tiny organ near the hypothalamus that made shifting possible never had a chance to develop.

She'd taken her supplement this morning, as Tala knew she would every day for the rest of her life. This ability was too wonderful, too powerful, to ignore.

It was frightening as well, knowing she had control over her body in ways she'd never imagined. Knowing she had the power to kill.

The image of Jimmy Cole's body remained insubstantial in her mind's eye. Tala honestly couldn't recall killing him, though she remembered the coppery taste of his blood. She didn't remember her shift, either, though it had felt oddly familiar at the time.

Just as running, now, felt familiar. There was an amazing freedom to life on four legs. The power, the speed, the knowledge of her world. Tala had often floundered as a human. As a wolf, she was complete. An alpha bitch, a leader in her own pack.

How quickly the men had accepted her! She felt her confidence grow with each stretch of her legs, each new experience that somehow fit into the puzzle that was Tala.

Scents were easy-to-read labels, announcing in the equivalent of bold print where mice scurried and rabbits hid. Noises her human mind translated as a vast cacophony and labeled simply *sounds of the forest* were filtered by her Chanku mind into individual voices with straightforward messages: *food, prey, fear, joy.*

Her broad, claw-tipped paws carried her at an amazing pace through thick shrubbery and dense forest, over rushing streams and across shaded meadows. She raced ahead of AJ and Mik, her wolven mind in the forefront, the fears and anxieties that constantly beset Tala buried too deep to slow her tempo.

All the while she ran, her intended mates raced at her side. Not once did either AJ or Mik take the lead. They deferred to Tala, their alpha bitch. Accepted her leadership no matter how new she might be to this form. Followed her without question, with undisputed loyalty.

Silently encouraged her. Welcomed her into their fold. Anchored Tala the wolf. Tala the woman.

They gave her courage and unquestionable love.

The sky was a dark bowl of diamonds when AJ suddenly caught scent of a deer. Three wolves turned as one and chased down the aging creature, one weakened from a long winter and unable to flee.

Tala made the catch, going instinctively for the animal's throat, though AJ and Mik helped her quickly finish the animal. In spite of their assistance, she snarled at them, stood over her prey and guarded the still warm body. When she fed, they deferred, snarling and pacing, but keeping well away while Tala ate her fill.

Finally, fully sated, Tala backed away and groomed herself, rubbing her bloodied muzzle in the damp grass, licking at her paws and the parts of her pelt she could reach.

AJ and Mik fed companionably, and the three of them raked their hind paws in the soft earth and kicked dirt over the carcass. After a final sniff, they trotted down the trail, tails waving like flags.

After a few yards, Tala halted, raised her nose to the night sky, and howled. Her humanity was almost completely buried, submerged in the lust of the kill, the scent of the two males beside her. The males joined their voices with hers, the mournful howls echoing through the forest, sending lesser creatures into hiding, bringing the more confident out to pursue their nightly routines.

The wolves had fed. There would be no more killing tonight.

Mik nipped at Tala's shoulder and led off down a narrow trail, heading back toward the cabin. Tala refused to follow. *Not yet. The night is still young and I want to run.*

Mik glanced toward AJ and his long tongue lolled from his mouth. *We're not going back. There's a place we want to share with you. A very special place.*

After a few minutes, they came into a small meadow. Steam rose from behind a tangle of brambles. Circling around, Tala found a small, crystal-clear pool surrounded with flat stones. Though it appeared almost manmade, it was obviously very much a part of nature.

She sat back and tilted her head, staring directly at Mik. He shifted, as did AJ. The two men stepped into the waters and sighed. "It's a natural hot spring, Tala. Much more comfortable without fur."

Silently laughing, Tala rose to two legs as a woman and joined them, finding a perfectly placed flat stone deep enough below the water level that she could sit comfortably with the steaming waters up to her neck. The minerals in the water soothed the persistent pain from raw skin on her healing back.

Mik sighed again and stretched out his long legs so they tangled with Tala's. "We're not all that far from Mount Lassen. This is probably heated by part of the lava pool that once fed the volcano. The temperature is the same even when there's snow on the ground. It's a great place to finish a run."

"It feels like a hot tub." Tala closed her eyes and let the water ebb and flow around her body.

"That's what we thought." AJ moved to sit on Tala's left, effectively sandwiching her between himself and Mik. "We built up the seats with stone when we realized what a treasure we had."

"Hmm . . . it is a treasure. I can't ever remember feeling this relaxed."

Mik's mouth found her right breast, his lips firm and almost cool against her heated skin. AJ nipped at the left, his tongue feathering the very tip while his fingers wound their way down between Tala's legs, tangling there with Mik's.

You ain't seen relaxed, sweetheart. Mik's soft chuckle made Tala smile. The sensation of two men suckling her breasts, two men pleasuring her sex while her body soaked in a steaming forest pool was almost more than she could bear.

Her orgasm, when it came, was almost a gentle caress, a rising tension topped with pure sensation, a soothing slide into satisfaction. Together, AJ and Mik took Tala to her peak once again, held her there, then helped her over. Again and again they repeated the sensual process until her body felt limp and unresponsive, until every muscle had the tension of wet noodles and her heart no longer labored with their touch.

When Mik crawled out of the pool and shifted, Tala barely found the energy to follow. AJ was close behind her and she sensed his shift as she once more regained her Chanku form. She stood still, blinking indecisively, her mind benumbed from the many climaxes the men had given her. The paw roughly scraping across her shoulder, when it happened, shocked Tala. She spun around with teeth bared.

She hadn't expected this. Not now, though she should have known it was coming. Tala wanted this bond. Feared it. Bowed her head and accepted that somehow, some way, the two she loved most of all would lead her through this necessary rite of passage.

Mik was the one who mounted her, his sharp wolven cock penetrating her sex, hips pumping as he drove deeper with each thrust. Some part of Tala's mind wondered how AJ would take her as well, but she'd not thought of the other option, the fact that AJ had entered Mik in the way they'd always had sex.

If she'd been human, she would have smiled. So much worry about nothing. Tala dropped her barriers and welcomed her mates into her mind. Welcomed both of them as the moment of climax grew near, as the tension within their writhing bodies built, expanded . . . exploded in a convoluted maelstrom of images—of pain and fear and overwhelming sorrow.

They'd shifted, reacting simultaneously to the powerful mind link with Tala. Still buried in her tightly spasming sex, Mik held Tala's shivering body in his arms. AJ lay against Mik's back, his cock still inside, the three of them huddled in a tangle of arms and legs while Tala sobbed uncontrollably.

It was AJ who moved away first, who leaned over and gave his hand to Mik, pulled his lover to his feet, then helped him carry Tala to the warm pool. Though she cried, her body seemed relaxed, almost boneless, and the men floated her between them in the steaming water. Mik supported her head against his chest while her buttocks rested in AJ's lap.

They sat that way a long time before Mik finally spoke aloud. "We were looking for you. That's why AJ and I were in that seedy little bar in the first place. We were looking for Mary Ellen Quinn."

Tala shook her head. Her voice was rough from crying, her words flat and lifeless. "Mary Ellen died three years ago. She didn't deserve to live or I would have remembered her."

"She was attacked and she killed. It was her nature, your nature. You are Chanku, whether you take the supplement or not. The beast is still a powerful part of who you are, what you do." AJ stroked Tala's arm, played with her fingers, finally raised them to his lips and kissed the tips of each one. "You know you're not the first to do this, to shift without warning, without the supplements, when your life was threatened. To kill without remembering."

Tala raised her head and stared at AJ. "What do you mean?"

Mik answered. "There's a pack in Montana, four Chanku who live together. One of them, a young woman named Keisha Rialto, was assaulted before she knew anything about her heritage. She shifted and killed her attackers. From what we've been told, it took months before she was able to remember what really happened. Thing is, once she remembered, she was able to move past it."

Tala shook her head, but she didn't pull away from either man. "I was already a whore. What were two more men? I'd taken more than that before. I was bought and paid for."

"No, Tala." Angry she would think this way, Mik shook his head and wished the images from Tala's mind hadn't been quite as vivid, the pain as intense. Those two bastards deserved to die for what they'd done to her and so did Jimmy Cole for knowing Tala's past and taking advantage of her amnesia. She was lucky to be alive and relatively unmarked.

"They didn't pay to torture you. They paid Cole to use you for sex, which, as a latent Chanku female, is something you could never get enough of." Mik kissed her soundly on the lips, reinforcing his statement. "When it comes down to it, prostitution was probably the ideal position for a woman with needs beyond the norm. But torture? No. Unacceptable. Your life force was too powerful to let them hurt you any more. What they did to you went way beyond what any woman should endure."

Tala turned her head away and buried her face against Mik's arm. "I'm a whore. That's what I do."

"What you did." Mik caught her chin in his fingers, turned her face back to his and kissed her. "Not anymore. You have me. You have AJ, and eventually other members of our pack. We'll be able to take care of everything you need, just as you do for us. Trust me. We saw what happened. That's the thing about a bonding link. We both know what you know, what you've experienced, just as you know us and our backgrounds. Those men would have killed you. That was their intent. You merely beat them to it, a lot more mercifully than what they had planned for you, I imagine."

"Mik's right, sweetie. Get over it." AJ laughed, breaking the tension with his flip remark. Then, kissing her lightly on the forehead, he added, "You know we love you. You're not alone anymore." He grinned again and shook his head. "I'm sorry, but you don't look much like I'd pictured Mary Ellen Quinn."

That brought a slight smile to Tala's lips. "Why were you looking for me? Because of Bay? I saw him in your minds, saw him as your lover." Tala blinked and seemed to bring her world back into focus.

A world that had suddenly exploded wide open. Baylor was alive! There was a chance she might even find her sister, with the help of these amazing men of hers.

"He's one of the newest members of Pack Dynamics. When he told us he had two sisters he'd lost touch with, we knew we had to find you." AJ shook his head and chuckled. "Unfortunately, we were looking for a plump little blonde."

Tala frowned as she searched her memories. "I haven't seen

Bay in about ten years. He described how I looked when I was married. I'd gotten heavier and I used to bleach my hair."

"That explains a lot." Mik kissed her.

"What about Lisa? Has anyone looked for her?"

Mik shook his head. "I don't know about your sister. Last we heard, she was in Tampa. One of the pack will find her. Right now, though, we need to get you back to the cabin and get you to bed."

"Why do I sense an ulterior motive beyond sleep?"

AJ stood up and pulled Tala out of the pool. "Because we rarely go to bed merely to sleep. We're Chanku. There are better things to do between sheets."

"Or on top of sheets, or even in the forest." Mik followed them out of the pool. Standing in the pale swath of moonlight, his long hair hanging in shimmering ribbons over his shoulders, across his broad chest, he looked like a god.

Tala swallowed back a moan and turned to AJ. Even more beautiful than Mik, he gazed on her with absolute devotion. His beautiful amber eyes glittered and, like his packmate, he was already massively aroused.

She could take them here, in the depths of the cool forest beneath a starry sky. Take them as wolf or as woman, whichever they chose. Or they could return, go back to the warmth of the cabin with a fire crackling in the big stone fireplace. After running as Chanku, she realized sex would be even more intense, and suddenly the violence, the levels of arousal she'd noticed earlier when they made love, made sense to her.

A cool breeze popped up and Tala shivered. Then she shifted, regaining her wolven form as easily as . . . ah, was it really all that easy?

Was anything? The thick pelt now covering Tala's body warmed her. The male wolves running at either side protected her. She was woman.

She was Chanku. Waving her plume of a tail in invitation to follow, Tala took off in a steady, ground-eating lope back to the cabin. She might be wolf, a creature of the forest and one with the night, but she was still civilized.

There was a lot to be said for hot sex with her own personal gods in the comfort of a warm bed. Thinking of the possibilities, Tala raced along the woodland trail toward the cabin.

Epilogue

"Hey, Tink. Take a look at this."

Martin "Tinker" McClintock grabbed the sheet of white paper his boss, Lucien Stone, ripped out of the printer. He stared at the brightly colored map and short paragraph printed below. "Lisa Quinn? Bay's sister?"

"Looks like. She's not in Tampa at all. I found her working at a wildlife center in Colorado, a place that's sort of a rehab for lost souls and injured animals. Everyone else is on a job, and AJ and Mik won't be home from the cabin with Mary Ellen or Tala, whatever she calls herself, for at least another week. I thought maybe you'd have the time to see if you can find her."

Tink tried really hard to control the broad smile that split his face. Tried and failed. He tipped a salute to his boss and grinned at the beautiful mulatto woman sitting behind Luc. Tinker'd bet his soul Tia had a part in this assignment, bless her heart.

"I'll do my best. Luc, thank you."

"Good luck, Tink. If she's out there, we know you're the one to bring her home."

Home. Tinker looked around the apartment he'd shared with Tia and Luc for so many months now and realized that, as much as he loved them, it really wasn't his home. Not his at all.

Carefully folding the information about Lisa Quinn and sticking the paper in his back pocket, Tinker headed down the hall to pack.

Fantaisie

Noelle Mack

To JWR, the best bête

1

The lion seemed to enjoy the attention. Good. This was one client who really could bite her head off if he didn't like her work. Tanya ran a large-toothed comb once more through the section she had just finished, and clipped it to one side.

The beast had a magnificent mane that would be the envy of a rock star. But it took forever to section and comb out. And even though the lion's trainer, a stocky guy in khakis, was close by, Tanya was careful not to pull or tug on the coarse locks. Closing its golden eyes, the lion allowed the grooming to proceed.

She fanned out a handful of hair across her palm, running the comb through it slowly. Money couldn't buy highlights like this. Overall, the lion's mane was black, but on close inspection it was streaked with russet and fine threads of pure gold.

Tanya had sketched and scanned a few styling ideas before she got to France, including a fantasy braids-and-beads look, and e-mailed them to Jean-Claude, the lion's owner, the creative director and founder of an unusual small circus, a man she had heard of once or twice before he contacted her through a friend. He was descended from nobility and he was rich.

She guessed Jean-Claude had liked the sketches. Without further comment from him, an invitation to his chateau and a reservation for a first class flight to Paris had popped up in her in-box the next day, waiting for her approval.

There had been only one possible reply, the only French word she knew. *Oui.*

A week later, she was explaining why she was bringing twenty pounds of crystal beads and two huge suitcases full of hair-styling products into France to a bemused customs official. He shrugged once she got to the part about the lion and slapped a sticker on her suitcase, waving her out to look for a sign with her name on the other side of the glass door.

The chauffeur waiting for her didn't seem to speak English, so she'd contented herself with looking out the window for the long trip to the chateau.

The mix of office parks, factories and dreary outlying sub-urbs that seemed to surround every city in the world had thinned out after a while and a gentler landscape of golden fields appeared. Glimpsing the first chateau she'd ever seen, she'd had the odd feeling of traveling back in time. It was much smaller than this one, nestled in trees and overlooking a placid river in which its reflection shimmered.

The stone walls were covered with lush green ivy that gave the chateau the illusion of fading in and out of the woods as they sped by. Tanya had been enchanted by the sight, racking her brains for the French word for stop, hoping to wander around the grounds and take a few pictures. She'd rapped on the panel that separated her from the chauffeur, but he'd ig-nored her, driving on at a pace that terrified Tanya, even though she was used to careening New York taxis.

She had been relieved to get out of the limo and surrender her luggage to the servants who came out of the massive wooden doors of Jean-Claude's chateau. They took her upstairs, brought a light meal on a tray, and left her to her own devices. She would have loved to explore the rooms she'd seen from the shadowy hall but had decided to save that for later.

A note in perfect English, signed by Jean-Claude with a calligraphic flourish that reminded her of old documents, had instructed her to meet the lion's trainer the next morning in the fenced field behind the chateau, and added that her room overlooked it. Tanya had pushed aside the heavy brocade draperies that covered one tall window of her chamber to see.

The field had been empty then. Of course. No one would let a lion just wander around. Judging by the size of his palatial house, Jean-Claude had the money to provide the animal with a little chateau of its very own. As far as she knew, his fabulous circus only gave private shows for Saudi royalty and reclusive billionaires and people like that. People who didn't want to mingle with screaming kids waving glo-sticks.

Once upon a time, she'd been one of those kids, impressed by the majesty of the big cats. But only once. The man inside their cage made the lions and tigers bat at striped balls and jump through hoops at the crack of a whip. She hadn't liked the show.

Tanya clipped back the hair she'd just combed out, and the lion turned its massive head suddenly to gaze at her. His golden eyes held a look that seemed as old as time.

There was a soulful intelligence and dignity in their depths that took her by surprise. Her lips parted in surprise and a soft oh came from her before she could think. Tanya turned to the trainer—and found that he had gone away.

And left her alone with a wild beast. She took a step back, clutching her comb like a weapon. The lion blinked and rested its head on its enormous paws. Tanya worked out and she was a fast runner, but a lion was a lion.

Continue.

Tanya stared at it, telling herself that the lion hadn't spoken. Her imagination was talking. She hadn't slept well last night, troubled by work worries and yesterday's long flight. Mesmerized, she looked deep into the lion's eyes and he looked into hers. The golden warmth of his gaze seemed to dissolve the tension in her body. Without another thought, Tanya obeyed the unspoken command to continue, wherever it had come from, and approached the animal without a trace of fear. She could swear that a catlike smile curled up the corners of its mouth as she did.

You put a spell on me.

"Same here," she said flippantly. The lion gave her an interested look. "Quit staring at me."

He shook his massive head and looked up at the sky. Well, if she was under a spell at the moment, it was a peaceful one. She began combing and sectioning again, just as if she were back in her Manhattan salon on East 57th Street, absorbed in the soothing rhythm of hairdressing.

An hour passed and then another without her realizing it. She was nearly finished and the lion seemed to be asleep. The trainer reappeared and nodded to her casually, as if leaving her alone with a wild beast was no big deal.

Maybe not to him, Tanya thought with a start. What had just happened? She should have run away screaming when she realized she was alone with the lion, but she . . . hadn't. Coming back to reality, she reminded herself of the main reason she'd taken this gig. She desperately needed the money. Spells, hah.

Her salon lease was up and the rent was being raised to a zillion dollars a month. An international coffee chain was eying the space even though they already had three franchised cafes on her block and they had deep, deep pockets. If she couldn't come up with the rent increase, the nice people who worked for her, including two single moms, were going to be standing in line at the unemployment office, which would break her heart.

Plus she would have to go back to Texas and live with her parents. She loved her folks but that thought was truly scary. One tame lion who liked to have a woman run her fingers through his mane, not so much so.

Absent-mindedly, she wound a coarse wisp of its hair around her finger and made a spiraling curl. Her signature touch. She pressed it into the mane and stepped back to admire the effect, wondering if she should hold up a mirror so the lion could see how he looked. But his beautiful golden eyes were still closed.

A young housemaid in a long dress and white apron came out of the side door and crossed the field, bucket in hand. She set it down, wringing out the towel in it, which she offered to Tanya, murmuring a few words Tanya didn't understand.

Tanya nodded her thanks. Since her arrival, she hadn't been able to make out what the servants were saying, although a word or two sounded familiar. She figured it was French but she couldn't be sure. They were unusually quiet and deferential, as if they would just as soon not be noticed anyway.

But they anticipated her needs. The maid must have been watching her work from inside the house and ventured out into the field when it seemed safe. Tanya took the towel as the maid turned around, calling to a little boy. He came through the field next, giving the sleeping lion an awed look. He was carrying a dish of tiny strawberries. Another thoughtful gesture. She was hungry. Someone must be reading her mind.

They looked like wild strawberries. Probably handpicked in the surrounding woods by the little boy. *Fraises des bois.* How very French. She scrubbed up, handed the towel back to the waiting maid, and popped a strawberry into her mouth from the dish the boy held up. The taste was exquisite, nothing like the flavorless mega-mutants from the supermarket back in the US.

She smiled at the little boy, who smiled back, blushing. Was he Jean-Claude's son? He was adorable in those handsewn wool pants tied at the waist with a drawstring and his little linen shirt. He mumbled something that sounded very polite, and the house-maid laughed, bowing slightly to Tanya as she and the boy withdrew.

The sound of a vast yawn made her turn around. The lion had arisen, stretching exactly like a house cat, its enormous paws extended and its rump up. She looked at the baroque curl of its long tongue and its gleaming white fangs, feeling a shiver race up her spine.

The lion gave her a sleepy-eyed look and moved to its trainer, allowing the man to guide him out of the field, its tail swaying lazily as they walked away. She could just see the top of a huge striped tent behind the trees. Pennants of bright silk fluttered from the poles that held it up.

Hmm. That hadn't been there when she began to work on the lion's mane, she was sure of it. And it wasn't possible to set up such a big tent so quickly and make no noise at all. Tanya took a few steps in the direction that the lion and its trainer had gone, before the soft sound of other footsteps on the grass stopped her.

"Ah. He enjoyed that," a deep male voice said.

She looked over her shoulder. Uh-oh. Talk about spells. This man could put one on her whenever, wherever. He was just about too sexy to be believed, with thick, dark, tied-back hair and a rugged face. His eyes were dark brown with sparks of gold in the irises, and his lashes were black.

The man had a masterful air. He was tall and powerfully built, dressed as simply as the little boy, but the old-fashioned effect was totally different on him. His linen shirt subtly re-vealed as much as it concealed, pushed against his body by the breeze and open at the neck. And he wore breeches of soft, sup-ple leather and tall black boots. Riding boots. Yeehaw.

Okay, so he's a ringmaster, she thought. He's entitled. Ring-masters wear breeches. Maybe he'd taken off his red frock coat for now. But not his black riding boots, lucky for her.

"I am Jean-Claude," the man said with a slight accent, ex-tending a hand. Tanya took it, yielding inwardly to strong fin-gers that clasped hers for a moment longer than necessary.

"Um, hi," she replied, hoping he spoke English as well as he wrote it so they could get past the usual guidebook conversa-tion starters. "I'm Tanya. Thanks for everything. I mean, for bringing me here to France and all that. Your chateau is beauti-ful." She paused to take a breath, telling herself not to babble.

"Thank you," he said. "It has been in my family for a long time."

So far, so good, on the mutual comprehension. "Really. How long?"

"Centuries."

"Oh. Imagine that." She barely could, having grown up in a Dallas suburb where the oldest house had been built only a year before she was born, and she was twenty-eight. A photo of her mom and dad, standing in front of their brand-new house with their brand-new baby—her—flashed across her mind.

She looked up at the immense stone house looming in back of Jean-Claude, letting her gaze rest on the windows of the room she knew was hers. There must be twenty rooms just like it in the main part of the chateau, and that wasn't counting the wings. Framed by louvered shutters and shadowed by draperies that hid the interiors, the windows seemed designed to keep the ordinary world out. A faint tremor ran through her. She would have to go back to that world soon enough.

"Are you cold, Tanya?"

She loved the way he said her name. Soft and low, lingering over the syllables. "A little."

Tanya rubbed her goose-bumpy arms, wishing he had a

ringmaster's red coat to offer her right now. She knew he would. Jean-Claude was obviously a gentleman. But he couldn't exactly whip off his linen shirt and wrap it around her shoulders.

"The sun is low. Shall we go inside?" Despite the formal quality of his speech—to be expected from someone who grew up in a chateau—his tone was warm.

"Okay."

"Perhaps a cup of *chocolate chaud* would take the chill away."

Tanya's eyes brightened. "Ooo. I love French hot chocolate. Nice and thick and gooey and—and I sound like I'm six years old."

"Not at all. Your eagerness is charming. I shall ring for the maid."

"Oh, you don't have to. Whisky's quicker anyway. But not before sundown." She winced. That sounded bad, but it was too late to take it back. "I prefer wine," she added hastily.

He didn't seem to notice her gaffe. "Very good. Then we will share a bottle or two over dinner. I would consider myself honored if you would join me tonight."

"Ah—all right. I'd like that very much." Interesting. He didn't treat her like the hired help or an annoying American. This gig could be exactly what she needed for more reasons than one. She studied the tall man who stood in front of her. Jean-Claude's hands rested just above his hips, his strong fingers spread out on either side. His stance was relaxed but there was something compelling about his physicality all the same.

Just like his big ole lion, he scared her a little. And you like it, she told herself. She'd bet anything he roared in bed.

She looked him over. He seemed so commanding. So virile. Those soft leather breeches showed everything. He probably had more women than he knew what to do with.

Hmm. A wicked thought flashed through her mind. Add a

riding crop to the breeches, boots, and aristocratic ponytail and she could have herself a really entertaining fantasy.

Jean-Claude smiled at her and something inside Tanya melted. Do not fantasize, she told herself sternly. Just because you're in a different country doesn't mean you can run wild.

She walked through the lower floor of the château, her footsteps echoing. It was alarmingly grand. Lined with mirrors in elaborate gilt frames, the hall through which she passed gave the illusion of being much wider. And she saw herself many times over, myriad Tanyas moving through rays of reddish light. The sun was setting.

People were talking in the room just beyond, and she hurried a little. Was she late? Were there other guests? Tanya looked at her watch, and realized she was still on New York time. She fiddled with it, setting it ahead by several hours, and looking around for a clock to get it right on the minute. There, on the mantel, in front of the ormolu mirror—that thing might be a clock. Three slender marble goddesses held up a glass sphere with a mechanism inside it that whirred silently. She went over for a closer look.

There were hours engraved upon the mechanism but she couldn't figure out how to read it. A sundial would have been easier. No doubt there was one in the formal parterres of the garden outside the windows, but she wasn't going to look for it now. Tanya glanced in the mirror and ran her fingers through her auburn curls, flinging them over one shoulder and batting her eyelashes at her reflection. The new shade of shadow brought out the green in her hazel eyes. You sexy thing, she told herself.

She went on to the room where the voices were coming from, standing just outside the door for a moment. A manservant in livery was setting out domed silver platters and a maid was arranging fragrant pink roses in the centerpiece. She was somewhat older than the maid who'd come to Tanya in the field, with a more delicate face. Her slender white fingers touched the petals of the roses, opening them more to show the deeper pink inside.

The set table was beyond elegant. Snowy napery. Antique silver and china. Crystal wineglasses. Her Texas grandmother would have fainted at the sight.

The servants cast a quick glance at her and seemed to vanish into thin air. The way they came and went so swiftly was a little unnerving but Tanya wanted to be with him and only him. If everything was already on the table, including the wine, she just might get her wish.

Jean-Claude rose to greet her with a bow. "Good evening. You are beautiful." The admiration in his eyes was as sincere as his tone, and she felt her face grow warm. She was glad Jean-Claude liked it, because it was the only dress she'd brought with her, figuring she'd hit the Paris clubs when her week here was up. With its plunging neckline, slinky black synthetic material, and jagged hemline, it was her favorite dress for dancing in.

"Everything looks so nice," she said. "Thank you. Your, uh, servants are amazing." Servant. That was a word to trip over. She didn't know how anyone got used to being waited on.

"Hmm. The aristocrats of the *ancien régime* invented a table that rose through the floor, fully appointed and laden with food so as to do away with inquisitive servants altogether."

La-di-da. Tanya wanted to pinch herself. Perching in a gilt chair and eating with antique silver seemed to require a towering powdered wig and a pannier gown that was too wide to get through a door unless you went in sideways.

He pulled out her chair and waited for her to sit down. The moment of truth. Tanya had never quite mastered this particular trick. She sort of slid and sort of sat, keeping her butt just above the brocade seat. Jean-Claude did the rest with a motion so subtle she barely noticed it until the immaculate white table-cloth enfolded her bare knees.

Good girl, she told herself. And how nice it was to sit on up-holstery this luxurious. Especially since she wasn't wearing underwear. She could practically feel the pattern of the taut brocade through her thin dress. Jean-Claude gave her an oh-so-European half-bow and moved to his seat. The courses had been set within easy reach by the manservant—or was he the butler? Tanya really wasn't familiar with the details of livery. If she re-membered her *Masterpiece Theatre*, footmen wore breeches, butlers didn't, and head butlers had more buttons than anyone else in the cast.

It was possible that French people didn't have butlers at all, or that they called them something else. Butlaires, maybe. No. Majordomos? That didn't sound right either. She took a sip of the wine Jean-Claude had just poured for her and smiled up at him. Not a question she was going to ask right now. The wine was so good that she planned to have a second glass and then she could ask him, when she no longer cared if she made a fool of herself.

He took off the domed cover of the dish nearest him, and sniffed the aroma that wafted up. "Ah. My favorite. *Boeuf bourguignon*. Allow me to serve you."

"Please do." Tanya nodded, grateful that it was beef and not something like tripe or other squishy inside stuff. The French ate unusual things, but personally, she had drawn the line in Texas long ago and she had drawn it at prairie oysters.

He took off the other covers and revealed a tempting array of courses, elaborately sauced and arranged on the platters. Apparently Jean-Claude could afford the best, and preferred the best. She studied him over the rim of the wineglass she was sipping from. The soulfulness she had noted in his eyes had deepened to a frankly sensual stare all of a sudden.

Animal instinct.

Oh, no. Now who was talking? Tanya quickly set down her wineglass, glancing away from him and catching a glimpse of herself in the mirror. The burgundy made her lips shine, and its complex flavor lingered very pleasantly in her mouth. Jean-Claude gave her a seductive once-over. As if he knew how she would taste if he kissed her right now: like wine and woman.

She gave him a demure smile. Tanya wasn't going to give in that fast. He sighed and went back to filling her plate with delicious food. She needed it. The first glass of wine had gone straight to her jet-lagged head and opened the door marked Wanton Behavior.

Tanya suddenly knew without a doubt that she was going to end up in bed with Jean-Claude. Maybe not tonight but certainly before the end of her weeklong stay. Okay, maybe tonight. They could skip the introductory small talk and pointless exchange of life stories. More than anything, she wanted to find out right away what he looked like buck naked. With that long, dark hair spilling over his bare shoulders and chest.

What about love?

Tanya shook her head to clear it. That was definitely her inner lonely-girl-in-the-big-city talking. She imagined herself drinking a shot of refreshing, ice-cold, pure cynicism and slammed the mental shot glass down on the table. Love wasn't what this encounter was going to be all about but at least she knew that she wasn't hearing talking lions.

"So," she said pleasantly, opening up a new topic of conversation, "it must be fun to run a circus. How long have you been doing that?"

"Since before you were born."

That didn't make much sense. Jean-Claude wasn't more than ten years older than her. He had great eye crinkles when he smiled but no other lines on his handsome face.

"Oh. Is it a . . . family business?" Oops. That sounded like a tire dealership or something. Jean-Claude was, as far as she knew, a nobleman and the inheritor of a venerable chateau. He certainly looked noble, dressed for dinner in black tie. Regal, even.

"In a way," he said.

Not a very informative answer. But then he was concentrating on the food. He finished a mouthful of savory beef, taking a true carnivore's pleasure in every molecule.

"Well, I'm sure you love what you do."

He inclined his head in a gracious nod. "And yourself?"

"I like it, sure. I've had my own salon for two years now."

"A friend forwarded me a copy of the article in *Vogue*."

Tanya shrugged. "That was mostly about Frederic Fekkai, not me. I only got a one-line mention."

"But it was a memorable line." Jean-Claude smiled and poured her more wine. "May I quote? 'When it comes to hair, Tanya Jones is the future.'"

"Yeah, they said something like that. Haven't seen a stampede of new clients, though." Which was yet another reason why she had responded to his e-mail. No matter what *Vogue* said, her salon was barely breaking even. She didn't feel like telling him about her lease being up.

"My dear Tanya, you have uncommon talent. And you understand fantasy. Your sketches were remarkably imaginative. No one in Paris is doing work like that."

Tanya took a bite of her food, pleased by his compliment. "Well," she said, "I hope the lion lets me do more than comb his mane."

"If not, then *c'est la vie*," Jean-Claude laughed. "A lion is a lion. But he likes you very much. And I suspect the rest of the company will too."

They approached the tent behind the trees an hour or so later, treading a path made soft by freshly strewn sawdust. A half moon hung low in the night sky, lighting the way. Tanya held the high heels she'd taken off, not wanting to twist an ankle. He took her hand in a way that seemed deliciously intimate, rubbing his thumb gently against her palm as they padded softly over the path. He didn't seem to be in a hurry.

Neither was she. The excellent dinner and fine wine had put her in a wonderfully sensual mood made more intense by their mutual self-restraint. No playing footsie under the table. No leaning over to reveal a glimpse of bosom. She'd sat up straight and so had Jean-Claude.

But Tanya'd had the uncanny feeling that he was reading her mind as they ate and talked. Chalk it up to fabulous burgundy that had been mellowing in the caverns under his chateau for decades. There was no way he could know that she was thinking about, oh, oral sex with him when all she was doing was passing the salt. Her own animal instincts had kicked in, though. Tanya sensed that he was as hot for her as she was for him. But he had been a goddamned perfect gentleman all the same.

Ahead of them through the trees the striped tent glowed and she saw shadows move across the fabric walls, one flying in mid-air.

Just outside the tent Jean-Claude paused to take her in his arms, looking down at her with an expression she couldn't quite read. "I must warn you. The rehearsals are usually private. The performers sometimes work in the nude, or nearly so. Their every move is captured by hidden CGI cameras and the animation artists take over from there."

Ah-hah. Computer-generated imagery and animation. Special effects and skin. So that was the secret. She was only surprised that rich people would pay so much to see it. Sex was no big deal in this day and age. But maybe Jean-Claude's circus offered more.

"Anything can happen," he was saying. "They won't notice you but you mustn't be shocked by what you might see. Do you understand?"

Tanya hesitated for a fraction of a second. "I think so. But why won't they notice me?"

He kissed her forehead very gently. "Because you will be standing in the dark and watching them. As if they only existed in a dream. Your dream—with a nod to Toulouse-Lautrec, one of my favorite artists. Poor fellow. But he found a happiness of sorts with his prostitutes and performers." For a fleeting second, his expression turned profoundly sad.

He took her arm before she could reply and led her inside. They stood to one side of tiered seats where they had a clear view of the center ring. A spotlight positioned at the top of the tent blinded Tanya for a moment. She heard the calliope before she saw it, then looked at the moving figures that decorated it. Jesters, kissing lovers, and plump cherubs popped out of hidey-holes in it on every fourth note, an eternal carnival made of painted wood.

A young woman was practicing a routine on double wires strung close together, suspended about five feet over the ground. Her hair was pulled back and she wore only a leotard almost the same color as her skin, finely knit. No tights. With one foot on each rope, she bent her knees and did a somersault, landing with ease and bouncing on the wires.

Her closefitting shoes were worn and dirty, with ribbon ties sewn by hand. Like a ballerina's rehearsal toeshoes, they were meant to work in, not to be pretty. But the tightrope walker's strong legs and the sinuous curves of her body were beautiful. Without a trace of makeup, without false eyelashes, without sparkly decorations in her hair, she was the picture of graceful femininity. The brilliant light poured down, giving her a shimmering aura that made her look like a hologram.

A strongman came swaggering into the ring to meet her. His outline shimmered, too, and Tanya wondered if Jean-Claude's CGI artists had already staged this scene, or if it was being created before her eyes. A few details seemed roughed in, but the strongman did look like a Toulouse-Lautrec sketch. There wasn't much to his costume, just a few artfully shredded scraps of fabric over his bulging crotch and muscular butt.

How nice that he wasn't the balding, beefy, wax-mustachioed type of strongman. This guy was young and sleekly built, with a lot of dark hair and a boyish grin. The woman on the wire flipped off and he caught her with ease, bending his head down to kiss her lovingly on the lips when she twined her arms around his neck.

She whispered in his ear and wriggled in his arms, laughing. Then, with a little assistance from him, she climbed up onto his shoulders, and from there, back onto the wires again. He stood underneath her, looking up between her legs. Jean-Claude stood behind Tanya, his chin just above her head and wrapped his arms around her middle, just under her breasts. The intimate contact felt amazingly right. Connecting with him sexually was what she wanted to do . . . and she knew it was going to happen tonight. But for now, she was willing to watch.

"Do you like my *tableau vivant*?"

"Is that what it's called?"

He brushed a warm kiss against her. "Yes. A living picture."

Tanya drew in her breath when the woman pulled aside her leotard, revealing a shaved pussy to her lover's ardent gaze. Okay, well, showgirls shaved. Nothing new about that.

The woman on the wire laughed and slid a finger between her labia, then touched it to her tongue.

Tanya hadn't been expecting *that*. Things were heating up fast.

"Do you want to watch?" Jean-Claude whispered.

She leaned against him. His cock was already stiff and it pressed against the small of her back. He held her closer still, and she enjoyed the feel of his muscular thighs against her soft ass.

Did this count as voyeurism? Did she care? She was sure the lovers in the ring weren't real. Three-dimensional, yes. But insubstantial. Definitely holograms. How nice of Jean-Claude to arrange an erotic after-dinner entertainment like this. "Yes," she whispered back.

The woman in the leotard balanced on one leg in an arabesque, stretching her arms out to the side and proudly thrusting out her breasts. The fine knit of her leotard showed her erect nipples to advantage and the strongman applauded. Then she came out of the position, setting a foot on each wire again. Even shaved, her labia didn't show much, pressed in too long, perhaps, by the tight leotard. Again she slipped a finger in between them, opening her sex in the same way the maid at the dinner table had played with the petals of the roses.

Hmm. Coming into the dining room and looking at the maid, Tanya had found the gesture sensual but not remembered the fleeting thought until this moment.

The acrobat bent her knees again and the strongman moved so that he could slip his tongue into her pussy. He thrust in and out, letting her bounce ever so slightly on the wire to take his tongue deeply inside her. She moaned with pleasure when he flicked the soft tip over her clit again and again. But in another minute she straightened, thrusting a fingernail through her leotard and unraveling it so that her bottom was bared too.

She turned around and flashed him, bending just enough so he could grab and squeeze her beautiful buttocks from behind while she pleasured herself with her fingers in front.

Tanya wondered how the woman could keep from coming. She didn't seem to be afraid of falling. Having sex on a tightrope came as naturally to her as walking. She watched the woman stand up again and step onto one wire with both feet, then slide down into a full split.

She's computer-generated, Tanya reminded herself. You could do it too if you were digitized.

The strongman just about licked his lips at the sight of the pretty acrobat. He steadied her on the wire by cupping her buttocks, and stared at the pussy that was stretched completely open, dark pink and juicy, before he got to work himself and made her come in his mouth. Once . . . twice.

Just what Tanya had been thinking about Jean-Claude doing to *her*. She was distracted by the acrobat's cry of joy at climax, and rapturous words of love in a language Tanya didn't understand. Not French. Who cared? The two were giving each other pleasure that any human being could comprehend.

The strongman kissed her between the legs one last time before she slid off, using his body for support. He turned around and then Tanya saw his erection. The tattered thing he wore barely contained the straining flesh.

The woman pulled down his scanty costume, and kneeled to lick his tight, heavy balls, fondling his buttocks and making him stand with his legs apart, stretching the fabric between his muscular thighs. She encircled his shaft with her fingers, then wrapped his hand around hers, sliding hers away to let him pump hard, waiting with open mouth for the first hot spurts.

It didn't take long. She stroked his scrotum as he gripped his cock, holding himself punishingly tight to make the strong sensation last. He moaned when he ejaculated, pulsing over her tongue. A few drops fell on her skin and she made him let go, closing her lips around him and sucking his cock, holding him tight in her loving mouth.

Shuddering, he balanced himself by holding on to her shoulders, taking deep breaths that hollowed his tense belly. He was beautiful. Tanya couldn't believe she was watching this, but she couldn't look away.

Jean-Claude released her and lightly, ever so lightly, cupped her breasts through the thin black material of her dress. He rubbed her nipples with his palms until she wanted to cry out with pleasure. But she couldn't. The couple in the ring might not be real, but their presence was most definitely felt.

Jean-Claude stopped what he was doing and dropped his

hands, clasping her just above the hips. All Tanya could think of was how it would feel to be naked, on all fours in his bed, being fucked from behind while he held her hard where he was holding her gently now, experiencing the deepest possible penetration.

"Thank you for sharing your fantasy, my dear Tanya," he whispered in her ear. "I am glad to be able to make it come true. Did you enjoy that show? The dancer on the wire and the strongman were amusing touches, I thought."

She turned around and gave him a startled look, remembering his words to her before they entered the tent. *You will be standing in the dark and watching them. As if they only existed in a dream. Your dream.*

"But I didn't share it. You must have—"

"Read your mind? Yes. We shared that *fantaisie*."

She blushed, feeling guilty. Not that she had anything to be guilty about, even if she had imagined oral sex with him. Six ways from Sunday. Had it been that obvious?

"Forgive me. I have perfected the ability over many years. My performers can improvise from very little—a few words, a fleeting image. And they are quite uninhibited. But none of what you saw is real."

"I figured that out. Cool trick. But let's get one thing straight: my mind is off limits."

"Why, if I may ask?"

The couple in the ring were caressing each other but Tanya suddenly wanted to slap him. "Because it's *my* mind. Not yours. Stay out of it." Being snapped out of an intensely sexual experience was bad enough. Finding out that her brain had literally been picked was worse.

"Very well. I do apologize. I only wanted to give you pleasure. And it is not as if all of your thoughts are an open book. But sexual desire is very easy to read."

Stirred up and angry with him, she gave him a scornful look, chiding herself for drinking so much wine and wondering whether he was crazy. Then, out of nowhere, another face came over his, like a transparent mask. The lion's face. The eyes looking through it were identical.

Tanya gasped and the apparition vanished. He was himself again. Handsome, rugged, exactly the same. Then the light in the tent went out. He took her hand and led her out of it as quietly as they had come in.

Some part of her wanted to pull away—and wanted to run. But she didn't. In the dark, out in the woods, she felt irresistibly drawn to him and that pull was much stronger. She was intrigued by the game he was playing, when it came right down to it, and very curious to find out what he would do next. But where he was taking her, she didn't know. The feel of the soft sawdust under her feet kept her on the path. She clung to his hand.

"Who are you?" she said in a whisper.

"Someone you have met before."

"I know we haven't."

"Allow me to explain—"

"Please do. I know those two weren't real, but the others—the trainer and those servants—what about them?"

He brought her to the edge of the field where she had groomed the lion. "Figments of my imagination also."

"Then where am I?"

"In another time. But you are safe here." He looked toward the chateau. Wreathed in mist, it was elegant—and eerie. A lit-up window on the ground floor radiated warmth, but all the others were dark. Was that the kitchen the housemaid had come out of with the little boy? She could always run there. But they were his servants. This was his house. She wasn't safe. Not with someone who could read her mind and make people appear when they weren't really there.

She turned to look at the tent. It too had vanished. Okay, so he could make things disappear too. She half believed in his magic and half didn't. Whatever. She was going to play along. His world, his rules.

"Is that why I didn't understand those two?"

He seemed reluctant to answer. "They talked in patois. Circus folk are from everywhere. Gypsies. Italians. Russians. Who knows what they say?"

She got the message: she couldn't communicate with anybody here. That wasn't good. It was night and she was alone with this guy. Reminding herself that she had been alone with the lion only a few hours before and survived to tell the tale did not cheer her up. She stopped and yanked her hand out of his. "Wait a minute. Is my Now your Then? What year are we in?"

"It doesn't matter. You would not believe me if I told you."

He folded his arms across his chest and waited for her to argue with him. She didn't want to. Damn and double damn. What the hell was going on? Never mind the wine she'd downed. Chalk it up to Jean-Claude's psychological acumen and intense animal magnetism. She could see *that* in his eyes. The transparent face of the lion? Blame that on the moonlight. Somewhere not far off she heard a lonely, deep-chested roar.

Tanya took a deep breath. "Let's begin at the beginning. I was picked up at the airport by—by someone who drove me here. In a limousine."

He shrugged. "I avail myself of modern conveniences when I can. And I could not send a coach and four to fetch you from Paris, my dear Tanya."

"I guess not. So you live in another time but—hey, you e-mailed me. I haven't seen a computer since I got here. How did you do that?"

He raised an eyebrow as if that were a very stupid question. "I have a laptop."

Of course. No doubt he kept it locked up in a Louis XIV armoire, next to his crystal inkwell and quill pen. She couldn't find the words to ask another question, although her mind was buzzing with them. What she had heard so far was beyond comprehension.

Jean-Claude gave a deep sigh. "The lion and I—"

She caught a flash of gold in his gaze and held up her hand. "Hold it right there. I saw the lion's face appear over yours. What was that all about?"

Jean-Claude smiled sadly. "He is my Other."

2

"I float in time and so does he. It might be more accurate to say that I am caught in its flow. I have not figured out how to escape."

Tanya felt a chill come over her at the desperate calm she heard in his voice. "What does the lion have to do with it?"

"He too is caught. In our youth we gamboled upon the lawns of this chateau. A cub and a child, without a care in the world. He was kept here, in a menagerie that no longer exists. I—I was the son of the duke who built this chateau centuries ago."

"That makes you"—she hesitated—"practically ancient." She looked him up and down. He was in great shape for a really, really old guy.

"Yes."

"I feel like I should curtsey. I mean, your father was a duke and your mother was a duchess—"

"She was not," he said softly. "She was a Bedouin, captured on the ninth crusade by my father."

"Uh-huh." Tanya tried to remember what she knew about

the Crusades. Not much. "You still haven't explained the lion part."

"Her tribe traveled in caravans. One day her kinsman killed a lioness in the grassy lands of Africa and my mother, a young and beautiful widow whose baby had died of a sudden fever, took pity on the tiny cub they found by the lioness's body. She suckled it at her own breast."

Tanya just stared at him without replying.

"The cub struggled to live. Little by little it grew—equal measures of her magic and her mother love."

Her eyes got a little misty. This was quite a story. She wanted to hear more about the magic part, even if it couldn't possibly be true and this couldn't possibly be happening to hard-headed her.

"So. The caravan made its way to Jerusalem, not knowing that a battle raged there. My father claimed her—or abducted her. He would not say. I am sure that he was determined to possess her, unaware that she was a sorceress of genius. She cast a spell that made him love her, lion child and all. Some months later I was born."

"What a beautiful story. I don't believe a freakin' word of it."

"Nonetheless, it is true. Her final spell bonded the lion to me as a blood brother—and made us immortal. She thought of it as a blessing. To me, it is a curse."

Play along, play along. "Why?"

"Because I am lonely. The lion and I have no other kin. You, however, emanate an intriguing aura that makes me wonder. I have never felt as attracted to a female as I am to you. Why is that?" He cast an appraising look at her that made Tanya squirm.

"Beats me. I don't have a drop of lion blood," she said, swinging her high heels by the strap. "Just your standard seventh-generation Texas mix of Irish-German-Mexican-Scots-Hungarian-Basque-French- Czech genes. And that's only my mother's side."

"Tell me about the French relations. What was the family name?"

Tanya couldn't remember. Then it came to her in a scary flash. "I think it was . . . no. Couldn't be." She pressed her lips together in case she blurted out the name. Deslions.

He smiled very widely. "Of the lions. Forgive me for reading your mind again."

He had. He really had. There was no way he could have known that. She herself had only seen the name once, written in the huge old bible her mother kept in a locked chifforobe. "That doesn't mean anything."

Jean-Claude put his paws—*his hands, his hands, his hands*, she chanted silently—on his hips and stood with his muscular legs apart. The bulge in his pants was bigger than the strongman's. She wanted to touch it. Must be the moonlight. Must be madness.

"Come inside." He beckoned to her. "Come."

Tanya had a feeling she was about to be mounted. And not on the wall. In his bed. By him. Repeatedly. The call of the wild was echoing through her body, damn it.

"What are you afraid of? I will show you the painting of my mother suckling her two sons. It is very small—a miniature, on ivory. I keep it under lock and key in my study."

She shook her head. "More computer-generated imagery. That won't prove anything."

Jean-Claude only shrugged. "Come inside anyway. Your feet are bare and the grass is damp. You cannot sleep out here."

She looked at the shoes in her hand, wondering if it was possible to stun someone with a pair of discount-shoe-store high heels. They would probably fall to pieces. "Uh, no. I'm going back to New York. Tonight."

"And how will you get there?" he inquired.

"I have a round-trip ticket. I'll call a taxi—" She fell silent, realizing that she hadn't seen a vehicle with an internal combustion engine since the limousine had driven away.

Jean-Claude sighed. "As you wish. I will not keep you here against your will. You may return to your own time tomorrow."

"Do I have to say thank you?"

"No. But I shall miss you. You are a unique woman, Tanya— and extraordinarily beautiful. You could stay, you know. We might as well enjoy each other's company for a few more nights."

There was no doubt in her mind as to his meaning. Despite her misgivings, she was actually tempted. He was playing games with her mind, but they were extremely interesting games.

"My dear Tanya . . . if you were to grant my wish—I suppose it is too much to ask. Never mind."

"I don't grant wishes. I'm not a fairy. I'm a hairdresser. And by the way, even if I leave tomorrow, you still owe me for the entire week. I have a payroll to meet."

He smiled slightly and walked ahead with long strides. "Come into my study," he called over his shoulder.

"No way."

"It is where I keep my accounts—and my gold. A man caught in time accumulates far more than he needs. I shall pay you now and be done with it."

"It has to be modern money," she shouted after him. "Not ducats or doubloons or anything like that."

"They are worth much more than euros."

Humph. If he was right, she didn't want to be wrong. Her financial problems weren't going to go away without a big pile of money to throw at them. She followed Jean-Claude back to the chateau.

Tanya settled herself on a rococo chair, and watched him carelessly scoop a handful of gold coins out of a drawer in a desk. He put them into a small leather bag and handed the bag to her. She folded her hands around it and kept it in her lap.

"Take those to a dealer in antique coins. He will wonder how you came by them, but there is no tracing their provenance. Tell him whatever you like. They are worth a fortune and you will be a rich woman."

Rich. That would be the day. She hefted the leather bag and listened to the faint clink. "How do I know these aren't, um, chocolate coins wrapped in gold foil or something?"

"Trust me."

She didn't. It occurred to her that he would overhear the thought but that was his tough luck.

He smiled slightly. "I trust you, although you have not fulfilled your side of our bargain."

Tanya hesitated before answering. "I—I can stay the rest of the week. Fair is fair." The little bag of gold was reassuringly heavy. "But you have to stay out of my mind. Agreed?"

Jean-Claude inclined his leonine head. "Agreed."

"You still haven't explained everything."

"That may not be possible."

She leaned forward in the chair. "The thought-reading—can you teach me to do that?"

He laughed. "You don't need to learn. You are remarkably sensitive to others, my dear Tanya. Your touch stirred the lion to his soul—it was he who summoned me to meet you in the field, you know."

"Oh." She remembered the moment she had seen Jean-Claude, just standing there, tall, proud, and virile. Would it be so wrong to jump in and have a sexually satisfying fling?

She looked up when he coughed discreetly. Jean-Claude was studying her pensive face. "It seems my answer did not please you, Tanya. Very well, I will explain as best I can. The thought-reading is like"—he searched for the right words—"like listening to the clicks of a complicated lock one must open by stealth. It requires acute perception and great patience."

He rose and closed the desk drawer, pacing about the room with long strides, restless as a wild animal. "But I had time. The descendants of the duke continued to live in this chateau, and so did I, among them in various guises. The circus you saw is one of many. My lion brother and I created diversions and entertainments in each generation. No one ever knew that we could communicate in our own way, without words. But we did and we do. Words have many limitations, Tanya."

He fell silent, but only for a moment.

"Like my father, most of the members of my family were intelligent and highly educated, and invited the great and the brilliant here. And sometimes, when they wished to be amused, actors and musicians were invited as well, or artists to paint their portraits and delightful scenes. Naked nymphs in bosky settings, that sort of thing. My family looked down on creative people, but found them useful."

"The paintings are wonderful," Tanya said. She'd admired several in the halls.

"Thank you. A few of them are my own work. I have some talent as a painter."

"I'm not surprised," Tanya murmured. No doubt Jean-Claude had actually known Toulouse-Lautrec.

"When one is immortal, one has nothing but time. I know seven languages. I studied the rational sciences: physics, biology, mathematics. I read the texts of alchemists, stargazers, philosophers—"

He stopped pacing and stood for a moment before her. "Pythagoras and Plato believed in the transmigration of souls, you know."

Tanya knew good and goddamn well she had nothing to add to *this* discussion. "Pythagoras," she said pertly. "Didn't he invent geometry and the hootchy-koo of the hypotenuse?"

The corners of his mouth twitched with amusement. "Something like that."

"And as for Plato—enlighten me, Encyclopedia Man."

"He believed that the material world is only a shadow of the real world."

"Hmm. I wouldn't know."

Jean-Claude seemed lost in thought for a moment. "But the Greek philosophers never answered a certain question to my satisfaction."

"And what would that be?"

"Whether love was real. What do you think?"

Tanya had no idea. Seemed to her he oughta know the answer after seven or eight centuries of existence. She sure as hell hadn't figured it out in her one lifetime on earth. "I don't know."

"Would you like to find out?"

She held up both hands. "Whoa. I'm having enough trouble comprehending the time travel thing. Plus you might be just plain crazy."

He smiled faintly. "You are refreshingly honest. But everything you have seen and experienced here is real in its way."

Tanya shook her head. "Maybe. Maybe not."

He clasped her outstretched hands. Without thinking, Tanya turned her face up to his and he pressed a brief, unexpected kiss on her forehead. "There is an unknown universe within every mind, Tanya. Will you allow me to take you where you have never gone?"

Something clicked in her mind. She heard it distinctly. Was that the click he had talked about? "Will I be able to come back?" she whispered.

"Of course." His look pinned her to the chair. Her thin dress might as well have been invisible. He raked her with his golden gaze, arousing instincts she could not deny. "We are kindred spirits, but you are not my prisoner and never will be."

"Thanks. I think."

He smiled, brushing the back of his hand against her cheek. The light hair on it tingled against her skin. "You are blushing. Was my erotic circus too much for you?"

"No," she lied. "But I would like to know where the tent went. And where I'm going to go. I don't want to drift around in your imagination or your memory. I want to go back to New York eventually and I want to stay . . . me."

"Of course, my dear Tanya. I would not dream of altering your reality. I am only inviting you into my own, for however long you wish to stay." He still held her hands and he helped her to rise.

"Not long."

He let her go. "Very well. But will you be mine for just one night?"

Tanya could not look away from his penetrating gaze. "Y-yes."

3

Once the word was spoken, there was no taking it back—because she didn't want to. When she said yes, she meant yes. One night. Just one night. And she had a feeling it was going to be unforgettable.

Tanya followed Jean-Claude, a few steps behind, not because she was feeling submissive, but because she liked to watch men walk. Eloquent as this one could be, his body said more. His long legs strode in a sensual rhythm, with an earthiness that reminded her of how the lion had sauntered from the field, his tail swaying in a lordly way.

Jean-Claude's butt was beautiful and muscular. She could imagine him giving her maximum pleasure with each tightening thrust of his manly ass—how long had it been, anyway? She couldn't remember much about her lackluster dates in the last year, besides yawning through dull dinners and skipping the routine sex afterwards. The Big Bunny, her vibrator with the clit-stimulating wiggly ears, was a lot more reliable.

But Jean-Claude looked like the real thing and then some. And if she really was in another dimension and time—Tanya planned to do some serious snooping around tomorrow to find out—she might as well enjoy it. Talk about no-strings-attached sex. He wasn't going to be hanging around her apartment or salon expecting to be taken care of when she got back to New York.

With her bag of gold. She curled her fingers around the soft leather and let it thump against her thigh. Whatever happened, her employees were going to make out all right. Flash forward to the future—she would make out all right too. Maybe open a salon in the Virgin Islands or someplace warm, where she could live in a bikini.

Jean-Claude stopped in front of a closed door, and she bumped into him. Ahh. He was hard all over. She slipped her hands around his back and brushed her fingertips over his taut nipples, resting her cheek against the back of his linen shirt. He smelled wonderful—like hot, sensual, kissable man.

"Our lips have not touched."

Laughing, Tanya let him turn around in her arms. "You said you wouldn't read my mind."

"My darling, I did not. It was simply a statement of fact." He made up for lost time by bringing his lips to hers for a sensual exploration of her mouth. His hand caressed her cheek while he kissed her, then traced a stimulating line from her chin to the side of her neck to her nipple. He cupped her breast and squeezed, drawing her hips against him with the other hand.

It wasn't long before he moved from her hips to her ass, rubbing and stroking both round cheeks with abandon but keeping his hand on the outside of her silky dress. "No underwear? You looked so prim at dinner and sat so straight . . . ah, I should have followed my instincts and slipped my hand under your dress . . . like this!"

He let go of her breast and grabbed her bare bottom with both hands, lifting her off the floor so she was kicking in midair. She held on to him by his hair, smooching him lustily.

Jean-Claude kicked the door open—so much for his patience with locks, mental and actual, she thought—and carried her into the bedroom, throwing her onto the grand gilt bed.

She sank into a down cloud, her legs open and her dress flipped up, leaving her bare to the waist. He stared hungrily between her legs as he shucked his clothes. She admired the fine dark hair on his chest and the narrow trail it made down his torso to where his thick, stiff cock bobbed between his legs. The big balls beneath it nestled in dark curls that she longed to get her fingers in, tugging on it gently so she could nuzzle and lick and enjoy his male scent. Tanya arched and wriggled out of her dress.

On all fours.

He hadn't said it but she heard it. He wasn't going to wait for the blow job she planned to rev him up with. Not a problem. Tanya got on her hands and knees, swaying her hips, enticing him with the sight of her sex, moving up to the headboard to make room for him on the bed. He pounced, kneeling behind her to lick her labia, spreading her ass cheeks so he could really go in deep with his tongue.

It felt so good to be fucked with something that was simultaneously soft and hard. She rocked a little, pushing her behind into his face, as unashamed as an animal and well aware that she was arousing him to fever pitch. He moaned against her slick flesh, nipping her ass and rubbing a fingertip against her tight anus. It pulsed in response and he growled.

Then his laps and licks got faster, until he stopped and mounted her, pulling her hips back hard and filling her up with the biggest cock she'd ever had inside her. Tanya gave a guttural cry of pleasure.

Jean-Claude dropped his body over her back, holding himself up on one straight arm and curving a hand underneath to tease her nipples, then slap her breasts gently so they swayed and bounced with his thrusts.

His hand moved all over her. He seemed to love everything about a female body—the soft abundance of her breasts, the frothy curls of pubic hair, and most of all, her womanly behind. His excitement intensified. He grabbed her around the waist with both arms, slamming into her cushy ass, that huge cock parting her pussy lips, and pumping harder and harder.

He was fucking her fast now, biting her on the neck in a way that thrilled her. The power of the male body sliding over hers, giving her deeper penetration than she would have ever thought possible, was overwhelmingly sensual.

Jean-Claude's muscular belly suddenly tensed and his cock strokes grew quicker still as he groaned with lust, pushing her hair aside to nip at her vulnerable neck. He dug his nails into her skin as a slow pulsing seized his cock—she could feel it against her snug, juicy pussy. He rammed into her, bucking and writhing on her back, filling her with an explosion of creamy cum, crying out her name.

His hands slid down and found her clit, which he rubbed between two fingers, teasing its tip with skillful sensitivity until an amazing orgasm hit her hard. Her pussy tightened around his still enormously erect cock as he prolonged her climax, stroking her cum-slicked clit until she pushed her buttocks backward into him, wanting more, more, more.

Male, female, human, animal—Tanya no longer knew at that moment who or what she was, and she didn't care.

They were one. Slowly coming down from the height of sexual pleasure, they rocked on all fours, he over her, until she eased herself down on the bed. Jean-Claude followed, curving his big body around hers with the utmost gentleness, strong and protective. His warmth, his silken strength, his lovingness were too much for her. Tanya fell fast asleep, cradled in his arms.

* * *

She woke up because Jean-Claude was chewing gently on her ear and because the sun was coming in through the antique lace curtains.

"You animal," she whispered drowsily.

"Yes, I am," he said. "And a hungry one. What would you like for breakfast, my lioness?"

Tanya opened her eyes and looked down at her body. She was still human, no claws or fur or anything. Smelling very loved. "What are you having?"

"Haunch of antelope. Raw."

"Ugh."

"I spoke in jest. My breakfast has not varied for a hundred years. *Brioche, confit aux abricots, oeufs en beurre, jus,* and *café au lait.*"

"Oo la la. Have your imaginary servants send up a second order of that."

He rolled away from her and pulled on a long rope adorned with a silk tassel. Tanya heard a distant bell ring twice.

"They know the signal," he said, rolling back and curling around her again. "Breakfast for two, served in silence."

Tanya pouted. "Huh. So you have had women in your lair before."

He shrugged. "I did not know you would come into my life. My previous amours are numerous but they mattered very little to me. There is no need to be jealous."

She settled her head on the pillow and looked up at him. "Hug, please."

"What?"

"The only rational cure for irrational jealousy. Works like a charm."

He enfolded her in his strong arms and she sighed with pleasure. "So what's on the agenda for today?"

Jean-Claude kissed her tousled hair. "I thought we might

visit the lion first. You can continue the work you started. He spent most of yesterday admiring his reflection in the lily pond. The king of beasts is vain, you know."

"All right. Sounds like a plan."

A knock on the door made him whisk the sheet over their naked bodies. A manservant came in, not looking at them as he set a huge round tray on a square table, not making a sound. Jean-Claude dismissed him with a wave, and he left, closing the door behind him. Jean-Claude jumped out of bed, gloriously naked, and filled plates for both of them, handing her a bowl of café au lait to sip while she waited.

It was strong, richly flavored, and laced with cream, and so good she wanted to lap it up. She tipped the bowl up to drink it faster, giving herself a coffee-colored mustache. Jean-Claude laughed when he saw it and bent over the bed to lick it off her upper lip. Then he stuck his tongue in her mouth just for good measure.

"Mmm." She held out the bowl. "More, please."

He refilled her bowl and sat down with his own, but not before he set the filled plates on the bed. They devoured everything, getting a little crumby and sticky in the process. Tanya decided she didn't have to feel guilty about letting someone else clean up after her when the servants were only imaginary. She said as much to Jean-Claude, who found it amusing that she would feel guilty.

Then he sent her off to bathe in a swan-shaped porcelain tub hidden behind a screen. She turned the winged spigot and filled it with steaming water, stepping in as daintily as a marble goddess. He came behind the screen when her toe touched the water, patting her behind where it was pink from sitting through a luxurious breakfast in bed.

"Enjoy your bath. I will meet you outside when you are done."

She treated herself to a long soak, using lavender-scented soap and a soft cloth on her skin, although she was reluctant to wash away his scent. It soothed and stimulated her at the same time. Tanya realized how much she was going to miss him when she went back to New York. One night with him was definitely not enough.

Jean-Claude met her in the field, where the lion was strolling around, whiffing the breeze that ruffled through the trees. The tent and the performers had not reappeared, Tanya noticed. Fine with her. She wasn't sure if a real woman could ever compete with a fantasy female invented by a man, but she told herself that the pretty acrobat in last night's erotic encounter belonged to the strongman, not Jean-Claude.

She adjusted the strap of the bag slung over her shoulder, filled with brushes, combs, and beads, hoping the lion would behave as well today as he had yesterday. The trainer was nowhere to be seen, but if the lion was Jean-Claude's brother, she figured his presence would be enough to keep the animal calm.

The lion sprang up onto a square-shaped rock just big enough to hold it, although its paws draped over the front. "He looks like the New York Public Library lions on 42nd Street," she called to Jean-Claude.

"Indeed he does."

She walked up to him and slipped her hand in his. "Have you seen a picture of them?"

"Not a picture. I visited New York decades ago with the lion. He wished to meet his stone brethren and I was inclined to oblige."

Tanya nodded. "You mentioned that he was lonely."

"Yes."

She thought about it for a moment. "But how much fun can a stone lion be?"

"Ah. You would be surprised. There is blood in their marble veins. The library lions are alive in their own way, although they cannot leave their pedestals. Such is the price of fame."

"Are you pulling my leg?" Tanya asked.

"Not at all. They like to watch the parades go by on Fifth Avenue, and see lovers meet on the steps. And they look out for those who only wish to enter the library and read in peace."

Tanya smiled. She loved the famous library lions and it was easy to imagine that everything he said was true. She had stood by the south statue during the last Veteran's Day parade, watching the soldiers, young and old, march by.

"I saw the oldest marchers nod to the lions," Jean-Claude said. "Some wave. Such men are closer to the next world and know that each year's parade may be their last."

"Do the lions nod back?" Her tone was light, but Tanya was touched. She knew what he meant about those old soldiers. Marching bravely on, more in remembrance of their fallen companions than for their own glory, and fewer of them each year.

"Always," Jean-Claude replied.

She stood on tiptoes to kiss him on the cheek. The lion turned his noble head in their direction, his eyes bright and golden. "Look at you," she called to him. "Your mane is a mess. Do I have to comb it out all over again?"

The lion nodded gravely as they walked toward the rock he sat on.

"Holy cow. He understands."

"Of course, my dear. He is rather better at mind-reading than I am, and he has a superior sense of smell. I am sure he knows exactly what we did last night."

They stopped at the base of the rock. Tanya reached up and tentatively patted one mighty paw. "Don't tell, okay?"

"Who would he tell?"

It hit her again that she was in another time and place, and very, very far from home. But with Jean-Claude by her side, that didn't seem to matter at all.

He motioned for the lion to jump down. It obeyed, landing with an almost noiseless thump that shook the ground all the same. Tanya was thrilled to find herself looking straight into his eyes, and only a few feet away. The lion closed that little distance, though, padding over to her and rubbing its gigantic head against her shoulder, catlike, and ridiculously friendly. She stumbled against Jean-Claude, who told the animal to stop.

The lion yawned disrespectfully and strode past him. For a moment Tanya wondered if the two would engage in a brotherly tussle on the grass. Strong as he was, Jean-Claude wouldn't win that one. But the lion circled around him and settled down in front of her. Tanya opened up her styling bag.

Even though his mane was mussed, it was in much better shape than yesterday, and she was able to begin beading the locks she twisted gently between her fingers. Jean-Claude stretched out on his side to watch her, twirling a stem of clover between his fingers. The lazy sensuality of his powerful body was something to see, and the memory of last night's blazing sex made her feel pleasantly hot for him again.

A few hours later she was done and her bag was nearly empty. She'd used hundreds of beads but the effect was spectacular. The crystal beads in the lion's mane caught the sunlight and sparkled as if the animal had come down from the starry heavens to strut his stuff on earth.

Just for the hell of it, she took a big mirror from her bag and held it in front of him. The lion squinted down his nose when he looked into it, and Jean-Claude laughed. "My brother, you are magnificent. But not when your eyes are crossed."

Looking annoyed, the lion got up and walked away, switching his tail.

Tanya laughed too. "Now what?"

"Now we bring back the tent."

"We?"

Jean-Claude scrambled to his feet and brushed bits of grass and clover from his clothes. "Are we not partners in this fantasy?"

Aww. She felt honored. "If you say so."

"I am hoping that our sexual energy will inspire fresh creativity."

Whatever, she thought, smiling at him. Tanya kneeled to tuck her brushes and gear back into the bag and slung it over her shoulder. He reached out a hand to help her up and they walked from the field, watching the tent rise up from nowhere, its poles topped with bright pennants as before.

Magic time. Ordinary life was never going to be the same after having this much supernatural fun. She heard the shouts of people inside—Jean-Claude had conjured up many more this time.

They went down the sawdust path and he held open the flap. As before, the performers didn't seem to hear or notice them. There were gymnasts—men, stripped to the waist, spanking excess chalk from their strong hands—and acrobats, mostly female, with supple bodies that she envied.

The lion had entered ahead of them, and a slender woman, Chinese, with flowers in her black hair, was riding on his back. Following them was a juggler dressed in motley colors, throwing rings in arcs above his head, not even looking as each ring seemed to return obediently to his catching hand. The arcs became higher and higher—certainly high enough to touch the tent, Tanya thought, which wasn't as large as modern ones. With a start, she watched the flying rings pass through the fabric of the tent's top without tearing it and come back down again. It was a very clever illusion—or just plain magic.

Each person the lion passed admired his beaded mane, toying with the beaded braids that Tanya had woven. He nodded regally to all, making the beads click rhythmically with each soft step he took. The Chinese woman slid off his back when he completed a circle of the inner ring and stood on her tiptoes to scratch him between the ears.

She couldn't reach. A muscular gymnast came over and lifted her by the waist to make it easier, and the lion closed his eyes, enjoying the delicate scratching, a blissful grin on his face. The gymnast set her down and she vanished in a puff of smoke and flower petals. The lion sneezed and a flower petal settled on his broad nose.

"Hey, that was adorable. Bring her back."

Jean-Claude shook his head. "Later, perhaps. I have in mind something darker—and more intense. Our bedsport has been gentle but I suspect you have a wild side."

Her eyebrows went up. "Wild? Who, me? Look, just because I got on all fours for you doesn't mean that—"

Jean-Claude patted her thigh. "Do not take offense. I have been working on an entertainment for a rich fellow who worships women and wishes to be thoroughly dominated by one. As before, the participants are imaginary and we are only spectators."

Tanya settled into a plush velour seat that tipped back slightly. "Rough play, huh? Sounds kinky. But I'm starving. Think you could conjure up a hot dog, popcorn, and cotton candy first?"

He made a face.

"Oh, don't go all French and snooty on me. Junk food is part of going to the circus."

Jean-Claude snapped his fingers and a basket appeared on the bench.

"Good going," she said. "What's in it?"

He didn't answer her for a moment, looking out over the troupe of performers absent-mindedly, as if he were figuring out which one he wanted to do what. She touched his shoulder and repeated her question.

"Hmm? Oh, cheese and bread. And chocolates. Pears. Champagne."

"Well, can't complain about that." She opened the lid of the basket. "This stuff looks tasty."

Jean-Claude nodded absent-mindedly, watching the circus performers mill around. He was communicating silently with each one, evidently, because most of them faded away into the shadows, along with the lion, until only three were left: two male gymnasts and a female acrobat. She was dressed, if you could call it that, in a black leather strappy thing that reminded Tanya of a Karl Lagerfeld creation.

The men stepped into an open cube about ten square feet, made of thin steel rods, facing each other on opposite sides with arms and legs stretched out and hanging on for dear life. With a flamboyant gesture, the woman signaled an unseen someone to lift the cube far above the ring. It hung there, spinning slowly, as if it had been drawn in space, an illustration of geometry and perfect human proportion.

"No net?" Tanya whispered.

"Have you forgotten that they are imaginary?"

"Oh, right." Still, the men looked incredibly real, with straining muscles in their arms and legs as their hands clutched the rods and their toes gripped them.

Another snap of Jean-Claude's fingers and the men's gym pants vanished, leaving them completely naked, their big cocks and balls clearly visible between their spread legs. Neither man was erect, but the sight was impressive enough to make Tanya suck in her breath. Jean-Claude looked down at her and smiled slightly.

"To your taste, mademoiselle?"

Tanya nodded. Her eyes widened when the cube revolved, giving her a look at each man's magnificent tight ass and the back view of what they had between their legs. Jean-Claude sat down beside her.

"Good. And now for the woman." He pointed up. The acrobat was coming down from on high, standing on a platform, unstrapping the black leather outfit to expose her breasts and buttocks. She held a many-tailed whip, Tanya noticed. Jean-Claude really was going to kink things up. No wonder this was adults only.

The cube revolved in mid-air and the woman inspected each man in turn, touching the buttocks of each with the handle of her whip as they passed in front of her. Looking at one another, then at the lovely dominatrix, the men got erect fast. Their cocks jutted out and their balls no longer swayed between their legs.

"They cannot pleasure themselves, you see," Jean-Claude whispered. "If they let go, they will fall. So they must submit to milady's will."

The cube stopped and one man was before the woman. Tanya saw the muscles in his back ripple with tension. He had no way of knowing when the dominatrix would begin, save to look in his partner's eyes . . . which widened when the whip licked through the air. The man in front of her took the lash on his buttocks without a sound at first, standing strong and scarcely flinching under each stripe. The other man watched intently, his gaze moving from his partner's face to the stiff cock that grew stiffer with each lash.

The man being whipped was shiny with sweat, his powerful body trembling with the strange pleasure he was being given. He moaned, hanging on to the rods, tensing his buttocks when his cock began to throb uncontrollably, ejaculating in a white spray that fell into the darkness below the cube.

Tanya sat forward in her seat. The cube revolved again, and the second man took his punishment like the first, begging the woman to give him more and do it harder. He too quickly climaxed under the whip, much to her satisfaction. Exhausted, they clung to the rods while the dominatrix was lifted on a wire, then let down between them in the middle of the cube.

She wound a leg around the wire and grabbed their cocks, one in either hand, rough and ready. Jean-Claude narrowed his eyes, Tanya saw, focusing mentally. The men again became erect, and the woman lowered herself on the wire so that she could take one cock in her mouth and the other in her pussy. She swung between them with skill, working the huge cocks of her submissive lovers for her own pleasure, in an erotic rhythm that didn't quit. Tanya was totally turned on. This was one hell of a show.

From somewhere came music—a heavy, throbbing beat that didn't quit either. Jean-Claude pulled her onto his lap, facing out toward the trio in midair. Tanya felt his hands slide up inside her top and arched her back, craving hot nipple play. He didn't have to take his cock out and she didn't have to get undressed. Straddling his thigh would do just fine. He seemed to know instinctively what she wanted and leaned back so she could ride his leg.

She watched the woman and the two men, who flashed in and out of her field of vision. Tanya squirmed in Jean-Claude's lap, pressing her pussy against his thigh as he reached around to tug at her nipples. The dominatrix reached climax seconds before she did, banging her bottom hard against the man with his cock buried in her pussy and letting go of the other one.

Tanya gasped and hit that high herself.

4

Jean-Claude stroked her back, letting her calm down a little before he turned her around halfway, still on his lap but resting against his chest. Tanya pressed her thighs together to stop them from trembling, still excited by the erotic act he had created out of thin air just for her. That hadn't been on *her* mind. Was it his hidden desire? Did her masterful lover secretly enjoy being whipped?

"No, my darling—ah, forgive me. I promised not to read your thoughts but I picked them up before I could help myself. My client will enjoy this trio. Your uninhibited response is proof enough of that."

Tanya had to wonder where her inhibitions had gone. She didn't seem to have a single one where he was concerned.

"Shall we invent another scene? Theme and variations?"

We again. She supposed she could change careers. Explaining to her parents that she was going to (a) move to France to live in a chateau and (b) fall in love with a time traveler and (c) manage an erotic circus would be a challenge. Her dad, the nicest guy in the world, might even look up over his newspaper.

Fall in love? Whoops. Had she really thought that? She looked up into Jean-Claude's soulful eyes and patted his cheek. He hadn't mentioned it again after his brief speculation on the subject.

Could happen, though. She knew that instinctively. He might very well be the one. Meaning *the* One. Because she didn't do anything halfway.

"Is something the matter?" Still cuddling her, Jean-Claude reached for the basket and took out a pear. He turned it around in his hand and took a bite, munching it thoughtfully. "You did not eat."

"Well, no. I was a little, uh, distracted."

He smiled. "Good."

Tanya sat up. "I didn't eat. And you didn't come."

Jean-Claude shook his head and finished the pear. "I can wait."

Flushed with happiness, Tanya got up and stretched. He ran an appreciative hand over the curving shape of her waist when her top rose and bared her middle. "Ah, my dear, you are woman incarnate. So sensual. So alive."

"Worship me. Go ahead. I like it."

He sat up and nuzzled her belly, making her laugh. "A giggling goddess. Tanya, Tanya . . . you were meant for me."

She stroked his thick, dark hair. "Speak into the bellybutton, please. And tell our studio audience how you feel."

He stuck the tip of his tongue into it and made her laugh even more. "Come. Let us go back to the chateau. There is a room I would like you to experience."

"And why is that?"

"You will see."

Tanya tiptoed in. The walls were covered with paintings—original paintings, not wallpaper, and probably worth a fortune. Figures from classical mythology, naked nymphs and nude youths, mingled with fine ladies in period silk gowns and their amorous lovers in imaginary gardens. It was a room made for love.

Every detail radiated tenderness, right down to the dewdrops on the painted leaves. The lovely women on the walls rested dainty hands on the thighs of their swains, who all seemed about to burst out of their breeches. The contrast with the darkly sexual scene they had just witnessed was extraordinary.

Tanya spotted a lion in the background of one, led by a nymph, by a pink ribbon around its neck. It had a slightly foolish expression, and its golden eyes seemed to be staring at the nymph's bare bottom. An amusing touch, as Jean-Claude would say.

Tanya had a feeling that he had designed this room himself, although she knew he hadn't painted it. The signature of the artist was one she remembered from the Frick, the most exclusive museum in New York, where paintings very like these adorned the walls of a room of their own.

But that room didn't have a bed like this, a spun-sugar fantasy of white lace and linen within the framework of a four-poster fit for Madame Maintenon. Like the paintings, like the room, made for love.

Jean-Claude stayed near her, not saying anything, letting her enjoy the art and the suggestive scenes within each panel. Tanya looked up at his handsome face. With his long hair drawn back and his old-fashioned clothes, he was raffish and elegant as the noblemen in the paintings. She looked down. Yes, he was erect. Undoubtedly picking up her response to the paintings but too sneaky to say so.

Without saying a word, he undressed her and carried her to the bed, setting her down in the middle of all that white. Tanya felt like she was floating on a cloud. Sweet. She watched him undress, longing to make love to him face to face this time. Naked at last, his hair untied, he turned his back to her, looking for something in an armoire—oh, my. He had lengths of silk in his hands.

"May I tie you? I want to pleasure you with my mouth and my body, but only with gentleness. It is the most incredible sensation, my darling Tanya. Allow me."

His voice was soft and sensual, and the hints of gold in his eyes shimmered under his downcast lashes. His hair spilled over his shoulders, a glorious dark sheen in it. "Yes," was all she said, spreading her legs far apart so that her toes nearly touched the bedposts. Slowly she reached over her head, extending her arms.

He savored the pleasure of tying her up, wrapping each wrist and ankle in silken bonds. Tanya couldn't move. She didn't want to. Exposed and bound, her body ached for the tender release she knew he would provide. Jean-Claude moved to the bed and bent over her, caressing her body in long strokes, his hands warming her skin. He parted her labia and looked long and lovingly at her there, running his fingers easily through her curls. Then he came over her, his head between her legs and his cock over her face. She couldn't move up to suck or lick him, and she knew he didn't want her to.

But he did want her to look. A dominant male, proud of what he had. And he had reason to be. Feeling his lips brush her labia and draw her clitoris into his mouth, she admired the huge, silky-hot cock and heavy balls that had given her so much pleasure her first time with him. Jean-Claude began . . . and proved to be a master of oral loving, bringing her close to climax within minutes, then pausing to nip the inside of her spread thighs, making her tremble.

He let her rest. And he started all over again. Tanya was wild with lust and something else that his subtle lovemaking unleashed deep within her. She strained against her bonds, and he stopped what he was doing to release her, slowly and surely. His deliberate expertise made every sensation that much stronger.

Tanya grabbed his shoulders when her hands were freed, pulling his head to her breasts, making him suck and suck until the feeling almost made her come.

But she needed his cock for that to happen. He knew. Gazing into her eyes, he moved her hand to his shaft, looking at her while she stroked it, murmuring words of ardent desire in French. She didn't understand it, but she didn't have to. She knew why it was called the language of love.

He released her ankles, rubbing them one at a time in his strong hands, rubbing her feet and kissing her toes. He lifted up her legs to her shoulders and tied her hands to her thighs. Then he buried his face in her pussy once more, giving her a lascivious tongue-fucking but staying away from her throbbing clit. She couldn't touch it. Couldn't touch him.

Moaning, she held her legs up, presenting her sex for his erotic delectation. He continued to pleasure her, but with his fingers now, eyes on her face, smoothing her sweat-soaked hair away from her cheeks as he thrust deeply again and again, touching her womb with infinite gentleness and pulling out slowly. "Feel me inside you, darling. Let me love you. Open to me."

"I—I want to come," she gasped.

"Not yet."

At last he stopped, touching fingers slick with her juice to his lips and then to hers. She licked her lips, and he kissed her, lingering long enough for her to calm down.

He sat up and stroked her thighs, pausing to untie her hands. She was finally completely free—and she was weak with desire. Tanya reached out her arms to him, and he came to her, touching his cock to her swollen, deeply stimulated pussy and making her wait for it a little longer still.

She clawed at his shoulders, at his buttocks, thrusting her hips up against his with a cry of wild desire. He was in her. Physically and emotionally.

"So . . ." he whispered. "Rough or tender. Fast or slow. Whatever you want, I will give it to you. Now and forever. Be mine. Be mine."

Intense sensations pulsed through her, opening her soul. Tanya moaned, lost in the feeling that he was the one. The only one. And she wanted him for always, as crazy as it was.

"Yes," she whispered. "Oh, yes. . . ."

They kissed again, long and deep, and she surrendered to his tenderness, almost wanting to cry as he stroked her hair back and touched his lips to her closed eyes. Jean-Claude nibbled lightly on her ear and Tanya heard a soothing growl that made her smile. She slowly came back to reality—the sweetest, most sensual reality she had ever known.

"Ah, you are lovely," he whispered. "But I fear I am asking for too much, too soon."

She sighed deeply and he rose halfway, bracing himself on his elbows. Tanya gazed up at him, loving the warm look of satisfied desire in his eyes. "Um. Maybe you are. But do we have to talk about it now?"

"No." He dropped his head to the side of her neck, biting lightly and growling again, louder, until she giggled.

"Do whatever you want. Just don't stop," she murmured.

Jean-Claude gave her a wicked grin. "Are you quite sure? Are you in the mood for an amorous adventure, my love? We need never leave this chateau to see . . . well, some things you may never have seen."

"Is that right? Don't forget I live in New York. I'm kinda hard to shock." She looked up at him, smiling just as wickedly.

"Hmm. I must confess, I have had many more affairs than most men. It was as good a way as any to pass the time."

Tanya wriggled out from underneath him and stretched lazily. "I don't care. Just so long as I know I'm the most beautiful, most intelligent, and most desirable of all."

He shot her a quizzical look. "But you are."

"Really?" She couldn't keep the cynicism out of her voice. "And I thought fairy tales were hard to believe. But I do like this one so far. Great interior decoration—"

He drew her to him and held her close, then nodded at the figures on the painted walls. "They have been observing us."

Startled, Tanya realized that the nymphs and shepherds and lords and ladies had changed positions. Their eyes were too bright to be painted, with a lively depth and sparkle that betrayed their interest in what Jean-Claude and Tanya had been doing. "Hey, no fair. You didn't tell me sex with you was going to be a spectator sport."

He kissed her hair. "I cannot always predict what these phantasms will do. I have not seen them move for, oh, perhaps a century."

"You mean you haven't had sex for a hundred years?"

"Ah—not in this room."

Tanya thumped him on the chest, not wanting to know much more about his amorous adventures, as he called them. He caught her by the wrist and kissed her hand, paying particular attention to each fingertip with his tongue. "Don't try to distract me, Jean-Claude. It won't work."

"Shhh." His voice was soothing. "They have forgotten about us. We can watch them now. It was the fashion then for noblewomen to play at being shepherdesses and dally with rustics. Ah, there is Chérie with a strapping young fellow—she preferred her lovers to be of considerable size in every way."

"I see what you mean," Tanya said in a soft voice. Chérie's man was hung like a horse and his erection was rarin' to go. "Wait a minute—why am I whispering? Can they hear me?"

He shrugged. "I do not think so. They are back in their world and time."

Tanya propped her head up on her hands and got comfortable, as Jean-Claude stretched out by her, warm and naked, and already semi-erect again. The feel of his swelling cock against her hip was quite pleasant and Tanya felt the stirrings of arousal deep inside her.

"Wait a minute—who is that watching Chérie? He sure looks like you."

Jean-Claude nodded. "It is me. Chérie loved to tease me by letting another man fuck her thoroughly while I watched from some hidden place."

Tanya twisted around to look at him. "So this is your version of X-rated home video. Do you know what happens when those things get posted on the Internet?"

He slapped her on the ass and Tanya yelped, even though it felt good. "What happens in the chateau stays in the chateau. Is that not what you Americans say?"

She turned back to watch the trio. "You really do get around."

Chérie was as pretty as a china shepherdess, adorned in a close-fitting bodice of pink silk, tied like a corset with criss-crossing black ribbon. The tight lacing made her breasts pop up. Her pink nipples were visible and she pinched them both, making them even longer, cock-teasing her big lover for all she was worth. He stared at her hungrily.

Tanya glanced at the Jean-Claude on the wall, who looked—um, not as interested in Chérie as the other guy was. More like he had done this before and enjoyed it well enough.

She strutted and preened, sweeping up her fancy skirt to show her man her bare ass. He reached for it and she slapped him playfully.

Okay, this was back when a big behind on a woman was all the rage, Tanya thought a little wistfully. Chérie was proud of what she had, and there was plenty of it. She waved her hand in an imperious gesture—so much for the shepherdess routine—and her big buck lowered his breeches. His enormous cock stood at stiff attention, stroked by her with a skillful hand. She gently stretched the tight foreskin down past the swollen head, and he gasped. Jean-Claude sighed—her Jean-Claude, not the one on the wall—as Chérie kneeled down, hoisting her skirts high to keep showing off her ass.

Others in the scene gathered in the shadows to watch as her wet pink tongue flicked over the head of his cock, darting into the hole and swirling around as the man she was blowing struggled to keep his balance. She cupped his balls, squeezing repeatedly and continuing to stroke and suck until he cried out and ejaculated on her bared bosom.

Chérie stayed kneeling as she rubbed the hot, creamy drops into her skin, resting her head against his thigh while he steadied her with one hand and slowly got his breath.

Tanya looked again at the Jean-Claude on the wall. *That* had gotten to him—he strode out from his hiding place, looking half-angry and half-aroused.

"That is how she liked me to be," he explained in a low voice to Tanya.

"Okay. Whatever."

The Jean-Claude on the wall pulled Chérie to her feet, protesting the interruption, then told her to get on all fours. With a very sensual pout, she promptly obeyed, and he straddled her, facing the other man. Bending down, placing both his hands on her bare buttocks, Jean-Claude spread her wide.

Her submissive posture and the sight of her plump, juicy cunny made her lover's cock throb and swell. But he would have to wait. Jean-Claude was spanking her ass and Chérie cried out with delight, shamelessly thrusting her bottom up for more of what he was giving her until he forced her back down on her knees again.

Jean-Claude kneeled in front of her and undid his breeches, good and hard from the pleasure of administering a spanking to a willing, wanton woman. His lovely Chérie took his thick length into her mouth, sucking greedily. The man she'd been pleasuring dropped to his knees too, and rammed his cock into her without waiting for permission from anybody, pounding hard against her soft ass and making her shake.

Tanya felt the real Jean-Claude press his hugely stiff erection into her side and slide it against her smooth skin. He seemed to be willing to wait and watch the show—oh, hell. He knew how it turned out.

But she didn't. As the men on the wall vigorously pleasured Chérie, Tanya wondered what would happen next. The other figures in the rustic scene watched also, sexually stimulating each other in a hundred different ways. Fingers probed between trembling legs, breasts were bared and buttocks squeezed as soft cries of lovers echoed in the room . . . where before there had been only the two of them. She marveled at the sight.

Both Jean-Claudes sighed at the same time. Tanya gave hers a soft kiss, slipping her tongue between his lips and deepening it. His eyes closed and so did hers—and by the time she looked back at the wall, the men were standing, their pants half-fastened. But Chérie was entirely naked and swinging on a narrow plank suspended from twining roses.

"That can't possibly hold her," she whispered. "She's a big, healthy girl."

Jean-Claude smiled against her cheek. "With big, healthy buttocks. Oft immortalized in verse, you know. A court poet wrote a famous ode to Chérie's beautiful derrière."

"I don't doubt it."

Chérie swung back and forth, her bare breasts bouncing. As the Jean-Claude on the wall watched, his arms crossed over his broad chest, her other lover pushed her to and fro, obviously enjoying the chance to fondle her behind with every fro and to. She kicked her shapely legs to help him out, spreading very wide so everyone got a look at her pussy, fringed with soft curls and juicy from being fucked so nicely.

A young woman stepped out from the crowd and Jean-Claude

caught her eye. He stopped the swing with one strong arm and nodded to her to come forward. She licked her lips at the sight of Chérie's most intimate flesh, and began by pressing tender kisses to the inside of her soft thighs. The other man used the swing to push Chérie into the young woman's mouth, tiny pushes that made her moan with delight.

Encouraged by the watchers, the young woman thrust her tongue deep into Chérie, again and again, pausing only to nip at her labia while Chérie hung on to the swing's ropes and let her head drop back. Her shimmering hair fell in waves nearly to the ground. Jean-Claude let the other man steady the swing as he lifted the skirts of the young woman who was performing cunnilingus on Chérie. Her buttocks were bare but she wore stockings held by beribboned garters, an added enticement that made her round behind look even more tempting. He couldn't take his eyes off it and his breeches came down again in about a red-hot second.

"Like it from the back, don't you?" Tanya murmured. "You animal."

He chuckled softly. "Indeed."

The Jean-Claude on the wall finger-fucked the woman first, getting her ready for his thick cock. Tanya could see the veins on it, throbbing just under the heated skin, painted with artistic precision—and she could feel them for real against her side as her Jean-Claude adjusted his position. His balls were tight and up, hot on her skin under his long shaft.

The man holding the swing braced himself and his luscious passenger for Jean-Claude's first thrust. He slid in as the woman bent forward and the quartet moved with practiced ease, sucking, pushing, thrusting with abandon. Jean-Claude's muscular belly tightened against the woman's behind as he sank deeply into her, growling and digging his nails into her soft flesh. Her tongue worked faster on Chérie's hungry cunny, flicking near the clitoris until Chérie grabbed the ropes and lifted her ass off the swing, craving to be sucked to orgasm. The other man cupped her lifted buttocks in his big hands and began to squeeze them as the standing woman, fucked harder still by Jean-Claude, took Chérie's clitoris in her mouth and sucked it in little pulses.

Tanya squirmed on the bed, totally turned on by the show. But it wasn't a show. It was something that had happened, however long ago, and that made it almost real.

Jean-Claude nuzzled her hair and ran a hand over her back. His touch was electrifying. "Ah, it is sweet to see the pleasure that women can give each other," he whispered into her ear.

Tanya didn't feel like arguing. But it was the men in this scene who were doing it for her. Jean-Claude's big rod was slick with pussy juice—she glimpsed it every time he pulled back almost all the way, teasing his lover with the sensation of the swollen head between her labia. He thrust a finger into her, folding his hand into a fist so he could get in all the way, and pulled it out, slicker and wetter than his cock. With just his fingertip, he touched the tight puckers of her anus, easing inside when she lifted her head from Chérie's pussy. The woman looked over her shoulder and nodded, excited by the sensation of him in her little hole too.

Piqued, Chérie caught the woman's hair and forced her mouth between her legs. She wrapped her thighs around the other woman's neck and back at it they went. The quartet reached climax at almost the same time: Chérie first, screaming; then her woman lover, pushing back to take it and give it hard and fast; then Jean-Claude as a pulsing pussy around his cock and tender little anus around his finger proved too much for his self-control; and then last of all Chérie's big buck, coming in his breeches, spurting uncontrollably and wetting the front.

Tanya was writhing on the bed without knowing it, until Jean-Claude got on his knees behind her and swiftly scooped her up with one arm around her hips. He spread her fully but he didn't ram in. No, he kneeled to worship her swollen, tight labia with his tongue, licking up every drop and making her more excited when he did. His soft breath warmed the inside of her thighs—he seemed to be relishing the female smell of her. He bit her buttocks with sensual skill, finding the right places to nip and then press soothing kisses to the spot.

She closed her eyes, moaning and rocking on all fours, aware only of him. The erotic tableau faded from her memory in an instant. There was only his body, his cock, touching her labia. There was no need for him to separate them, but he penetrated her carefully. The silky-hot head went in and then he stopped. Tanya imagined him looking down at her pussy, the head of his cock swelling her labia, the hot shaft behind it sticking out straight from his body into hers—but just an inch. She begged him for all of it but he stayed where he was, resting his strong hands on her buttocks and waiting. The desire built and built within her body, yet she held still.

"Do you want me, my love?"

She didn't remember saying yes. But she said it over and over when he was suddenly deep inside her, possessing her completely, making her cry out—wild for him. Totally wild.

5

There was more to come in the next few days. With uncanny ease, Jean-Claude moved with her back and forth in time, through the many rooms of his chateau. At his silent command, the servants appeared and whatever need they had—food, drink, baths—was fulfilled.

She glimpsed his Other through the centuries, regal and proud wherever he was, but with a look of faint sadness in his eyes. But then the lion didn't get much in the way of loving, at least not from his own species. Jean-Claude said he had arranged for a lioness to visit now and then, but there were few to be had in France.

Right now they were curled up in another bed, idling away the afternoon with conversation. She'd seen the lion that morning, but only for a moment, being groomed by the stocky trainer she'd met the first day. "You know, your brother still looks lonely. Have you ever thought of sending him back to Africa?"

Jean-Claude shook his head. "How would he survive? He has grown accustomed to having his meat served on a silver platter."

"But don't lionesses sort of do that anyway? They hunt, not the males. As far as I know, lions sit around a lot and try to look magnificent. Whoever has the biggest mane gets the girl."

Jean-Claude laughed. "Then, my dear Tanya, you may be the best thing that ever happened to my lion brother. His trainer told me that he spends hours gazing at his beads and braids."

"Uh-oh. Does he suck in his stomach too? Maybe he's having a midlife crisis. But he's immortal. It might never end."

He took her hands in his. "You have done your best. We must hope that he is happy enough. I know that I am."

Tanya snorted. "You got to fuck away the centuries. He didn't have that option."

"I amused myself," Jean-Claude said flatly. "What else was I to do? I never expected someone like you to come into my life. Seeing you was rather like seeing a unicorn. I was not quite sure you were real."

"Hmm. I think I'm becoming less real every day I'm here." Tanya rose from the bed in the medieval chamber, draping herself in a sheet of white linen dripping with handmade lace.

"How beautiful you look in white," Jean-Claude said softly. He rose up on one elbow and reached out a hand to her. "Come here."

Tanya avoided his gaze. "Not now. I hate to say this, but we do have to think about wrapping up this crazy affair. I gotta get back to New York eventually."

He fell back into the pillows, pulling the covers up over himself. "I don't want you to go."

"I have a life, you know. Just one."

Jean-Claude frowned. "I have lived a thousand lives. Too many."

"Don't knock it. You've had a lot of fun, pal. I'm sure you'll keep on going after I leave, come to think of it."

"Hmph."

She glanced his way. He was sulking, his arms crossed over his brawny chest. "I have responsibilities. I have employees. I have to get back to my salon."

Tanya looked on the floor for her jeans and T-shirt. His breeches and flowing shirt were on top of them. He liked to undress her first, was why. The way everything was tangled up, it almost looked like his clothes were making passionate love to her clothes.

Tanya retrieved her stuff, letting the linen sheet drop to the floor. Without a sound, he came up behind her, warm hand on her bare butt, stroking her voluptuously. The skin-to-skin contact stopped her where she was, jeans in hand. Sex with him was just too damn good not to enjoy it every chance she got. She straightened and arched back against him, letting him reach around to caress her breasts.

He was erect—she could feel his stiff cock at the small of her back, his big balls resting just above her ass. God, tall men were fun to play with.

"Where are you taking me now?" she murmured. One minute ago, she hadn't been interested. Now, held in his sensual embrace, she was. "I think I've seen everything."

"Not my first time."

Tanya turned inside the circle of his arms, facing him. "Now that could be interesting. Just tell me that you were of legal age."

He laughed. "I was twenty."

"And how old was she?"

"They were older."

Tanya's eyes widened. "They?"

"Two ladies-in-waiting to the queen."

"My, my. How much older?"

"Oh, perhaps five years—six years. I do not remember. They were cultured, highly educated women, whose beauty and elegance awed me. I had been sent to court by my father, who wished me to acquire a measure of sophistication and further his own connections there. But I was unsure of myself, having been raised in the country in this distant chateau. They decided to teach me everything they knew."

Tanya patted his ass. "Nice of them. I'm sure it wasn't just a public service. I bet you were tall and terrific even then."

He inclined his head and brushed a brief kiss on her lips. "I was tall, nothing more. And excruciatingly shy."

"I bet that turned them on."

He seemed a little surprised. "How did you know?"

"I know women," Tanya said. "Young man? New in town? Handsome? Attentive? Adoring? Eager to be touched for the very first time? Oh boy, what a fabulous fantasy."

Jean-Claude's amber eyes glowed with newly awakened memories that made his cock stir. "Then come back to bed and I will tell you all about it."

"What the hell." Tanya dropped her jeans and let him lead her there.

He got in first, then swooshed the covers over her, indulging in a few moments of cuddling and stroking before he began his tale. The lengthening shadows of afternoon made the room gloomy and a little chilly, but his nearness warmed her.

Jean-Claude pointed a finger at a candelabra across the room and, one by one, the candles on it flickered with tiny flames. Their combined light revealed a tapestry on the wall that she hadn't noticed when she'd come into the chamber. The weaving was as subtle as a finely colored painting, in hues of madder yellow and indigo and scarlet, and infinite gradations of those hues mixed to make many more. In its center were two noblewomen, sitting on a tasseled divan side by side, with two small dogs playing at their feet.

They were attended by a troubadour playing a lute. Singing songs of courtly love, Tanya thought. Or perhaps something more risqué. The polite smiles that curved their small mouths did not quite go with the sensual look in their heavy-lidded gaze. These medieval ladies were clearly eying the troubadour. Tanya squinted at the tapestry. The troubadour was handsome, with black, curling hair, but he bore no resemblance to Jean-Claude.

"As you can see, they were beautiful."

"Great hair too." She noted the style on the woman on the left: her waist-length, rippling golden locks flowed down her back, kept off her oval face by a delicate jeweled filet across the forehead. The other woman was a brunette, who restrained her equally long tresses with a transparent veil and a velvet band. Pearl drops hung from her ears and more pearls nestled in her bosom. Their dresses were simple in cut, with narrow bodices that flowed into cascades of silk.

As Tanya studied the tapestry, the figures in it came to life and she could hear the rich baritone of the troubadour. If she had to guess, she would say he was singing in Italian.

"Such men wandered from court to court," Jean-Claude explained. "They stayed for a season or two in each place. If they pleased milady and her companions, they sometimes stayed longer."

"I see. And when do you come into this scene?"

"Look closely."

The tapestry was now three-dimensional, and in the background Tanya glimpsed a heavy curtain hanging across the back of the room in which the threesome sat. The curtain stirred slightly—and she glimpsed a familiar face at its edge. Jean-Claude's. Much younger.

"I had no idea at that time that such elegant women could be more wanton than town trollops," he murmured. "Let me assure you that I had no intention of spying. That day I had fallen asleep on the deep stone ledge of the castle window where I had been looking out towards home, which I could not see. The alcove was warm and a kind maid drew the curtain to let me slumber. The singing woke me."

Tanya nodded. She watched as one of the women pulled her silk skirts up above the waist, revealing her pussy to the troubadour, who winked at the other lady. Neither seemed surprised. He set the lute aside and went to her, saying something in Italian. He traced his fingertips over the tender flesh and gave her a taste of herself, anointing her small lips with her own juice before he kissed her.

Not wasting a second, the other lady got her skirts up and showed her pussy too. So much for the music, Tanya thought. The troubadour was hot-looking. She couldn't blame them. He pleasured them in turn with his fingers and his tongue, and they ate it up. They seemed to enjoy watching each other receive his erotic attentions, directing him to do precisely what they wanted, taking advantage of his skill.

Still side by side, they sat upon the divan, composed and ladylike if you didn't count the shameless display of pussy between spread thighs. As he kneeled and got busy, the ladies caressed each other's breasts, pulling and tugging on nipples freed from tight bodices by expert hands.

Jean-Claude's hand slipped between Tanya's legs and he slowly finger-fucked her, keeping time with the talented troubadour. "As you can see, I was safe enough behind the curtain but I could not escape. Young and inexperienced as I was, the trio mesmerized me. I didn't make a sound."

But one of the dogs sniffed him out, yapping. A woman turned around and spotted him—the brunette, whose demure expression and veiled hair made Tanya think that she was not as wanton as the other. Hah. The brunette shooed the dogs away and called him over without bothering to drop her skirts. In fact, she invited him to look his fill by spreading her legs even more.

Jean-Claude stared at her swollen sex. His cock rose upright and he forced it down by grabbing it, but nature won out and up it came again. The noblewoman beckoned him. He didn't refuse and he didn't run.

She ran slender white hands over the hard rod beneath his clothes, rubbing and rubbing until the stimulation made his body shake. Then she unlaced him and freed his cock, encircling it lightly and sliding her fingers over it until her amorous companion looked over to see. The handsome Italian stopped to wipe his mouth and took his own cock out, handling it with pride and stroking it to maximum length. But Jean-Claude's was bigger. He blushed and the women laughed at him.

"Were you a virgin?" Tanya asked.

"Yes."

"Not for long. Not with this bunch."

He grinned. "You are right, as usual."

The brunette let go and took his hands in hers, pulling her down to him for his first taste of womanly heaven. Awkward but eager, the young Jean-Claude knelt between her thighs and applied a tentative tongue to her pussy, then licked avidly. The blonde woman rose to allow the brunette to recline and reach out her arms to her novice lover, guiding him all the way.

With a cry of sensual surprise, Jean-Claude thrust inside her, closing his eyes, rocking back and forth, cradled in her thighs. The Italian troubadour watched intently, then put a hand on the younger man's behind, stroking the sensitive skin of his tight buttocks and running his fingertips over the tense hollows at the sides.

Tanya heard her Jean-Paul gasp. "That was him? And I thought it was my lady."

She laughed a little. "So some guy was patting your butt. You didn't know. And you enjoyed it."

Jean-Claude blushed as deeply as the young man. "I was lost

in the sensation . . . and about to come. Ah, he was a Florentine—
they are notoriously fond of young men."

They both watched as his former self pounded into the first
woman he'd had, rolling his hips in a way that made the
brunette moan with pleasure. Between the firm hand caressing
his buttocks and pushing him down with each thrust of his cock
and the brunette's undulating embrace, young Jean-Claude came
explosively, crying out and almost collapsing on her. Sighing
with lust, the troubadour gave him one last good squeeze and
had the blonde bent over the divan seconds later, positioning his
cock tip on her asshole and waiting a few more seconds for her
to thrust back and take him deeply in her behind.

Probably wishing he was doing Jean-Claude, Tanya thought.
She turned to gaze at the real man, feeling like she was falling in
love with him all over again. His expression was bashful, almost boyish. A scene from his endless life had revealed more
than he'd thought it would, and he had reason to blush. She
looked from him to the youth he had been, loving his long-
lashed innocence, and then back to the experienced, hand-
somely lined face he had now.

"What is it?" he asked softly. "Am I less of a man in your
eyes now?"

She kissed his nose. "Don't be silly." She kissed his lips.
They stopped looking at the naughty noblewomen and concentrated on each other.

Yes, the tableau was erotic, but it was the openness of his
younger self that truly touched her. Once upon a time, he had been
vulnerable . . . and virile, of course. That quality had endured.

Two days later . . .

But mere virility wasn't enough to base a relationship on.
Okay, tripping through time had been the adventure of a life-

time, but she would have to be crazy if she thought it was going to last. Falling in love for a week was an exhilarating experience, nothing to take seriously. Tanya tossed her things into her suitcase, much lighter now that she'd used up twenty pounds of hair product on the lion. The adventure was over, she was going straight to the airport and skipping the Paris clubs, and returning to sanity.

How depressing.

Wild men and sexy beasts were much more fun. She picked up the little sack of gold coins he'd given her, swinging it, enjoying the clink of real money—the realest money she'd ever seen. No dead presidents, no live queens with funny hairdos, no holographic-calligraphic decorative doodads to stop counterfeiting. Just solid gold.

Like his heart. Tanya looked around the room. Was he standing behind her, putting thoughts into her mind? No—she was alone. She let out a sigh of relief and kept on packing, until she realized that it had been a sad sigh and not a sigh of relief. She was going to miss him. Big time.

A knock on the door snapped her out of it. "Come in," she called, hoping it wasn't him.

The knob turned and Jean-Claude walked in. "Is your mind made up?"

"You can read it. You tell me."

He looked into her eyes and the expression in them floored her. Soulful intelligence. Dignity. Longing. Love.

Stay.

"I can't. Like I said, I have a life."

He watched her throw things into her suitcase at random. Neither of them spoke for several minutes.

"Would you mind very much," he said cautiously, "if I were to share it?"

She opened her mouth to reply, then shut it and tried to think of an adequate response. "Look," she said at last, "I know a lot about you—and thanks for the guided tour through French history and your entire life, it really was a blast—but you know almost nothing about me. You can't just follow me to New York."

He crossed his arms over his chest and gave her a blasé look. "Why not?"

"Oh, about a million reasons. You can't walk a lion down Fifth Avenue, for starters."

Jean-Claude shrugged. "I shall create a safari park just for him. He will have more lionesses than he knows what to do with."

She pointed a finger at him. "You know, that approach didn't do you a lot of good. You're never going to be satisfied with just one woman or just one life."

"I disagree." His tone was calm.

"Please don't be so reasonable. I hate it when men get reasonable. It makes it very hard to fight with them."

He threw up his hands. "Why would you want to fight with me?"

"Because."

"Why, Tanya?"

She zipped up her suitcase, gritting her teeth at the faint shriek it emitted. "Because it's the fastest way to end this affair."

He came around it, taking her by the shoulders and giving her the golden-gaze routine. Tanya looked deep into his eyes, then turned her head away. He was good at it. It almost worked.

"But I know you are the right woman for me. I knew it the second I saw you. Animal instinct."

"Yeah, yeah, you said that. I mean, I heard you say it inside your head that first day."

"Then trust your instincts, Tanya. Remember, you're one of my kind."

"In your world, maybe. Not mine." She had forgotten to

pack her sneakers and squatted to cram them roughly into a side pocket. "Look, Jean-Claude, love isn't about magic shows and unbelievable hot sex and sleeping late and having tiptoeing servants attend to your every need—I mean, the instant gratification aspect of it was great, and the sex was amazing, and I still haven't figured out the CGI thing or the time travel, but . . ." She trailed off, catching her breath.

"Then what is love about? Is it real?"

"Love is . . . love is about volunteering to go out in a New York snowstorm for the Sunday paper and coming back with the last bagel in the bakery too. Which you split with your honey so no one goes hungry. Love is sitting socks to socks on the couch and reading that paper aloud to each other. Love is ordinary. But it endures. And yeah, it's real."

He pondered that for a moment. "Very well. If that is what you want, then that is what I will do."

"You don't know me!" she burst out. "Yes, you turned me inside out, sexually speaking, but that doesn't mean as much as men think it does."

Jean-Claude gave her a worried look. "It doesn't?"

"No!"

He squatted next to her, carefully tucking the laces of the sneakers into the side pocket. "So our story is not to have a happy ending?"

Unbalanced and upset, Tanya fell back onto her butt. "How the hell should I know?"

He straightened, looking down at her. "Allow me to accompany you to New York. Although I cannot conjure up a real snowstorm, we will buy this last bagel if it means so much to you and we will split it. And we will share the newspaper. We will sit socks to socks."

It sounded so ridiculous to hear him say it in his grave voice that she had to laugh. "All right. I really can't say no. It has been one hell of a week. I just needed to make sure that—I don't know. I'm not sure about anything anymore. You kind of blew my mind. In a good way."

He pulled her to her feet and enfolded her in a huge hug. "Perhaps we should start over."

"Okay. You're on." She rested her head against his chest, listening to his heart beat. As happy endings go, that sounded like a pretty good beginning.

Call of the Wild

Kathleen Dante

1

Shifting to a lower gear, Deanna Lycan took yet another S curve in the endless mountains with more caution than was her wont. Laden with all her worldly belongings, her sporty CR-V was less nimble than usual and she didn't want to push it.

Anyway, there was no rush. No one was expecting her. No one would mind if she got to Hillsboro tomorrow or next week instead of today. She stifled the familiar pang of loneliness the thought evoked. That might change, if her inquiries proved fruitful. She could only hope she wasn't off on a fool's quest.

Few vehicles shared the winding two-lane highway, allowing her to snatch an occasional glance at the scenery.

On one side was steep mountain covered by hardwood and pines, but the other side was a drop-off that plunged to a rushing stream hundreds of feet below. Every few turns revealed another breathtaking vista of blue mountains stretching rank upon rank into the distance, seemingly untouched by the summer heat.

The sight of all that open space soothed something inside her, calmed the restlessness that for the past year had made her miserable in Boston. A strange development for the city girl she knew herself to be. But she couldn't deny the sense of homecoming she felt at seeing the panorama, after nearly a decade since she'd last beheld its like.

The endless double yellow lines unrolled along the middle of the road before her, faithfully snaking along the curves, dividing the narrow highway into equal lanes. Rather like the way her future had looked before she'd decided to pull up stakes. Steady, static, sterile . . . and ultimately stifling.

Who would have thought that Boston with its picturesque neighborhoods echoing with history, and its concerts and plays and museums—cultural activities she enjoyed—would now encroach on her?

Too little room, too many people, too many strangers—and no family.

Suddenly, it had been like she couldn't breathe.

It had gotten so bad that she hadn't allowed a man in her bed in months. Couldn't stand the thought of sharing her space.

Well, hopefully, all that would change in Hillsboro. And she was taking the first step toward making it happen.

Deanna made a face. Jumpstart her dismal love life? Who was she kidding? Just because she was relocating didn't mean she'd find someone who'd awaken her dormant libido. Which was a pity, since the horizontal tango used to be a lot of fun.

She took a tight turn and hard plastic rattled in the back seat—maybe her measuring cups. Since whatever it was sounded loose, not broken, she ignored it.

Except for that, the humming of the CR-V's tires filled the silence. She'd turned off the radio sometime back, after the mountains started interfering with reception. The cell phone in her purse was just as quiet, which was fine with her.

She'd put everything on hold. All her clients knew she was on vacation—her first in years. Anyway, it wasn't as if web design generated that many emergency calls.

Hoping for a whiff of green, Deanna lowered her window to let the wind play through her hair, making the wavy locks dance across her shoulders, and angled her body so the breeze blew down the front of her tank top. Despite being on a highway, there was barely a hint of exhaust fumes in the flow of warm air that caressed her body, a welcome contrast to urban smog.

The next turn unveiled another panorama of mountains and clear sky, an infinite palette of blues she couldn't hope to capture in her designs. If it weren't for the wide steel guardrail, it could have been the same sight first beheld centuries ago by the colonists who'd settled the area.

She smiled at the romantic notion. That's what came from knowing nothing of her ancestry: trying to connect with some history greater than her own. Growing up in an orphanage, knowing nothing much about her parents, save that they'd died in a car accident when she was four, had given her a thirst for heritage. Deep roots. But, somehow, she didn't think anything she might learn about her parents could live up to such fantastic pipe dreams.

A loud, protesting *Blat!* from behind broke the tranquil afternoon drive.

She shot a glance at the rearview mirror and stared.

Reflected there, a black pickup swerved onto the highway, cutting in with utter disregard for traffic and safety. To her dismay, it was speeding up as it weaved unsteadily between lanes, repeatedly crossing the double yellow lines and gaining on her.

Deanna forced her attention back to the road in front. It would do her little good to avoid the danger behind her, only to drive off the highway or get into a crash herself.

The road curved away from the mountainside onto a short viaduct that cut across a narrow valley. In the straightaway, she opened the throttle, coaxing more speed from her faithful CR-V, her heart in her throat, the steering wheel biting into her white-knuckled hands. Behind her, the roar came on like an unstoppable nightmare, loud and getting louder.

Beeeeep!

The car behind her fishtailed across the road as its driver lost control, leaving nothing between her and the weaving pickup.

No matter how hard she looked, there was nowhere she could turn off to let the truck behind her pass, and no cops when she needed one. She could only stay ahead or hope its driver came to his senses.

The uneven race continued off the viaduct and back on another mountainside, the truck rapidly making up the distance between it and her car.

Deanna stomped down on the accelerator. The CR-V responded sluggishly, weighed down by her belongings. Plastic rattled, the disparate odors of cinnamon, paprika, and fennel swirling through the car. Her spice rack must have fallen over.

The road twisted once more, another picturesque valley unfolding to her right. But she didn't have time to appreciate its beauty or to wish away another metal guardrail so rooted in the modern day.

Veering across the double yellow lines again, the black pickup charged on with the roar of a revving engine.

Time seemed to stop. All sounds vanished as if Nature held its breath.

As Deanna watched with horror, the truck's silver grille and massive bull-bar glinted in the afternoon sun, headed straight at her.

THUNK!

The door slammed into Deanna's side, a scarlet starburst of pain that drove the breath from her lungs.

Tires squealed.

The CR-V slid toward the shoulder, gravel pinging on its undercarriage. Another impact threw her in the opposite direction, to land on top of her bulky purse. There was a long screech, like the wailing of the damned, as her faithful car jounced around her.

Another metal shriek filled the air, then silence.

For a long moment, the world stood still. Then the bottom dropped, dragging Deanna with it.

On most days, Graeme Luger enjoyed his job as a deputy sheriff in Woodrose, West Virginia. The town was perfect for his needs. It gave him a forest to run wild in, good people worthy of protection, relatively quick access to clan with a few hours' drive—and a steady stream of potential mates in the form of hikers and other tourists. Not that he'd had any success to date, but there was always tomorrow.

Today, however, didn't look to be one of the good days.

Pulling onto the gravel shoulder, he parked behind another patrol car and took in the situation with a quick glance, noting skid marks, the broken guardrail, and the black pickup opposite lying on its side up the mountain. Several vehicles were abandoned in disarray along the grassy verge, their erstwhile drivers crowding the edge of the road.

His lips twisted in an automatic snarl at the sight.

Henckel again. He ran a hand through his wiry crew cut. If he weren't prematurely gray already, the scene would have given him white hairs. This time the sheriff couldn't turn a blind eye to the young drunk's shenanigans. *Go straight to jail. Do not pass GO. Do not collect two hundred dollars.* Just because Henckel had led the high school football team to state victory was no excuse for this.

The prospect would have cheered him if it weren't for the cost. It shouldn't have been permitted to get this far.

Getting out of his patrol car, Graeme hotfooted over to join his fellow deputy by the guardrail, weaving through the rubber-neckers crowding the narrow shoulder.

"Gray!" The audible relief in Mitchell's voice made his gut tense.

"Henckel?"

"Over there. He'll keep." The older man jerked his chin at the fallen pickup. "More's the pity," he added in a mutter that Graeme's sharp ears caught. "This one won't." Mitchell pointed downhill through the break in the guardrail as Graeme reached his side.

On a small ridge nearly a hundred feet below, a battered gold Honda CR-V was snagged on a young pine bending under the strain. Its driver—a woman—was bashing at the windshield, clawing shattered glass clear of the frame, not waiting to be rescued. The massive dent on the driver's door and streaks of black gouged on its paint said Henckel's truck had rammed the car. The damage must have jammed the door.

Graeme reined in the flicker of admiration he felt at her initiative, knowing he probably didn't have much time. Even in the brief seconds he'd taken to study the situation, the car had slipped noticeably. It was up to him to save that woman.

Grant Mitchell was a good man to have at his back, but *agile* was the last word anybody would use to describe him. Short, with most of his weight carried in a thick potbelly, the other deputy wasn't one for scrambling down mountainsides. He left that to the younger guys like Graeme, who were in far better shape, contenting himself with providing support.

As he did now, bellowing at the crowd to stand aside and clearing the way for Graeme to sprint back to his patrol car.

Popping the trunk, Graeme snatched up the climbing gear he kept there for such emergencies. He raced back, rope slung over his shoulder. No time for anything fancy. Every second counted, as the tortured creaking from below attested. He wound the rope around a bent guardrail, tied it off on a nearby bumper, then started down the steep slope. The post creaked under his weight but held. Dislodged by his hasty passage, a minor avalanche of hard soil accompanied his rapid descent, clattering fit to startle wildlife.

Adrenaline had his heart pounding, sharpening his awareness until he could pick out the pungent bite of crushed wild-flowers, the sour sweat of the milling rubberneckers, and the nauseatingly sweet stench of hot rubber from forty feet away, even in his human form.

Graeme had to pause to shake his head clear. Times like this, his heightened werewolf senses were a danger on the job.

An updraft of warm air brought him the scent of flowing sap and something else that raised his hackles and—inexplicably—set his cock twitching. What a damned inconvenient time for his hunting instinct to raise its head! He ignored his reaction, focusing his attention on getting down to the trapped driver. If he wanted to save her, he couldn't afford any distraction.

As he continued down the sharp incline, he passed broken trees scarred with gold paint. Marked by the Honda's passage, they must have slowed its fall, which probably explained the driver's good condition.

At the top of the ridge, Graeme released the rope and turned to the battered car. His heart skipped at the lack of motion that met him. The woman had stopped trying to clear the windshield. All he could see of her was light brown hair. Had she passed out?

To make matters worse, the pine groaned, an audible warning of impending failure.

Brushing aside the remains of the shattered glass still clinging to the frame, he tried to get a better look at the driver and assess the situation.

Her head snapped up, revealing startled hazel eyes.

Relief washed over him at her reaction. "Come on!" He stuck an arm through the hole in the windshield to help her out.

"I can't. The seatbelt's jammed!" She'd twisted out from under the diagonal chest strap, but the lap band kept her trapped. Several frayed threads bore testament to her efforts at cutting the seatbelt.

And he could barely reach it from where he stood.

He'd have to go through the buckled window.

Taking a deep breath, Graeme braced his hands on the twisted metal.

A stirring perfume fogged his senses. It set his cock springing to steel-hard awareness, made his shoulders bunch with instinctive aggression that bypassed intellectual control. The scent honed his temper to razor edge, outrage flaring in his heart. How dare Henckel endanger this woman!

Gripping the two sides of the window frame, he pushed, drawing on his werewolf strength to bend the steel to his will. It bit into his palms, resisting his efforts. But slowly, with shrill creaks of protest, the metal gave way.

As if in sympathy, the tree groaned.

The woman squeaked as the car shuddered around her.

Finally, there was enough space for him to fit.

"Let me at it." Leaning forward, Graeme managed to wedge his head and shoulders inside and grab the strap. The position blocked her view of his hands, but it nearly stuffed his face between a damned fine pair of knockers and nose-deep in female ambrosia that practically short-circuited his wolf brain.

Her! That mouthwatering, blood-hailing scent was hers! Only long training kept him from howling. But, damn, she smelled oh so good.

"Sorry about this." His apology was muffled by the high mounds but she must have heard him; at least she didn't slap his mug while he worked at freeing her.

Confident his hands were hidden, he Changed one, a tingle of heat flooding it as his fingers contracted and claws emerged. He slashed down, the band parting easily with a brief rip.

He bumped his head on the frame as he jerked back, the jarring contact little more than a distraction. "Come on."

Pushing a large purse ahead of her, the busty brunette scrambled out of her seat, one hand clutching his biceps as she squeezed through the window.

Wrapping an arm around her waist, Graeme secured her to his chest, one unprofessional corner of his brain registering the soft breasts plumped against him. Gripping her—*firm, round*—ass with his other hand, he yanked her clear, scrambling backwards as the ground shook.

And not a moment too soon.

As he set her on her feet, a loud *crack* announced the tree's demise. With the loss of its support, the car slid off the ridge, tumbling down the steep ravine.

"Oh, God!" Deanna clung to her rescuer, chilled by her close call. If it hadn't been for him, she'd still be trapped and might have accompanied her car even farther down the mountain. She pressed closer to him, craving safety. Still feeling unsteady, she wrapped her legs around his, anchoring herself against the fear that threatened to shake her apart.

He stroked her back, crooning wordlessly, his gruff voice reaching deep inside her, enfolding her in reassurance, his big body a shield against the horror of her brush with death.

It had been a near thing.

Shivering with an uncharacteristic craving for support, she buried her face in his solid chest, soaking in the aura of strength that he radiated. The scent of fabric softener, sweat, and male filled her nose, calling to her like precious perfume.

Her empty sheath clenched, raw need coiling in her belly, sudden and unexpected. Unbidden and almost unfamiliar. It pinned her in place with a spine-tingling, knee-melting intensity that banished all thought. It had been months since she'd felt arousal, and never with such carnal violence.

Her rescuer wasn't immune to it either. His erection surged against her belly, swelling to an undeniable ridge, hard and thick with promise. All male hunger she wanted inside her.

Breathless with sensual awareness, Deanna stared up at him, into blue eyes gone silvery with desire. She clutched his belt, wanting to undo it, to release the turgid flesh caught between them. To take his cock into her wet pussy and ride him to blissful exhaustion. Her thighs practically quivered with need.

Her breasts tingled and firmed, her nipples poking through her thin bra and tank top. She wanted his mouth on them, sucking them, nibbling them until they ached. Her core pulsed with the strength of her desire.

"Gray!" The distant yell shattered the breathless moment.

Taking a deep breath, her rescuer turned his grizzled head to the shout. "We're coming!"

If only!

2

Graeme pulled into the clinic's parking lot the next day, still wondering about the wisdom of what he was about to do. He could tell himself it was only neighborly to help out, but he knew his intentions weren't that innocent. He could hardly pretend otherwise when the merest thought of her made his cock twitch like a flea-ridden cub.

What was it about Deanna Lycan that got to him so quickly? Sure, he'd practically buried his snout in her cleavage, but that didn't mean he had to mount her the first chance he got!

What did he know about the busty brunette besides that she was single, pretty, steady in a crisis, heterosexual—and smelled like his most carnal dreams come to life, especially after she creamed in his arms? Nothing much, except she was headed elsewhere and hadn't exactly chosen Woodrose as a stopover.

But he sure wanted to learn more . . . like whether her legs would be just as tight wrapped around his hips as they'd been around his thigh. Or if her breasts were really a nice handful; he hadn't felt any padding when she'd pressed against him, but that didn't mean much these days. The only way to find out for certain was to get her naked.

Just the thought sent a shudder of desire shooting through Graeme.

He scrubbed his face in disgust. You'd think he was a bird dog, the way his cock went on point around her.

Right. Just because she smelled like the next best thing to fresh venison was no reason to act like a wild beast. He'd be polite, helpful, and attentive, and if one thing led to another, great! But he wasn't going to pressure her into anything, wasn't going to imply in any way whatsoever that he'd accept sex in lieu of gratitude . . . even if it was true.

His intentions set to rights, Graeme got out of his Jeep and headed for the low, rambling building that was the town's sole medical facility.

The sight that met him at the front desk made him swear under his breath. Wrinkled pink shorts hugged taut, round globes tilted up in offering, the crease between them practically begging for his touch.

Damn it, Luger! The talking-to he'd given himself out in the parking lot went up in smoke. His cock promptly went on point, springing to rock-hard attention, quivering to be set loose and demanding immediate access to tight pussy.

Deanna Lycan looked more than fine to him, though he knew from the evidence photos that she had severe bruising on her left side from the accident.

Vicious, atavistic rage stirred in him at the memory, urging him to wring that idiot Henckel's neck, reminding him it was his duty to serve and protect. He restrained it with difficulty, knowing he couldn't allow that side of him out of leash. At least this time, the sheriff was leaving Henckel to cool his heels in jail.

She shifted her weight, her firm ass swaying in enticement.

The eye-popping vision him helped soothe his inner wolf. He couldn't do much about Henckel, but perhaps servicing her wasn't out of the question.

Deanna scrawled her signature across the forms, her mind preoccupied with her aching ribs and the problem of how she'd get around town. She had to remain in the area until the police salvaged her car, so she could reclaim her belongings. Not that she was ungrateful, since she wouldn't be alive if it hadn't been for that deputy. But it was a good thing she'd managed to take her purse with her when she was rescued; at least, it meant she had identification and some funds.

"Mary Lee tells me you're good to go."

The gruff, unexpected drawl gave Deanna a jolt, made her nipples tighten to aching points.

As though conjured by her thoughts, the deputy who'd saved her life stood behind her, his big body displayed in a moss-green T-shirt that clung to his rippling musculature faithfully and faded jeans molded to legs that could have doubled as tree trunks. He was built like a tank, his broad shoulders easily twice hers.

Despite the liberal dusting of white in his short-cropped black hair and bushy eyebrows, he couldn't be that much older than she was. He had the body of a man very much in his prime—as she well knew—and his face only had a few laugh lines.

Good heavens! Taking in the masculine eye candy, Deanna licked suddenly dry lips, her libido waking with a good old college cheer. She'd thought her carnal desperation the result of her narrow escape, an anomaly that was unlikely to recur any time soon. Obviously, she was mistaken.

She straightened slowly, careful of the bruise that made sudden movements chancy. "Deputy, um . . ." Her mind blanked, unable to pull up his name. Surely she knew it from yesterday, but for the life of her she couldn't remember what his name was.

"Luger. Graeme Luger." The deep bass voice that matched his physique so well did unspeakably intimate things to her body, made her wonder what he sounded like in the bedroom. "Just call me Graeme." Large hands surrounded hers, made her feel smaller than usual—even delicate.

She inhaled sharply at the unmistakable sexual interest in the bladelike smile that accompanied his introduction, and the heat pooling in her belly in answer. "Uh, Graeme. Has something happened? My things . . . ?" She forced down irritation at her uncharacteristic breathlessness. A lifetime of depending on no one but herself had left her wary of emotions that smacked of neediness.

Graeme immediately eased her concern with a quick shake of his silvered head. "I came by to drive you around." He lifted a bushy brow. "Unless you have a car waiting?"

Warmed by his consideration, Deanna shook her head in turn. "The rental agency can't bring a car until Monday. Even then, I can't leave without my things. Any idea when they'll be recovered?"

"It'll take at least a week." He shrugged, making his corded shoulders ripple. "There's no easy way to get down to your car. We'll need to borrow some equipment we don't have and that takes time and paperwork." The slow flow of words caressed her ears, almost distracting her from their content.

She sucked in her lower lip. It wasn't that grievous a setback. Her work files and other records were in storage in Boston. Her laptop could be replaced. Only her few treasures left over from childhood were irreplaceable. And those were at the bottom of the gorge. The delay simply meant she'd have less time to settle down in Hillsboro . . . and less time to devote to her inquiries about her parents before she had to get back to business. But the sooner she left Woodrose, the sooner she'd get to Hillsboro.

"If you need a place to stay . . ." He hooked his thumbs on his pockets, his arms akimbo, in a casual display of beefcake—a rare delicacy these past few months.

Deanna had to smile at the direction of her thoughts. "I've already made arrangements." Despite its picturesque scenery, Woodrose didn't have much by way of temporary lodgings. From what Mary Lee, the clinic's friendly clerk, had said, there were no motels or even a B&B nearby. Deanna had ended up reserving a log cabin outside town that—according to the woman she'd spoken to—was popular for fishing and fall color, the main tourist attractions in the area. But first she had to get to the rental office to pick up the keys . . . and find out where the cabin was.

"But not for a native guide."

Wrestling with her independent nature, Deanna forced herself to admit his help was necessary. After all, if she refused his offer to drive her around, how would she get anywhere, especially when she didn't know where she needed to go in this little mountain town? It wasn't as if she could download a map off the Internet, and Mary Lee had also informed her there were no local taxis and no means of hiring one. Until the rental car arrived, she'd have to accept help or limit her travel to her own two feet.

"But not that," she admitted reluctantly, trying to ignore the clerk's bright-eyed interest in their conversation.

"I'm free until five." His low drawl made it sound like they were discussing something more intimate than just his driving her around. Strangely enough, when she'd heard Mary Lee's accent, it had only registered as the voice of home, nothing more.

"What happens then?" Deanna forced down a flush as her body responded to his intonation.

"My shift starts."

"Then I guess we'd better get going." Fighting for a casual demeanor, she slung her poor, badly scarred purse—which now looked like a candidate for the trash bin—over her shoulder. "Thanks for the offer."

At her acceptance, Graeme flashed her a slashing grin that sent a shiver of awareness darting up her spine.

His car turned out to be a battered Jeep of indeterminate masculine color, a weird shade of green-brown that couldn't have been the manufacturer's original choice. She didn't think the name existed in her color palette.

To her surprise, he opened the door for her; she'd forgotten some men still held to such courtesies, used as she was to his counterparts in Boston. As she steeled herself to reach for the grab bar, he wrapped his hands around her hips and lifted her into the Jeep with solicitous care, clearly aware the bruise in her side made raising her arms above her head painful.

Deanna held her breath, supremely conscious of the heat of his hands through her shorts. She appreciated his help, yet her heightened awareness of him did little to put her at ease. Setting her battered purse at her feet, she tried to mask the strange turmoil swirling inside her with speech. "I don't think I've thanked you for saving me."

He shrugged, a surprising blush touching his cheeks with pink. "No thanks necessary. Just doing my job." He quickly shut her door and rounded the hood of the Jeep.

When Graeme got into the driver's seat, the already Spartan proportions of the vehicle seemed to shrink further. His back was so broad, his arms were scant inches from her own. And— healthy male that he was—he radiated a palpable heat that caressed her skin as he drove, like seductive fingers inviting her surrender.

Trying to ignore his allure, Deanna turned to the window to get a better look at Woodrose. The first time she'd passed through, the ambulance had been going too fast and she'd been in too much pain to pay attention.

Crammed between mountains, the town was a haphazard agglomeration of wooden buildings clinging to the steep slopes, laid out in no discernible pattern. Its roads were more like paved trails, rather than the orderly street grids she was accustomed to. But there was a rough charm to it all that harked back to simpler times.

They descended one slope and ascended another, winding between stands of deciduous trees and topping a ridge, before going down once more. Unable to pick out distinct landmarks, Deanna soon found herself disoriented by the switchbacks and crisscrossing streets unmarked by anything as obvious as a street sign. She was suddenly grateful for Graeme's presence beside her, dreading the time she'd have to navigate the town on her own, once she had a car again.

Despite their convoluted route, the drive didn't take very long—it only felt that way to Deanna's taut nerves. The cabin rental office turned out to be a long building filled with fishing gear, with lifelike mock-ups of large—presumably local—fish festooning its walls.

"Hey, Gray! You droppin' by the Hogg Wylde tonight?" The plump woman with glossy blue-black skin behind the counter gave the deputy a wide smile of welcome.

Acknowledging the hail with a casual wave, Graeme nodded. "Have to make sure there's no trouble."

"Good. Once those hotheads get liquored up, there's no tellin' what they might do." The woman shook her head, making the beads at the ends of her cornrows clatter.

Deanna ignored the irrelevant exchange for the one detail that interested her. "Gray?" she repeated softly.

"It's the obvious nickname." He ran a hand over his short crop of salt and pepper, a wry smile tilting his lips.

There was nothing overtly suggestive about his gesture, yet the speculation it gave rise to was inescapable: was he equally grizzled below, over his chest and groin? Heat flushed through her body at the thought of discovering the truth for herself. Her hands literally itched to find out.

"What can I do for y'all?" the plump woman asked, smoothing the front of her skirt as she looked at them expectantly.

"Betty, this is Deanna Lycan."

"The one Fred ran off the road yesterday." Betty nodded to herself. "Well, now, you don't look too bad, honey. Good thing Gray here got there when he did."

Deanna fought not to squirm while the other woman chatted on. Listening to platitudes about the recklessness of youth today was difficult when her body tingled with awareness, but she must have managed the feat—at least, neither of her companions looked at her as if she had spouted nonsense.

"Well, he's young," Betty finally concluded, setting out a register and a pair of keys on the counter. "Hopefully, this will teach him a lesson."

Deanna stifled a snort. As far as she knew, the drunk driver was less than ten years her junior! More than old enough to take responsibility for his actions. Not wanting to get into an argument, she managed to keep her opinions to herself while dealing with the rental paperwork.

"You sure you don't want anythin' else?" Betty asked as she put away the register and the credit card slips. "Nothin' much to do up there, what with no TV. You could try your hand at fishin'. We rent poles out. Give you a good deal on that. The creek out back's got some trout that's good eatin'."

More than ready to escape the good-natured stream of words, Deanna declined politely. After garrulous assurances that the cabin's power and water were on, and that fresh linens had been put in, they finally got away with Deanna clutching the keys.

Since it was approaching noon, Graeme brought her to a

small, unprepossessing diner. The outside of the building didn't look like it'd had the benefit of fresh paint in more than thirty years. The inside fared little better, the floors covered with scuffed linoleum. But the food promised to be good, if the number of patrons was any basis. It was early for lunch, but more than a dozen people were already seated in various stages of dining.

Everyone seemed to know the deputy by name. Deanna couldn't help but wonder if that was what life had been like for her parents in Hillsboro. But if that was the case, why hadn't there been family to take her in when her parents were killed? Did that mean her inquiries were doomed to failure?

Beneath the interested gaze of the townsfolk, they ate a simple lunch of salad and flame-broiled burgers, and discussed what she needed to buy.

"Okay, clothes, some supplies and food."

Deanna nodded. "Uh-huh, and some books. Enough to last me until my things are recovered, or at least until my rental's been delivered and I can get around on my own." She bit into the thick sandwich with unaccustomed relish, savoring the juiciness of the meat patty with some surprise. No wonder people were lining up to eat in the diner! She normally didn't pay much attention to food, but the hamburger just seemed to melt in her mouth and the beef was especially tasty.

Before she could ponder her sudden liking for meat, two grandfatherly types at the next table stood up and walked over, chatting all the while. They stopped beside Graeme—one lanky, the other stocky and balding—and bestowed genial smiles on him.

"So, Gray, is she The One?" the thin older man asked in an innocent tone.

The One? Deanna paused in mid-chew. Were they matchmaking?

His shorter companion didn't wait for an answer. "Where's she staying at, anyway?"

"Haven't you heard?" the lanky codger answered for Graeme, who wore a tolerant smile as he chewed in silence. "Betty rented one of the cabins out. That'd be to her."

"You mean that one by the creek?" The stocky man pointed a finger sideways, as if they could see through the diner's walls to whatever he was indicating. "A bit isolated for a city girl, don't you think?"

Deanna had been enjoying the ping-pong conversation between obviously old friends that didn't seem to need much outside input, but it looked like they would stand by the table all day if she didn't say something. Swallowing her mouthful, she injected: "Betty said there was a creek."

"Well, there you go! It's that cabin all right." The lanky one bent down to whisper in a conspiratorial voice, "Don't mind him. It's a great place to relax, lose the aches and pains from the crash, soak up the wildlife. Why, up there you might even see a wolf. No harm done, right?"

She blinked. *Wolf?*

The stocky man harrumphed disagreement. "The only way she'd see a wolf up there is if she's snorting something. There hasn't been a wolf in these mountains for more than a century—not since my great-grandpa's days—and you know it. It don't do to go around scaring people like that." The old codger continued his harangue as he and his companion walked on, clearly having forgotten Graeme and her in favor of retreading a favorite argument.

Deanna smiled at Graeme. "Wolves?" she asked with a healthy dose of skepticism. While wolves had been successfully reintroduced in Montana and Yellowstone, they hadn't reached West Virginia—at least as far as she knew.

He shook his head ruefully, sunlight picking out the silver in his crew cut. "You heard him. There hasn't been a wolf in these mountains in generations."

The rest of the meal went by without interruption, as the other diners chose to satisfy their curiosity from a distance.

Their next stop was a small store offering casualwear that ran to short shorts and crop tops. Since Graeme didn't evince any impatience, Deanna took her time browsing through the clothes on display, in no particular rush to bring her time with the rugged deputy to an end. She got a few simple tops and shorts, automatically choosing complementary colors, plus cotton sleep shirts. "These should be enough."

The deputy's bushy brows knit. "Enough for what?"

"To last until I get my clothes back. Then I can continue to Hillsboro."

He seemed to frown at her answer, but his expression cleared too quickly for her to be sure.

Despite the pleasure of Graeme's company, it felt strange to have a companion while shopping. Deanna had gotten used to doing most things alone. Certainly, her web design work wasn't conducive to face-to-face interaction; most of her business was handled online.

What was more, she hadn't been alone with a man in months, ever since her restlessness started.

Now, she had difficulty thinking of anything else but being alone with a particular well-built deputy sheriff, especially since he didn't leave her side while she shopped.

Dragging her mind back to what else she needed to buy, Deanna headed for the small lingerie section. Most of what was on display were strictly utilitarian cotton briefs. About as exciting as her grandmother's flannel nightgown, or so she imagined, if she'd had a grandmother.

She made a face, riffling through the sparse selection and resigning herself to the plain merchandise. All she needed was two sets; she could make do with that plus what she was wearing until she got her things back.

Only there weren't any bras in her size.

Deanna searched the racks repeatedly, a sinking feeling in her belly. While she wasn't that big, she wasn't small enough to go without support either. Especially not while wearing the T-shirts she'd chosen—and anything else would be too thick for the summer heat. But the prospect of wearing the same bra day after day was too much to contemplate on a full stomach.

"What's wrong?" The growled question came from Graeme, who was standing patiently at one side, out of her way.

"I can't find anything in my size."

Efficient man that he was, Graeme waved a clerk over and consulted her on the state of their inventory. Unfortunately, she could only confirm Deanna's conclusion.

When Deanna chose a smaller size than she normally wore, he plucked the bra from her hands to study it with a critical eye. "This can't be your size."

"It's better than nothing."

"You don't have to settle for that." He snorted. "Miss Ginnie might be able to help."

Miss Ginnie?

Though Graeme urged her toward the cashier, Deanna planted her feet, wondering who the woman was. "How?"

"She does direct sales for this kind of thing."

Understanding dawned. "She's an Avon lady?"

"Something like." Graeme shrugged, the muscles of his shoulder bunching attractively. "She's the town librarian and does direct sales out of her house as a sideline."

Satisfied with his explanation, Deanna paid for her clothes, conscious of the curiosity in the cashier's eyes.

Graeme drove her to a relatively newer neighborhood lined with prosperous-looking houses. He rang the bell of a two-story house and introduced her to the spry, elderly woman with blue-rinsed hair who answered the door.

Miss Ginnie showed them to the living room, an old-fashioned parlor with delicate lace curtains, a curio-filled china cabinet, and frilly cushions competing for space on the cabbage-rose–printed, overstuffed furniture. Strangely enough, Graeme looked quite comfortable in the overwhelmingly feminine space. She refused to discuss business until she'd served them sweet tea and cookies, waiting to see them take a bite before listening to their explanations.

"What size do you wear, dear?" The elderly woman took a measured sip of her tea after asking, seemingly oblivious to the impropriety of such a question in mixed company.

Conscious of Graeme beside her, his virility magnified by their surroundings, Deanna mumbled an answer. On the pretext of drinking, she hid her warm face behind the glass of cold tea, wistfully remembering the tin of Earl Grey in her car as she tried to swallow the near-lethal dose of sugar without flinching.

"No wonder you couldn't find any. That's one of the most common around here. Never fear, I have some in stock." Saying so, Miss Ginnie patted Deanna's hand and left the room, hopefully in pursuit of said stock.

The elderly woman returned carrying a colorful mound of satin and lace that she set on the coffee table. "Now," she announced with a cheerful smile, "let's see what suits you."

Deanna stared at the frothy lingerie before her, uncertain where to start. When Graeme had told her about Miss Ginnie, she'd hoped to find a few basic pieces, but this surfeit of feminine luxury far exceeded her expectations.

She stole a sidelong glance at her stoic companion. Was basic and utilitarian really the impression she wanted to make on such an incredible man?

Of course not. While she wasn't about to invite him into her bed right there and then, a woman had her pride to consider.

"Many of these are matching sets. I thought you'd like to see the lower half to get the full effect." The elderly woman paired together several bras and panties with finicky precision, setting them aside for closer inspection.

Deanna's eyes widened involuntarily at the selection presented. These weren't just the ultrafeminine undergarments she'd come to expect from seeing Miss Ginnie's living room; they were deadly weapons, an arsenal for seduction.

She fought to keep her gaze trained ahead and not to peek sideways to check Graeme's reaction. Her newly revived libido tantalized her with images of her standing before him wearing only the sexy garments. Her nipples tingled, tightening reflexively, as heat pooled in her belly. If she truly wanted him in her bed while she was in Woodrose, Miss Ginnie's wares could only help.

Graeme eyed the flimsy scraps of lace displayed before him, hard pressed to maintain an expression of calm disinterest. If Deanna knew he was imagining how she'd look wearing nothing else but that itsy-bitsy red number she held up, she'd probably run away screaming.

Little had he known when he suggested going to Miss Ginnie's that he'd set himself up for torture.

He'd heard some female deputies refer to the librarian as a "passion consultant," but he hadn't realized just how seriously they'd meant that description. Good God, he now couldn't help wondering if they wore that stuff under their uniforms—as a matter of scientific curiosity, of course. He'd never thought of them that way before and didn't want to start now.

Deanna, on the other hand . . .

He was more than willing to imagine her in any of the naughty numbers displayed on the table. But it still shocked the conservative wolf in him to learn that the little old librarian who baked him fudge brownies for Christmas peddled the stuff.

Not that he was about to say anything. It had been his idea to come here, after all.

"Why don't you try them on?" Miss Ginnie suggested, nothing about her manner indicating that her invitation or his presence was out of the ordinary. With an aside to him that they wouldn't be long, she led Deanna down the hall to another room, carrying some pieces in which Deanna had apparently expressed interest.

Graeme followed their progress through a mirror in the hall, delighted when they didn't close the door. The two women clearly hadn't noticed the mirror's strategic location. Well, he wasn't about to tell them.

Deanna winced as she pulled off her tank top with Miss Ginnie's help, slowly revealing a large, violently purple bruise on the left side of her ribcage.

The librarian clucked at the sight, too softly for Graeme to make out any words but definitely outraged.

He scowled in agreement.

If Henckel hadn't been in jail, uninjured despite his role in the accident, Graeme would've been tempted to share the hurt . . . with interest. As it was, it took everything he had to stay on the couch and not charge into the next room to check Deanna's condition up close.

All thought of wringing that young idiot's neck vanished, however, when Deanna shed her bra.

Forgetting about stealth, he stared at the bounty revealed in the mirror. High round globes with just the slightest hint of sag. Pale and creamy, like the underbelly of a mountain lion. His palms itched just looking at them—and looking from a distance, at that.

With a feeling of unreality, Graeme watched as Deanna tried on one sexy confection after another, twisting and turning as she checked the fit. Each one seemed designed to showcase her assets to their throat-drying, cock-hardening best advantage.

He shifted his weight against the too-tight fit of his jeans. Damn, but she looked edible! She smelled it, too. He resisted the urge to stroke his hard-on; Deanna wasn't prancing around to tempt him deliberately, and he knew very well he couldn't finish himself in Miss Ginnie's living room.

Deanna changed to another bra that plumped up her breasts, raising the mounds as though presenting them to a lover. The two women broke into conspiratorial giggles as Deanna scrutinized the result from various angles.

Graeme's inner wolf growled approval of the lavish display. He hurriedly reached down and adjusted himself. All he needed was for his circulation to get cut off for his torture to be complete. But still he couldn't tear his gaze from the mirror, not until Deanna and Miss Ginnie made to rejoin him.

By the time they did, he had his hands clasped together over his belt, trying for the innocence of a choirboy. There was something crude about flaunting an erection in front of a woman old enough to be his granddam. He couldn't do it. The mere thought of that formidable woman was enough to melt the steel of his hard-on.

But Deanna came away with a sizable bag of new lingerie. Just the sight of it made his cock twitch with renewed interest as soon as they were back in the Jeep; it didn't help that the smell of her excitement was stronger than ever, marking the interior with her presence.

Unless he wanted to sport a woody for the next several weeks, he'd have to give the Jeep a deep and thorough scrubbing after she left. Though if he had anything to say about it, she wouldn't be leaving anytime soon.

The rest of Deanna's errands stretched her nerves to humming anticipation, although—or maybe because—she now wore a fresh bikini panty and its matching bra. The fact that Graeme knew what her underwear looked like had her squirming with an inconvenient awareness. The knowledge that she had several sets of the lacy stuff was sufficient for her libido to concoct titillating fantasies of parading them before him.

It didn't help knowing that Graeme reciprocated her attraction. Despite his gentlemanly demeanor, the bulge tenting his jeans was unmistakable. Since it hadn't been there before, that most definitely was not a gun in his pocket.

They stopped by a small store that turned out to be an old-fashioned grocery that sold a little bit of everything, its goods displayed on weathered shelves with charming artlessness. There was something unbearably intimate about shopping for food together. Even a simple choice between apples and pears took on new meaning, as though she and Graeme were weaving the strands of their lives together at a deeper level than mere sharing of bodies. It was like his saving her had forged a bond between them that was being tempered by the everyday activities and growing stronger.

She didn't know what to make of it. An affair was one thing, but a relationship was out of the question when she didn't plan to stay in Woodrose for long.

Unnerved by the trend of her thoughts, Deanna tried to dismiss them as she filled her basket with food, books, and supplies. She bought enough to last her a few days, hoping she wouldn't have to depend on Graeme to help her restock.

It didn't do any good.

Her libido insisted on remembering how his arms had felt around her shoulders when he'd plucked her out of her car, how the hard slopes of his broad chest had flexed under her hands, how his thigh had pressed on her mound when she'd straddled him. Just that one embrace had seared him in her memory.

Trying to avoid reliving it only brought back more details. His faint sweaty scent that was all male. The warmth of his body and the heat of his embrace. The bass rumble of his voice, like a mountain given speech, crooning reassurance.

By the time Graeme took a turnoff onto a dirt road that climbed the mountainside, Deanna was in a pother of need. The bumps on the uneven track as it wound among the trees only made it worse, rubbing her clenched thighs together and rolling her mound around her aching clit as the Jeep bounced onward.

Wondering how he was taking their extended companionship, Deanna stole a glance at the muscular deputy. If anything, his erection had only grown more pronounced, the taut ridge extending to mouthwatering proportions.

She swallowed with difficulty, pure lust tightening her throat. When they got to the cabin, would he do anything?

Would she?

Deanna trembled, poised at a decision point, wondering which way was best . . . and which way she'd jump.

A weathered split-rail fence was her first indication they were nearing their destination and that their time together was running out. It paralleled the dirt road for a short distance, then disappeared into the woods. Shortly after, the trees thinned, giving way to a small clearing dominated by a lone structure.

The log cabin looked more than a century old, its roughhewn timber silvery with age, the alternating stripes of light and dark wood giving an interesting, if basic, pattern to its walls. Two small windows pierced the side facing their approach but there were none on the empty porch that spanned the bare frontage. Deanna's instincts told her the interior would be just as austere.

Still, the prospect didn't distract her libido from more important things. Like whether Graeme's cock lived up to the promise of his large hands and feet.

She flushed at the erotic image that conjured.

Should she ask him in? He might take that as an invitation to her bed . . . which it could be.

Graeme brought the Jeep to a halt before Deanna could make up her mind. While she was distracted by her warring impulses, he got out and quickly rounded the hood to open her door for her. "Let me help you with those," he offered, relieving her of her heavier purchases.

"I can manage," she protested, sliding out of the Jeep to gather the few remaining bags.

"I'm here anyway, so you don't have to," he replied in a reasonable tone.

Since arguing would only have been ungracious, she let him have his way. "Thank you." She couldn't think of anything else to say that wouldn't sound stridently stiff-necked; it wasn't as if *he* was injured and needed to take it easy.

Deanna's breasts throbbed as they walked the short distance to the porch together, Graeme carrying the bulk of her purchases and matching his stride to hers without comment. He'd leave soon. If she didn't do anything, he'd go his way and she'd be left with this aching desire and no relief.

She didn't want her hand, as easy and uncomplicated as that would be, eliminating the issue of a relationship versus an affair. She wanted him, wanted Graeme inside her, that powerful body between her thighs, fucking all her questions out of her mind. Her mouth dried at the mental picture. *Oh, yes.*

After unlocking the door, Deanna turned to him, her nerves singing with tension. Did she ask him in? Ask him to kiss her? Something. Anything to prolong their time together.

His mouth descended on hers in an aggressive kiss—a frankly carnal one of possession, hungry and dominant. Taking what she offered freely and claiming more.

Her wits fled, shredded as need clawed at her, demanding satisfaction. Here. Now.

Yes!

She tore at his shirt, itching to have her hands on his wide chest, craving the feel of skin on skin. Pulling at it, she found the hem and pushed it up to bare his chest. The crisp hairs that met her questing fingers made her purr with anticipation. That against her cheeks and her breasts! Her breath hitched at the thought.

Equally impatient, Graeme disposed of her shorts, shoving them down her legs, along with her panty. Hard fingers probed her slit, plunged into her wet pussy.

"Oh, yes." Groaning, Deanna widened her stance to take him deeper, to let him touch her however he wanted. She'd never known she could need anything so much. His fingers stretched her, filling her as she hadn't been filled in a long time. "More," she begged. "Deeper, Graeme."

He stroked her, pumping strongly, sending sparks of delight dancing along her nerves. He cursed fervently when she gushed hot cream on his palm.

Moaning wordlessly, Deanna scrabbled at his belt, desperate for more. She needed his cock inside her; as good as he was with his hands, it wasn't enough.

Graeme hissed when she rubbed the hard ridge of his erection. Brushing her hands aside, he unzipped his fly and freed his cock. It rose out of his jeans, thick and flushed, a bead of clear fluid on its broad tip.

Impatient to have him, she wrapped her hand around his proud flesh and aimed him at her slit.

"Wait," he choked out, catching her wrist. "Condom."

Oh, God! She'd nearly forgotten. "Hurry!" He was so hard, hot and smooth to touch, like velvet and peach fuzz to her restless fingers, she was tempted to forgo protection.

He reached behind and pulled out a familiar packet, obviously prepared for emergencies. Which was good since Deanna felt like she'd explode if he didn't take her soon. She snatched it out of his hands and tore it open, to sheathe his thick cock with its veined shaft in thin latex.

The condom only served to emphasize his girth. The sight whetted her desire, making her core spasm with need.

Backing her against the rough wall, he shoved his cock into her dripping pussy, as impatient as she.

With her nerves wound to the breaking point by the prolonged buildup, molten rapture erupted through Deanna at his welcome invasion, her orgasm like fiery lava in her veins. She gasped his name, helpless to deny her response.

Graeme wielded his body like a blunt instrument of brutal pleasure, pounding her into exquisite and utter submission. With tender ferocity, he rode her up another precipice to a greater, more devastating climax.

She clung to him, helpless in the face of all that ecstasy. All her imaginings through the long morning spent with him hadn't prepared her for the raw fury he unleashed in her body.

Unfazed by her release, he drove her higher, faster, climbing further into the soaring peaks of carnal rapture.

Pleasure crashed through her in wave after overwhelming wave, demolishing all her previous definitions of the word. Her shattered senses fled until all she knew was an endless rolling orgasm that swept her away.

Deanna returned to herself with a whimper, an unfamiliar, rhythmic sensation nagging for attention. She blinked her eyes open to find Graeme stroking her cheek, his blue gaze turned silver with concern. Slowly, her senses came back online, reporting various discomforts: a sore throat, the rough wood against her back, crisp hair rasping against her breasts, her body stretched and still impaled on his, her legs locked around his hips.

"You back now?" His subterranean rumble flowed through her, reaching down to rock her quivering core.

"Yeah." For some reason, her voice was hoarse.

"Good." He took her lips leisurely this time, exploring her mouth and tangling his tongue with hers. Enticing her to play. As though he wasn't already deep inside her.

Replete with pleasure, she reciprocated, content at the slower pace, needing time to recover. The multiple orgasms had been impossibly mind-blowing; she'd never imagined herself capable of experiencing such ecstasy.

Graeme's hands started wandering, his hard fingers tracing patterns on her sensitized flesh. They found her breasts and teased them to greater firmness, tweaking and rolling her tight nipples. His gentle play stoked the fire in her belly, sending hot need coiling through her responsive core.

Suddenly hungry for more, Deanna clenched her thighs, grinding her mound on his pelvis, trying for an angle that got her clit. She moaned as sweet delight washed over her in a gush of liquid heat.

He probed between them and found her erect nub, coaxing a greater response from her body.

She cried out in wordless disbelief as ravenous lust speared through her, an aching void that demanded filling, that craved carnal satisfaction. Good God, hadn't those incredible orgasms been enough?

"Ready for more?" He resumed thrusting, his hips pistoning in a slow, measured pace, pumping her to a silent meter. Despite her previous climaxes, he felt larger than before, thicker than ever. *Didn't he come earlier?*

His cock shuttled into her, the flare of his head rasping against her inner membranes. In and out. In and in and in until he was snugged against her core. Then out . . . out . . . out, holding to his timing with steely deliberation. He did it over and over. Endlessly. Building her desire higher and higher, but not allowing her release.

Until Deanna was nearly out of her mind with need, begging for relief. "Graeme, please!"

Clawing his shoulders for traction, she writhed in his arms, trying for that perfect angle, the slightest more pressure to tip her over the edge. If only she could make it!

But he had her trapped against the wall, could control just

how much of him she got. And he wielded his thick cock with ruthless skill.

Deanna howled as the tension in her core scaled a few notches higher. "Let me come, Graeme!" Her world seemed to narrow down to her body, to the erotic friction of his chest hair on her breasts and nipples, and the conflagration between her thighs.

Flexing his buns, he grunted as his balls kissed her thighs. "Not just yet."

Oh, God! How much longer could he last?

His head dipped to her shoulder where teasing nibbles added shivers of delight to her predicament. "Damn, you smell so good!" He sucked on her earlobe, the shocking sensation like a live wire plugged directly into her core.

It shattered her.

"*Yes!*" Graeme was suddenly pounding into her, taking her beyond anything she'd known before. His hips jerked, his cock pulsing and twitching inside her.

Pure incandescent rapture exploded in her core, a runaway steam engine pouring scalding heat through her body. It flooded her veins with unspeakable ecstasy too potent to deny.

She screamed in wordless relief, her voice mingling with Graeme's as he gave in to his orgasm. The moment spun out endlessly, an eternity of breathtaking pleasure that blinded her to everything else.

Wrung out by her release, Deanna floated in his arms, waiting for restlessness and panic to close in on her. But nothing came to disturb her peace.

3

A hard band suddenly tightening across her waist startled Deanna out of well-earned sleep. Wondering where she was, she lifted her head off a thick hooked rug in front of a cold fireplace. At some point, Graeme had carried her into the cabin. She hadn't been paying much attention since he'd been inside her at the time, his motions too stimulating to ignore.

A warm mouth fastened on her shoulder, nibbling and licking fit to wrest a carnal response from a stone statue—which she certainly wasn't. Large hands joined in, capturing her breasts with hard palms.

Desire stirred inside her, far livelier than she expected. Surely all that pleasure should have lasted her body for months? How could she want him again, and so quickly?

Her libido paid no mind to such reasoning. Whatever he had, she definitely wanted—and soon—especially after a strategically placed nip sent fire darting down her spine.

Deanna arched her back in encouragement, tilting her hips back and discovering his ready erection. Wanting her hands on him, she tried to roll over.

Graeme's arm tight around her waist prevented her from completing the motion. When she squirmed in his grip, impatient at its constriction, he growled at her.

She froze in surprise. She'd heard him distinctly—he'd *growled*, low and almost menacing. She looked over her shoulder at him. "Graeme?"

There was a sharp—even feral—light in his eyes when he met her gaze. A predator ready to pounce.

Instinctively, Deanna raised her chin in challenge.

Then he blinked and it was gone. But his erection remained pressed against her bum, communicating his intent. Before she could shift mental gears, he lowered his head to nibble along her throat, stealing her breath with little kisses.

"Don't move." His hold on her relaxed slightly, but not enough for her to turn over. Anyway, his weight pressed down on her, the hard ridges of his abs gliding over her buns and thighs, effectively pinning her in place with his sheer mass. There was no way she could budge him from that position until he let her.

Graeme continued to lick her shoulders, moving from side to side. He blanketed her with heat, his musky scent surrounding her until every lungful of air was filled with him. His hot hands painted tingles along her ribs and down to the tender skin of her groin.

Deanna moaned in disbelief as now-familiar delight spiraled up from her belly, dark hunger making her womb clench like a tight fist, hot cream spurting in welcome. Her breasts throbbed, protesting his neglect.

A hand slid farther down to cup her mound. Burrowing deeper, he found her clit and strummed it to quivering erection.

Lightning struck, sparking off a bonfire of raw need. "Oh!" Deanna gasped as heat spurted through her body, her nerves suddenly buzzing with anticipation.

"Oh, yeah," Graeme rumbled above her, his fingers gliding over her wet slit. "You want more, don't you?"

"Please!" She couldn't deny it, couldn't deny her response. Shifting beneath him, she rubbed her tight nipples on the rough pile of the rug, hoping to ease the throbbing ache in the hard tips.

Caressing her folds, he teased her with shallow, nudging probes of her sheath.

"Deeper!" She needed more! Needed him stretching her to aching fullness with his thick girth.

He thrust two fingers inside her, his palm grinding down on her mound. He homed in on her G-spot with uncanny certainty, honing her need with playful taps that upped her desire to quivering desperation.

"Take me, Graeme!"

"Open your legs for me," he ordered in a guttural tone.

She did so and felt him settle between her thighs. A hot brand slid down her bum to nudge her wet sex.

Then he parted her lips with his fingers, holding her open while he pushed into her, delving into her creaming channel with short digs that jolted her sensitized nerves. "Damn, you feel so good."

Deanna clawed the rug, groaning with each shallow thrust as he drove home, sheathing his hard cock in her welcoming body. He reached so deep inside her from this angle that his complete possession nudged her womb, sending a fierce jolt of delight through her.

Held in place by his grip on her upper arms, she could only lie there and take him . . . and that sure knowledge thrilled her. For once, she didn't have to think, simply feel. The freedom left her breathless.

Graeme rocked over her, his motions pressing her into the rug, each thrust drawing her climax nearer. Gradually, he increased his speed until rapture loomed like rolling thunder, heralding her imminent orgasm with rumbles of delight.

Straining for release, Deanna thrust her hips back, meeting his lunges, the wet slaps of their bodies blending with her gasps and his grunts. Pleasure eddied in her belly, a delicious foretaste of explosive release.

Just a little more!

He ground his cock inside her, his thick shaft swirling over her sensitized inner membranes. His motion shoved her mound against the rug, jolting her clit.

Pure lightning seared her.

The tension snapped. Heat burst through her as the dam broke, spilling rapture in a roaring freshet of sensation that swept everything in its path. She gasped, overwhelmed by the sheer ferocity of her orgasm. "Graeme!"

As Deanna tumbled in the aftermath, he made a guttural sound above her. Then she floated in velvet darkness, lost for a time from all the world while pleasure continued to resonate through her.

"You okay?" A large hand stroked her back, the constant repetition somehow soothing to her sensitized nerves.

"Oh, yeah," Deanna couldn't help purring, the languor suffusing her body more than compensating for the gentle ache between her thighs. Lying flat on the rug, she panted, feeling devastated by her response to Graeme's lovemaking. To think that all this time she'd never believed herself capable of so much passion, only to be proven wrong with such irrefutable evidence.

He got up and dealt with the used condom, discarding it in a trash can under the sink, his motions smooth and controlled, even graceful—unusual in such a big man. She hadn't even noticed when he'd put it on. As he returned from the kitchen, he plucked some foil packs from a box on the couch, then stretched out beside her.

Rolling over, Deanna blinked at the paperboard container. "They supplied the cabin with *that?*" Maybe fall color and fishing weren't the only attractions of Woodrose.

Graeme laid the packs on the hearth, his expectations clear. "These? I got them from the Jeep. I keep a box on hand for emergencies."

"You plan for emergency sex?" She frowned, wondering how many women he'd rescued and bedded before her.

His snort interrupted her musing. "'Course not. Sex isn't the only thing an unlubricated condom is good for. You can use them to keep small things dry, for example. Just plop whatever in and tie it off." He caressed her hip, a possessive stroke that nevertheless sent a thrill of excitement speeding through her. "Do you really want to discuss alternative applications for condoms right now?"

With desire once more stirring in her belly, Deanna had to admit she didn't.

"Ooooooh!" The feminine groan of exhaustion, complete with a breathless hitch that said "rode hard *and* put up extremely wet" to Graeme's heightened senses, had his limp cock stirring with determined interest.

He pried his eyelids up to stare at his impetuous member with disbelief. *Again?* He'd lost track of the number of times he'd taken Deanna that afternoon. It was a good thing they'd had lunch earlier or they'd have starved.

The strength of his need for this woman, the sheer intensity of it, had Graeme gritting his teeth. After hours of mind-blowing sex, he was still as ready on the trigger as a randy buck. If his werewolf metabolism didn't make short work of most drugs, he'd have suspected someone had doped his morning coffee with Viagra.

Damn, what was it about her that got to him so quickly? The way she'd fought to survive when she'd been trapped in the car? Her quiet determination to get things done? Was that what he found so attractive? Or was it something more basic?

Surely it couldn't be that pheromone thing his father had told him about? *The scent is unmistakable, like a shot of pure wanting straight to the gut, bypassing the brain and short-circuiting good judgment.*

But that sounded exactly like what happened to him around her. He couldn't deny her scent got to him exactly that way.

Could she be?

Was that it? As basic as female to male? Survival of the species?

He frowned, uncomfortable with the possibility. Like many of his agemates, he'd struck out on his own, moved away from the pack, because there was no hope of finding a mate within the clan. His female cousins all smelled like kin. Then, after all his hunts, he just happened to stick his snout between the breasts of a suitable female? The first solid candidate he comes upon turns out to be one with valor that appealed to more than his cock? That didn't happen in real life.

The sense of Fate taking a hand in random events was a hair disconcerting. He'd always thought of himself as someone in control of his own life. Now this?

Could she really be—

Deanna turned in his arms, her gentle curves gliding over his chest. A potent distraction. Her nipples hardened to stiff peaks, poking at him insistently, the sweet contact touching him with fire and banishing all logical thought.

The smell of sex and sweat and pure Woman wafted past his nose and zinged straight to his groin.

Who cared about Fate? Here and now was fantastic, and that was all that mattered.

Graeme bent down to take a tight, rosy nub between his lips, coaxing it to greater extension.

Their earlier bouts of lovemaking had passed in an intoxicating haze of pleasure. Now, he took the time to appreciate his good fortune.

He'd always been a breast man and—despite his already high expectations from his first up-close and personal encounter with her pair—Deanna excelled on that front. She filled his hands sweetly, soft and high and firm. Just the right size. Perfect.

Bending down, he brushed his cheeks against her, reveling in the velvety feel of her mounds and their hard tips. He plumped them together, burying his nose in her cleavage, and inhaled her marvelous scent. Damn, but she smelled so good. His cock twitched in definite agreement, swelling as his blood and judgment rushed south.

He toyed with her nipples, watched them tighten further, flushing red under his manipulations.

Moaning softly, Deanna squirmed under him, her scent strengthening, sweat beading between her breasts.

Another deep breath had his head swimming, his cock aching to be held. But not yet. He wanted to enjoy the moment a little longer.

Tracking the source of her musk, he slithered downward, rubbing his face over her smooth, so feminine body, admiring up close the gentle curve of her belly with its even, pale-gold tan, until finally he reached the light brown curls at the top of her thighs, the crisp hairs tipped with cream.

The potent spring of everything he wanted.

He spread Deanna's delicate ruffles to find her clit beneath its hood. Dipping his thumb into her cream, he stroked the little nub to erection, grinning to himself when a choked gasp sounded above him. He thrust a finger into her slit, groaning as her wet flesh welcomed him with a tight squeeze.

Keeping his thumb rolling over her shaft, he coaxed more cream from her pussy, breathing deeply of her musky perfume. He'd never imagined anything could smell so wonderful. He pumped her, drawing out more cream, the sight of her obvious arousal capturing all of his attention. Adding more fingers, he experimented with other strokes.

Her hips rolled as he caressed her. "Graeme!"

Smiling at her response, he panted to rein back his need, ignoring the throb of his aching cock as he redoubled his efforts, but it only drew more of her entrancing scent into his lungs. Unable to resist, he took her swollen clit between his lips and sucked it, using his tongue to play with her nub.

She shrieked in surprise, her hips jerking gratifyingly. Cream spurted from her slit, covering his palm with her passion—a blatant invitation he couldn't ignore.

Mindful of the risk, he grabbed a condom, tore the pack open with his teeth and sheathed himself single-handed.

Deanna tightened around his fingers, squeezing them urgently, her slick walls sliding around them like wet silk.

Unable to resist the summons any longer, he rose above her, aimed his cock at her slit and thrust hard, working into her until he was hilt-deep and wrapped in hot, wet pussy. Honeyed pleasure shivered through him as her inner muscles fluttered around his length, gripping him firmly.

Deanna wrapped her thighs tight around him, her back arched in the extremity of her need. As she met his thrusts, she chanted his name in a husky contralto that was just short of a growl. Her sexual flush painted the slopes of her breasts with red, the wash of color sweeping up her throat and deepening the pink of her lips and cheeks. The very picture of femininity. Absolutely lovely.

Yet he knew there was more.

Had to be more.

Instinct told him she had yet to reach some nameless peak. And only he could get her there.

His hands locked around her ass, Graeme drove into Deanna, pumping his hips to the roaring drumbeat in his ears. Wildfire gathered in his balls, streaking up his cock with each thrust. It burned down his control to bare threads, scorched by the ecstasy that threatened to break free.

And still she wasn't *there*.

Beneath him, Deanna sobbed, the tension in her pussy ratcheting tighter by another notch until she quivered around him, right at the brink of release. Almost scalding him with the intensity of her hunger.

His gut said she was almost *there*, would get to that peak . . . if only he could hold out.

She writhed around him, her sheath touching him with heat lightning all along his length.

The electrifying friction destroyed Graeme's control. The fire in his balls burst free, boiling up his cock like a geyser flashing over. Raw pleasure rocketed up his spine to explode in his brain.

The edges of Deanna's form shimmered briefly, like a mirage on a hot day.

What the—?

Her scent strengthened, sweet and full of carnal promise, an intoxicating whiff that made the room swim around him. His cock throbbed, the pounding of his blood a roaring in his ears.

Later. He'd consider the implications of what he'd seen and everything else that needed thinking about later. Right now, all that mattered was the feel of Deanna melting over his cock, squeezing him for all he had, fluttering around him as she convulsed in rapture.

Graeme gave himself up to the moment and over to the firestorm raging in his balls, letting it blow through his body as he pumped Deanna to ecstasy.

But as he floated in the aftermath of their passion, the image of her blurring in his arms clung to his memory.

4

Deanna's sheath fluttered again, the latest wave from her most recent orgasm wafting her higher. She moaned wordlessly, lost in sublime satisfaction. No matter how many times Graeme pleasured her, she still couldn't get enough of him.

Pip-pip-pip. Pip-pip-pip. Pip-pip-pip.

The shrill sound came as a rude shock to the senses. "What's that?"

"Ignore it." The muttered command came from chest level where Graeme was nuzzling her breasts.

The insistent beeping continued, its urgency unabated. Too insistent for her to ignore despite the toe-curling incentive her lover continued to provide.

She turned her head, searching the room for the sound's source. Eventually, she narrowed it down to somewhere under the sofa, then spotted a black watchstrap sticking out. "Yours, I think," she gasped, around a sudden dart of pleasure that streaked from her nipple to her core.

By the merry rumble she got in answer, Deanna wasn't sure

he'd heard her. She grabbed the short bristles of his hair. "Graeme."

Releasing the tingling bud reluctantly, he looked up. "What?"

"It's your watch," she answered, reciprocating his lack of enthusiasm for the interruption. But the least he could do was turn the blasted alarm off.

He gave the beeping device on the floor a look of grim dislike. "Shit." But instead of merely reaching over, he rolled off her and snatched it up.

Grunting something imprecatory, he searched the room, then went out to the porch, returning with clothes in hand. He tossed some in her direction, then started dressing.

Feeling exposed in her supine position, Deanna sat up, hugging her knees to her chest as she watched all that eye candy disappear under knit and twilled cotton. "Where're you going?"

Graeme pulled his T-shirt down over his head. "Work. I've got to go now or I'll be late."

It was going on five already?

"Will you . . . ?" She stared up at him, feeling awkward. How to ask if he'd be back when what they'd shared that afternoon didn't qualify as a one-night stand or a quickie? And should she invite him back when she wasn't even sure what she wanted from him?

"My shift ends at two. That's probably too late . . ."

"That's okay. I . . ." Could she tell him she wanted to see him again when they weren't even dating? Would saying so automatically mean sex? Even though it was true, she wasn't comfortable admitting it, just like that.

Disregarding her bra in the interest of haste, Deanna separated the pieces in the pile of clothing he'd thrown down and put them on, tucking her tank top into her shorts just as Graeme slipped his socked feet into his shoes. When she looked up, he was at her side, reaching out to tilt her chin up and claim her lips.

She sank into the kiss, closing her eyes as his heat enfolded her senses. Sure, she was leaving for Hillsboro as soon as her things were recovered, but this was wonderful for now.

Pip-pip-pip. Pip-pip-pip. Pi—

Deanna recoiled, startled by the sudden noise. Heard almost next to her ear, the beeping was even more jarring. "Go!"

Shaking his head as though trying to clear it, he stepped back and opened the door. While crossing the porch, he said over his shoulder to her, "I'll be by tomor—"

He stumbled, caught himself with a hand on a post, then swore. Deanna had started forward at his misstep, but relaxed when he chuckled ruefully.

"We forgot your things."

The porch was littered with bags, her purchases dropped helter-skelter when they'd given in to passion. She stared at the disarray, taken aback by the proof of her atypical abandon. "I guess we were distracted."

He helped her bring the bags in, then finally took his leave, his long legs covering the short distance to his car in a ground-eating lope.

Deanna stood by the door, fighting the selfish urge to call Graeme back. Was it merely sexual attraction or could it be insecurity that made her want to cling to him as the one rock of stability she had? Her heart tripped at the thought. Surely it was just the situation, a vulnerability left over from her close call, reinforced by her dependence on him to get around town? Once she had wheels again, she'd feel less fragile.

She turned away gingerly, her knees still shaky from that last vigorous bout of lovemaking. Good God, was she turning into a spineless doormat just because of a scare?

If you could call a nearly fatal accident a scare. That was like saying Godzilla was a hapless little gecko.

The low growl of the Jeep's engine started up, then faded into the distance, announcing Graeme's departure. The hours until his return suddenly stretched before Deanna, empty of activity when she was accustomed to keeping herself busy.

Needing to do something, she explored the cabin, curious now that he wasn't around to absorb her attention.

It was a spare structure, all rough wood bearing the obvious signs of hand-tool marks, but well kept for all that. There was only one room: the front door opened directly into the kitchen, which flowed into the main cabin furnished with a long wood bench smelling of lemon polish, a battered settee, and a modern recliner. The stone fireplace she'd noted earlier took up one wall with small windows on either side that matched the one in the kitchen. An economical toilet and shower were located under narrow stairs that gave access to a loft over the kitchen.

The second level proved just as Spartan. A utilitarian bed sat beside a small window, with a single closet at its foot, built in under unpainted rafters. The loft had enough space for another bed or two, and overlooked the living area, but other than that, it had little to recommend it.

Betty hadn't been kidding when she'd said there wasn't much to do around here.

Overall, a cozy sort of place with—her heart dropped at the realization—no air-conditioning.

All of a sudden, Deanna felt the urge to bake. Needed to bury her hands in soft yielding dough. Wanted to slap it down, pummel it, make something out of unpromising flour and yeast.

Returning downstairs, she gave the kitchen a closer look. There was a modern microwave that was useless for her purposes and a wood stove that might have been part of the cabin's original fixtures. She stared at it glumly, knowing that anything she tried to cook on that relic would be doomed.

It didn't help to remember that her precious mixer lay at the bottom of a ravine, along with her laptop and other worldly possessions.

Frustrated, she paced to the hearth with its soot-darkened stones and neatly raked ashes—incongruous, given the summer heat—and avoided looking at the hooked rug in front of it that had been center stage for much of that afternoon's lovemaking. Wood was already laid on the andirons, just awaiting a flame on kindling. More firewood was stacked under the bench, making a pleasing pattern she was in no mood to contemplate.

She opened the windows to let fresh air in. But there was hardly any wind stirring the heat and little enough to cut the thick odor of exuberant sex that permeated the room.

The reminder was too much. She fled the cabin's confines, hoping to find relief in the outdoors. Perched as it was on the mountainside, the porch turned out to have a commanding view of the valley and the town nestled in it; she could make out the fire station and, in the distance, the roof of the clinic. Framed by the treetops and by blue ridges in the distance, it was probably breathtaking in morning light. But she was in no mood to appreciate the scenery.

Giving her back to it, Deanna skirted her temporary home, needing to move to release the tension building up inside her.

Behind the cabin, she found a small picnic area complete with table and benches. From the rear, the wooden structure presented a blank face, except for a hutch that probably opened to the space under the bench inside. Near its small double doors was a large, old stump, its flat top marked by straight scars—it apparently served as a chopping block for firewood. There wasn't much else to see, besides trees and bushes. From the picnic table, though, she could hear the faint sounds of water tumbling—probably the creek Betty'd mentioned.

Curiosity stirred, but her feet remained planted on the dry grass. She couldn't avoid the issue any longer.

What had gotten into her—besides the obvious? Deanna blushed at the thought. She'd never been one for jumping into bed, yet here she was, less than twenty-four hours after meeting Graeme. Who would have thought her sexual drought would end so abruptly, and with such a man?

Her womb throbbed at the reminder, the pleasant ache between her thighs a potent memento of his lovemaking. Giving in to weakness, she sat down on one of the rough benches, folded her arms on the table and rested her head on them.

He was so different from the other men of her acquaintance.

Deanna sighed, running her thumb over rough, pale wood meditatively. Maybe it had been the danger, but from the very first, Graeme had made a strong, unshakable impression.

He'd been like an avenging angel seen through the hole in the shattered windshield, a halo of light around his head. In hindsight, it had probably been the sun glinting off his hair, but that logical explanation didn't lessen his impact on her.

Then, there was the way his arms had bulged when he pushed the warped frame of her car window open, his muscles thrown into stark relief by the massive effort. He'd rivaled the models and Classical sculpture she'd studied in college . . . and he'd been doing it to save her.

Surely that explained part of his attraction? How many men did she know who'd risk so much for a total stranger?

Wind blew over her, stirring her hair and rustling the leaves above her, as she pondered that.

No one else came to mind.

Only Graeme.

What was it about him that drew her so strongly? His easy manner with the townsfolk? His casual thoughtfulness? His energetic lovemaking and the care he took to make sure she enjoyed it, too? All of the above?

Deanna sighed, closing her eyes to the dancing sunlight that dappled the table. She wanted to *know* him—not just in the carnal sense of the word but in every other way.

Don't forget you're leaving soon. Hillsboro was where she might discover something about her parents, maybe even family.

Heritage. That's why she'd left Boston, and what she'd hungered for, ever since she'd learned what "orphan" meant. And Hillsboro was where she might find it, not Woodrose. Just because she'd met a man who intrigued her didn't mean she'd give that up.

And she only had so many days to do it, if she didn't want her business to suffer. It was one thing to take a week or two for herself to drive down; it was another thing altogether to let her projects hang fire for a month.

The breeze died down, leaving sunlight streaming down on her arms and face. Without the whispering wind for competition, the ripple of the creek sounded louder, punctuated by the occasional splash of water.

All at once, the sweat from the afternoon's activities made her skin itch. Since the clinic hadn't been set up for long-term patients, she hadn't been able to take a proper bath. Reminded of that deficiency, she decided that a shower sounded like a wonderful idea.

Deanna retreated to the cabin, then stripped off her limp clothes, which were the worse for wear from more than a day's use plus a few hours on the porch.

She stepped into the shower and turned the tap. Though the water was tepid, the pressure was strong enough to sting, a refreshing contrast to the humid heat. Soaping herself, she washed off the sweat and the lingering memory of the accident with a will. The foamy massage of the washcloth over her sensitized skin brought to mind Graeme's caresses. Her hands slowed as she savored the memory, retracing his strokes. Across her breasts, her thighs and belly, her neck and shoulders, even her back and bum, touching her all over with a hunger that couldn't be denied. She shivered with desire, her core almost convulsing in rapture.

He'd been insatiable. A fucking madman.

Deanna smiled at the description.

He'd made her scream and beg for release, and she wanted

more of it. Could barely wait until his shift was over and he returned to her. True, she was sore from his attentions, but that didn't matter.

She felt alive, free, and safe. More so than she'd felt in months. More like her old self, before the city had started closing in on her. Even though she'd only have these few days with him, she wasn't going to pass them up. When Graeme returned, she'd welcome him with open arms.

The issue settled in her mind, Deanna quickly finished showering. She dried herself with a thin towel from a stack on the shelf, the effort leaving a sheen of sweat across her shoulders. Her ease of motion surprised her. She'd forgotten to be careful of sudden movement, yet her body barely complained.

The mirror mounted on the back of the bathroom door provided another surprise: her bruise looked better. It had faded somewhat and was no longer so luridly purple. Of course, the splotches of green and yellow that remained weren't *that* much of an improvement, but stretching almost didn't hurt, which was a blessing.

She stared, dumbfounded by the rapidity of her recovery. Now that she thought about it, she hadn't been in any pain while making love with Graeme earlier. Not that that could have had anything to do with her healing.

Graeme spent most of his shift fighting his gut, which was bawling him out for leaving Deanna free to be claimed by some other male. He ignored it as the territoriality of his inner wolf, knowing better than to give instinct free rein when it had already run wild most of the afternoon.

The highlight of the evening was seeing Henckel behind bars, awaiting his bail hearing on Monday. By the time they'd brought him in on Friday, court had been out and the judge off for some weekend fishing—much to Graeme's satisfaction. He was of the opinion it would do the idiot good to have a fore-taste of jail to see if he had a liking for the institution.

Seeing Henckel also reminded Graeme to drop by the Hogg Wylde during his patrol to make sure the weekend revelry hadn't gotten out of hand. He made a point of checking on the idiot's teammates; with classes out for the summer and months to go before they dispersed to whatever colleges would take them, they'd taken to treating the bar like a second home. September couldn't come soon enough to break up that pack of yahoos.

The bar was a low building on the edge of town that catered to a rough crowd of drinkers. The owner spent the minimum on upkeep, leaving the weathered sidings bare and only a bat-tered and faded sign depicting carousing porkers to advertise its business. A graveled clearing served for parking, while picnic tables clustered closer to the bar.

By the time Graeme drove by, the heat of the night had forced the drinkers outside. Beer was flowing freely, as evidenced by the number of empties surrounding the group that worried him. With summer break, time lay heavy on the young idiots nor-mally led by Henckel. And from the sound of it, all that drink wasn't improving their belligerent dispositions.

"It's all her fault. If she hadn't been there, Fred wouldn't be in jail right now." The night air carried the complaint to Graeme's straining ears as he brought his patrol car to a halt on the road. The chorus of grumbled agreement that followed said this was a popular refrain.

Others picked up on the theme, elaborating on it and blam-ing Deanna for other imagined offenses.

Then someone broached the idea of getting even.

The group erupted with raucous, predatory laughter, the dis-cussion devolving into vainglorious boasts of how they would "punish" Deanna.

Over my dead body, Graeme snarled inwardly, wishing he

could throw the whole lot into jail for the duration of Deanna's stay in Woodrose. Unfortunately, he couldn't hang around to ensure Henckel's bunch didn't cause trouble; he still had the rest of his patrol to finish.

He assessed their condition with a critical eye. For once, he hoped they'd drink themselves to oblivion—they were halfway there already. If they did, he wouldn't have to worry about them for the rest of the evening.

It galled Graeme that the sheriff's orders forced him and his fellow deputies to ignore the idiots' very public consumption of alcohol. He couldn't even penalize the Hogg Wylde for serving minors.

And almost everyone in town excused the drinking as typical high spirits—boys will be boys, never mind that it flouted state law. After all, they'd done the same when they were teenagers and hadn't come to any harm.

His subsequent rechecks later that night found them embroidering on their notion of punishment. What was particularly worrisome was their restraint. At any other time, a few fistfights would have broken out by now. That they continued to huddle around the table drinking made for a change in pattern that didn't do much for his peace of mind.

Back at the station at the end of his shift, Graeme still couldn't put the boasts at the Hogg Wylde out of his head. What if there was more to it than a bunch of hotheads letting off steam? He knew from past experience Henckel's bunch didn't see anything wrong with roughing up people they didn't like.

"Heard there's a cold front coming." Mitchell heaved his bulk out from behind his desk with a grunt of understandable weariness. The heat and the full moon had brought out the mischief-makers in force, resulting in more than one house papered and several complaints of rowdiness and public indecency. They'd been run off their feet in the latter half of their shift.

"'Bout time we had some. It might cool things off a mite."

Graeme typed up the last of his reports, carefully punching keys that were too small for his fingers. Damned sexist typewriter makers never seemed to consider that men did their own typing these days.

He returned Mitchell's wave absently just before the other deputy disappeared out the door, his mind playing back the beer-fueled discussion he'd overheard. The more he thought about it, the more he didn't like it. Henckel's bunch was liquored up enough to make trouble for Deanna. And everyone in Woodrose knew where to find her.

Staring blindly at the report he was typing, Graeme imagined the damage those muscle-bound yahoos could do to Deanna without even raising a sweat. He gritted his teeth. Not if he had anything to say about it. She had enough bad experiences to turn her off Woodrose without those idiots giving her more reason not to stay.

Pounding on the typewriter, he finished the report. Once he'd signed them and turned them in, he'd be off duty. Then he could see what he could do about safeguarding Deanna.

Deanna lay on top of the bed, her limp sleep shirt clinging to her body, the crispness of her new purchase having quickly succumbed to sweat. The loft was like an oven, roasting her to a crisp. Even keeping the small window completely open didn't bring relief from the sweltering heat. She wouldn't have minded so much if Graeme had been the cause of it. But he wasn't.

She turned over, trying to find a cooler position, but the mattress had soaked up the heat of the day. The only cool spots were damp from perspiration.

Unable to stand it a moment longer, she escaped downstairs, but it was little better. The air was stagnant, a heavy blanket that clutched at her body. A second shower bought only a brief respite from the heat. Sweat beaded her back even before she'd finished toweling herself dry.

Deanna paced the Spartan room restlessly, a familiar tension like a clamp around her ribs. The same disquiet that had sent her fleeing Boston. She gritted her teeth against the sensation, dismayed to feel it again.

But it wouldn't go away.

The cabin closed in on her. Constraining. Like a cage when she wanted to roam free.

Deanna spun on her heel, the hair slapping her cheeks a poor imitation of the stinging bite of a strong gust. She needed to see nature surrounding her, to have grass under her feet, to breathe fresh air.

Outside, the trees rustled, as though calling to her, whispering of the wind blowing through their branches.

Finally, it was more than she could bear. She took up her beddings and picked her way through the cabin with the help of moonlight streaming through a window. In the clearing behind, she laid the sheets out to make a pallet on the grass.

Graeme turned off the track, dry leaves crunching as he drove past some bushes to park the Jeep under a sycamore. He stared up at the tall tree with its patchy bark reflecting moonlight, breathing in the hot, heavy air.

Nothing stirred in the night, almost as though the animals knew a predator was in their midst.

Switching off the interior light, he left the Jeep, closing its door gently, knowing better than to tempt Fate with loud noises. While traffic was unlikely at this time of night, Murphy played fast and loose with the odds. He stripped out of his uniform and left it folded on top of his shoes to await his return.

The heat of the night left a thin layer of sweat on his shoulders. Thankfully, he didn't have to stand it for long.

Reaching for his other self, he Changed. Heat shimmered through his body, bathing him in waves of power. In less than a heartbeat, an eye-blink too quick to register, he was on all fours with gray-speckled black fur covering his wolf body.

Graeme shook himself, settling his fur into place as he waited for the tingling afterglow of his transformation to fade. His mouth gaped in a lupine grin. No matter how many times he'd Changed since puberty, it was still a heady rush to take on his other form.

Then he stretched, feeling loose muscles answer his command, his claws digging into the soft ground. The scent of flaking moss and dead leaves teased his nose, then danced away, the heat leaching most odors from the wind. He'd have welcomed a little rain to help him track but doubted the gods who watched over good werewolves would let some fall right when he needed it. It was still a few hours before the predicted cold front would hit, supposing the meteorologists got it right.

The full moon starting its descent to the west cast more than enough light for him to travel with some speed. In no mood to explore the forest, he loped through a bank of maidenhair ferns, heading for the creek that passed close to Deanna's cabin. All that water would make it easier to track by smell. If Henckel's mob of swaggerers had passed anywhere near it, he'd find their trail.

Stronger odors and a soft gurgle announced the stream's presence long before he saw its banks. Skirting the dense vegetation at the waterside, he paralleled the creek for a distance, scrambling down slick rocks when it descended in a series of cascades on its winding way toward the cabin. He ignored the dancing waters glittering in the moonlight, more interested in the scents carried by the night breeze.

Nothing man-made was in the air. *So far*, he cautioned himself, wary of overconfidence. He sniffed again, just to confirm what his senses reported. It wouldn't do for the locals to see him by accident.

Closer to the cabin, Graeme checked his surroundings more carefully. In his wolf form and in favorable conditions, he could pick up scents from over a mile away and sounds several miles distant. With his Jeep parked downwind, he didn't detect any vehicles. *Yet.*

Then something else grabbed his attention by the scruff and shook it, demanding his complete and undivided focus. An irresistible scent that shot straight to his wolf brain, bypassing reason, reducing him to three hundred pounds of pure instinct.

Enticed by the olfactory ambrosia, he sniffed the wind for its source.

There! It was close. Strong and getting stronger. A low sob floated on the night air, coming from the same direction.

Heedless of all else, he sprang forward to hunt down the scent.

It called to him, a summons that couldn't be denied. A siren song he felt in his bones, singing to him of hunger beyond imagining. Evoking a response that was instinctive, bred into countless generations of werewolves long before Man had built his first city.

The pressure in Deanna's chest lessened immediately, now that she was out of the cabin. But she still couldn't stand still.

Restless in the heat, she paced the clearing, the soft knit of her shirt irritating her nipples, which were slightly sore from Graeme's lovemaking. She knew she ought to be worrying about her things and how much longer it would take before she could continue on to Hillsboro, but all she could think about was Graeme.

She wanted him again. Despite their enthusiastic and energetic lovemaking just hours before, she wanted him again.

Deanna turned back, trying to derail that line of thought. From picky celibate, she was becoming a sex maniac—albeit a picky sex maniac, Graeme being the only one to trigger this craving in her. None of the other men she'd met today had provoked anything stronger than appreciation for the male form. She'd never experienced anything like the carnal hunger that burned in her, that demanded the driving power of Graeme's possession.

Was it just because of that incredible rescue? Surely it couldn't be more than that. As out of character as today's actions were, surely they were understandable in light of her close brush with death.

Shoving her uneasy thoughts out of her mind, she settled on the pallet to court sleep. Though the ground was hard, it was better than indoors. Certainly, it was no harder than the floor when she'd been under Graeme and meeting his thrusts, or the side of the cabin when he'd first taken her on the porch.

Her nipples beaded at the memory, the stiff peaks rubbing against the thin cotton and aching from the gentle chafing. It was more stimulus than she could bear.

Throwing off her sleep shirt impatiently, Deanna lay back down on the pallet, unmindful of her nudity in the darkness and determined to finally sleep. A cool puff of air dried the sweat from her breasts, making her nipples tingle. She rubbed them, trying to soothe them so she could rest. But the sensual friction only made need pool hot and heavy in her belly, her sheath's emptiness another lingering irritation.

She made a face at her body's sensual hunger. Despite the lateness of the hour, Graeme was probably still at work; she couldn't wait for him to come and feed this outrageous craving he'd awakened in her.

Realizing she wouldn't get any sleep until she eased the ache, Deanna rolled her palms over her breasts, sighing when they throbbed. Her womb clenched, restive with need.

Why on earth was this happening now? She'd have thought all that sex with Graeme had sated her body. God, how could she want him again?

Want him still.

She finally allowed herself to remember what she'd been tip-toeing around all night.

The memory of that first time surged to the forefront of her thoughts. He'd lifted her into his arms without any difficulty or obvious exertion, pinning her against the rough wall in a forceful show of strength that was as attractive as it was unsettling. He could so easily overpower her. Hanging in his arms, she'd felt . . . defenseless and out of control.

When all her life she'd striven for independence.

Yet she wanted him. How perverse was that?

Heat seized her at the thought of just how much she'd craved his touch—and still wanted more. Her sheath gave a traitorous flutter, cream trickling between her thighs.

Deanna cupped her swelling flesh, the sweet ache of Graeme's possession fresh in her mind.

He'd been so big, the blunt head of his cock velvety beneath her fingers and crimson with his desire. When he'd taken her, he'd been relentless, pushing into her clamoring body with an insistence that couldn't be denied.

Helpless to resist the call of desire, she thrust her fingers into her pussy, gasping as the sudden friction evoked Graeme's power. Her hips rose involuntarily, driving her fingers deeper. "Oh, God!" How could she want him so much, crave his touch like this?

A warm breeze blew over her, a gentle puff reminiscent of Graeme's breath on her skin just before he took her nipples into his mouth. Groaning, she stroked her breasts with her free hand, her palm tingling at the memory of the feel of his short, wiry hair scraping over it. She plucked at her nipples, rolled the tight buds the way he had just hours ago. To have him do that again . . .

Sweet delight spiraled through her, fueled by the contact and her fantasies. Spurred on the sparkles flooding her veins, she forgot where she was, dismissing everything except her recollection of the raw ecstasy of Graeme's lovemaking.

Need speared her as she stroked herself, the thorn of a dark rose blooming in her empty core. The slender columns of her fingers barely stretched her sheath, a paltry substitute for Graeme's thick, hard cock. Pumping the depths of her weeping sex, she writhed on her thin pallet, carnal hunger driving her on.

It wasn't enough.

Deanna sobbed wordlessly, straining for release. The tension in her core wound tighter, glittering pleasure hanging just a heartbeat out of reach.

She wanted.

Graeme!

Drawing her fingers from her quivering sheath, she circled her clit, smearing hot cream over the erect nub. A spike of delight rewarded her, pushing her that miniscule step over the edge. Her orgasm washed over her in a gentle wave of sweetness, euphoric in its blissful power—and still she wanted more.

Needed more.

Heat answered her desire.

An agile tongue laved her slick folds, gliding over tender membranes with lavish strokes. It swirled around her clit in teasing circles, flicked over the turgid flesh and rolled it with breathtaking subtlety.

Groaning, Deanna raised her hips in encouragement, craving more of that sweet seduction. "Oh, Graeme . . ." For it couldn't be anyone else but him; she recognized the sudden fillip he gave her clit, arousing in its unexpectedness. He'd used it to good effect earlier that day.

He licked her swollen flesh over and over, fanning the flames of her desire to greater heights, drawing more cream from her sex.

Lightning arced through her core, sparked by his swirling tongue. She sobbed for breath, shocked anew by the strength of her response to him. It had her arching off the pallet as her heels dug into the hard ground. The tension in her core coiled tighter, threatening to explode.

Not yet. Not just yet. She wanted to make it last.

Her legs spasmed, tensing as she fought back her orgasm. She wanted to savor the buildup while she could.

Hard, rough pads pushed insistently on her inner thighs, pressing them apart. Sharp points prodded the thin skin, biting deeply enough to penetrate the dense fog of carnal delight blanketing Deanna's senses.

Something wasn't right.

Struggling against the sweetness lapping at her nerves, Deanna opened her eyes.

A gray wolf watched her with Graeme's piercing arctic blue stare, trapping her gaze as he licked her dripping sex, the curves of his fangs hard against her swollen flesh.

She gasped, nerve-jangling shock holding her motionless. Flat on her back and totally naked, her legs splayed open before the wolf, she was painfully aware of her vulnerability to its long, jagged teeth.

The impasse stretched on, neither of them moving.

Then hot cream spurted between her thighs, unbidden and irrepressible, as involuntary as the shudder that streaked up her spine. Good God, surely she couldn't be aroused!

A low growl rumbled in that deep chest. The wolf pressed forward. Its tongue darted into her, flitting against sensitized membranes, lashing her sheath with delicate swipes.

The intimate contact sent a shiver of pleasure washing over her, carnal need coiling tight in her belly. *Oh, God!* Each swipe reverberated through her, a fresh thrill that left goose bumps on her arms and made her nipples tingle with fierce delight.

How could she be responding to its actions? Surely it was merely the stimulation? She couldn't be so far gone as to find the danger exciting.

And yet she was aroused.

She couldn't deny the raw pleasure sweeping through her body like a wildfire blazing out of control. Couldn't ignore the rough tongue dancing over her tender folds. Couldn't escape the thrum of treacherous delight growing in her fluttering core.

How can this be happening?

Knowing better than to startle a wild animal, Deanna could only surrender herself to the inevitable, caught between exquisite sensation and self-preservation. No wolves in these mountains? What a bizarre way to discover otherwise! But if she survived the experience, she wasn't sure she'd correct the locals' misconception. Who would believe her? Even with the toe-curling delight from the wolf's lavish attention on her pussy, she had difficulty believing it herself.

A sharp spike of pure rapture forced a harsh gasp from her, but the wolf ignored the sound, intent on licking her. Still, she pressed her fist to her lips to silence the desperate moans that threatened to spill forth. Pleasure wracked her body as fire burned in her core and sizzled, building on her earlier desire. A carnal fever ate away her restraint, edging her closer to abandon.

What would happen when she lost it?

Another hot wave of dark delight splashed through her, making Deanna's legs twitch despite herself.

The wolf gave a low growl, pressing down on her thighs and holding her wide open to its ravishment. Its tongue lashed out, licking her juices from its narrow muzzle. It stared up her body, gazing at her with a sentient light in its pale blue eyes as it lowered its head back to her pussy and resumed lapping cream from her throbbing flesh.

A thundering outpour of molten lava scorched her senses.

Oh please, oh please, oh please. Rapture loomed, her climax inevitable in face of the torrent of forbidden delight. Her teeth dug into the back of her hand as she fought not to scream.

The wolf flickered, wavered like an image in a laser light show or a hologram switching angles. Heat seared her where its paws pressed on her thighs. Then Graeme lay between her legs, the intent look in his pale blue eyes identical to the wolf's.

The creature was gone!

Deanna couldn't think. Didn't know what to think. Didn't want to question her deliverance. The only thing that mattered was that Graeme was there. She grabbed his shoulders, her fingers barely making an impression on his hard muscles. The solidity beneath her hands assured her, more than anything else, that he was truly there.

Holding her shocked gaze, he crawled up her body, his turgid cock making his intentions clear. Placing the blunt head at her wet folds, he pressed against her. But instead of taking her, he merely stroked his cock over her slick pussy.

"What—Why—"

"No protection," he grunted, rocking against her, his hips pistoning with a sure steady rhythm, but never penetrating.

Only the faintest voice of good sense kept her from insisting they take the risk. She was so far gone that she wanted him inside her, filling her exactly the way she craved.

The scalding contact drove it out of her mind as he rolled over her clit.

It was too much.

Fire surged in her core, shot a tongue of flame up her spine. Still poised on the pinnacle of desire the wolf had built up, Deanna shattered. Clawing the blankets, she convulsed from the rawest of ecstasies, unable to prevent a scream of pleasure as she climaxed. A low howl of delight joined hers as Graeme took his release.

Finally, she floated in pleasure, covered by hot, hard male, the restless tension that had driven her all night banished. Even the memory of the wolf's ravishment didn't have the power to alarm her.

* * *

Graeme watched Deanna sleep with a gentle smile on her lips, the sweaty brown curl clinging to her cheek lending a misleading look of innocence to his lover. Despite her recent experiences, she looked more than fine. The livid bruise on her side was almost gone; only the faintest traces of yellow were left. Another benefit of all that sex—for a werewolf.

Such a valiant woman with hidden depths. To open her eyes and see a wolf nuzzled against her sweet pussy and not go apeshit, that took exceptional nerve. Just as it had taken nerve to fight her way out of her doomed car, instead of waiting for rescue. And to pull up her roots and relocate to another state, which was what she was doing, to judge from her Massachusetts license plates and fully loaded car.

He could only hope he wasn't wrong about her, that her nerve would withstand his disclosure . . . and that the knowledge wouldn't scare her away.

5

Deanna shivered as cold wind chilled her bare breasts. She opened her eyes, blinking in confusion at the moonlit bushes that filled her gaze. Where was she? The thin pallet and hard ground under her slowly registered. *Oh, right. The picnic area behind the cabin.*

She'd dreamt . . .

A wolf with Graeme's arctic blue eyes crouched between her thighs, its muzzle pressed against her pussy. Then it was Graeme lying between her legs, watching her with carnal intent.

An arm tightened around her waist, hot and hard and infinitely familiar, pulling her against an equally familiar, well-muscled body.

Graeme's.

Oh, God. It hadn't been a dream.

Despite the goose bumps rising on her arms, the sudden realization sent a spurt of hot cream trickling down her thigh. His hand wandered down, sliding between her thighs to probe her wet folds.

She caught his wrist, preventing a deeper penetration. The

bones beneath her fingers were large and strong—and altogether human. The crisp hairs on his arm were the furthest thing from the dense fur of a wolf. How could she even entertain the possibility that Graeme was anything but what he seemed?

Deanna slipped out from under his arm to study his face.

He returned her gaze, his arctic blue eyes steady and intent—the exact same look the wolf had given her as it licked her pussy. What other explanation could there be for its sudden disappearance?

"You're a werewolf?" Said aloud, it sounded crazy. Werewolves were myths; sure, they were popular in fiction and horror movies, but no one really believed they were real.

"So are you."

Deanna stared at him. That sounded even crazier. "*What?!*"

"You're a werewolf, too." The expression on Graeme's face was serious, lacking even the slightest tilt to his bushy brows.

Her stomach churned as she tried to laugh. "I know Lycan supposedly means wolf, but that doesn't mean . . ." She'd left Boston meaning to find out if she had any relatives, maybe discover something of her heritage, but she'd never have imagined anything like this. It was impossible!

"No, it doesn't. *Lykos* means wolf. Lycan comes from *lykantropos*—werewolf." He took her hand and brought it to his face. "And you smell like one."

He sniffed her, his eyes closing as he seemed to savor her scent like some fine perfume. "My father always said you could tell, but I never believed him until I met you. All my female relations just smell like kin." His cock stirred against his hip, thickening to semi-erection.

Deanna snatched her hand free. "I've never turned into a wolf in my life."

He merely blinked at her, his blue eyes glinting silver. "That's because a female's first Change is triggered by prolonged—and intimate—exposure to male pheromones." The way he said "change" made it sound significant, like it was written with a capital C.

She inched away from him, stopping only when her bare bum touched rough grass. "You mean—" All that sex she'd had with Graeme could make her a werewolf?

"Um-hmm. That's why I'm sure you're a werewolf. I've felt the start of it, the fever in you." Unconcerned by his nudity and obvious arousal, he flexed his shoulders.

Deanna stared at him across the meager pallet between them. She licked her lips, struck by the distracting picture he presented, with moonlight gleaming on his slabs of muscle. It was unfair how he could derail her train of thought with a simple motion like that. Taking a deep breath didn't help much in dragging her mind back to business, not when the air smelled of sex and male, but she managed to force her mind back to the gist of his outrageous statement. "It's biological? Don't you have to bite me to make me a werewolf?"

Graeme snorted. "It doesn't work that way. Werewolves are born, not made. Lycanthropy's not some kind of infectious disease, no matter what popular culture says. Either you have the potential to Change or you don't. No two ways about it."

She sat up and folded her arms around her bent legs, pulling them against her chest. "You're saying my parents were werewolves." She couldn't wrap her mind around the concept. When she'd started on this trip, she'd hoped to learn something of her family history, but this was too bizarre to take in all at once. *Werewolves!?*

"At least one of them," he agreed. "With your last name, probably your father."

Reeling from his revelations, Deanna shook her head. "I wouldn't know. He died when I was really young. I don't remember him or my mother." As an orphan, she'd been too old for easy placement, yet too young to recall her early childhood. "That's why I'm going to Hillsboro, to find out what I can about them." And why she'd ended up a ward of the state.

A sudden gust of cold air blew through the dark clearing, rattling branches and whipping her hair across her face, raising goose bumps all over her body. It brought with it the smell of green and rain and other things she hadn't been aware of before—small animals hiding in the brush. *Prey.*

Deanna shivered, feeling lost in a strange world.

"Why don't we continue this indoors where it's warmer?"

She welcomed his suggestion, snatching up her sleep shirt to cover her body from his hot-eyed stares. Maybe surrounded by reminders of the real world, his statements would be revealed for the fantastic babbling her mind insisted they ought to be. Werewolves didn't really exist! Not in this day and age.

Deanna rounded the cabin, knowing she ought to be afraid of being alone with him—someone who might actually turn into a large predator. He walked behind her, close by her side, as though herding her. She looked over her shoulder and saw him scanning the shadowy forest. Or maybe protecting her?

It was a potent reminder of what he'd done for her. How could she fear him when he'd risked his life to save hers? Werewolf or not, he had a streak of honor that ran soul-deep. But that didn't mean she could believe him.

Once inside, Graeme closed the door behind him and leaned against it, looking entirely normal, albeit completely naked and aroused. Nothing about him even hinted at anything unusual.

He didn't turn on the lights and she was just as happy to leave them off, not ready to face him under their glare.

"You can't ignore the signs."

She turned away to pace, her agitation needing an outlet.

Lycan means werewolf? Wasn't that a leap? She'd never felt less wolfish in her life!

"And Luger? Does it mean werewolf, too?" Deanna challenged, spinning on her heel to face him.

Still leaning on the door, his arms hanging easily, Graeme nodded. "It's a corruption of *loup-garou.*"

His answer took her aback, the quiet confidence underlying the reply shaking the wall of denial she was trying to build. Wrapping her arms around herself, she clutched at the soft cotton of her shirt. "Why are you telling me this?"

"Because you deserve to know." He inhaled sharply, then let his breath out slowly, as though bracing himself. "Because if we continue having sex, you'll Change."

His words hit her with unexpected force; her lungs actually seized in response. Could she have been considering continuing to have Graeme as a lover? An avowed werewolf?

An involuntary shudder of desire swept her body. No matter what her mind thought, her libido had its priorities set.

Pacing in front of the fireplace, Deanna forced herself to give his statement serious consideration. What if he truly was a werewolf? What if she was?

Was the chemistry between them as simple and powerful as that? And what of it? Couldn't the same be said of any sexual attraction?

Don't go blaming it on biology.

What if she broke things off and he was right? If she left for Hillsboro without ever exploring this, she'd always wonder. Even if she found family, they might not be able to answer her questions. They'd probably think her crazy for contemplating such an absurd possibility.

It was madness to entertain it.

Yet the wolf had had Graeme's eyes. And Graeme had appeared where the wolf had crouched—between her thighs. There was no way he could've moved that huge animal so quickly without her noticing, not when its paws had been set on her thighs just an instant earlier. Not when its fangs had been pressed against her sensitized pussy.

Her womb clenched at the memory, pure heat flooding her body. Stopping before the bench, she forced herself to focus on ends of the firewood stacked under it, to hold the random pattern in her mind and drive back the need clawing her belly.

Once she had herself under control, she looked over her shoulder at Graeme, who was now sprawled on the settee, quite unconcerned by his nudity, his heels propped on the coffee table. His big body reduced the sofa into a single-seater, his broad shoulders nearly spanning its length, his bulging forearms resting easily on its armrests. A generous pelt covered his chest, as speckled with gray as the hair on his head. It thinned into a vee that rippled down his belly and thickened around his hardening cock.

The sight sent a pang of hunger slashing through her, drawing her nipples into aching buds. Desire fought the bonds she'd set on it, her avid libido howling for another chance to have him pounding into her, riding her to rapturous oblivion.

"You really turn into a wolf?"

Not saying anything, Graeme pushed himself to his feet, his expression conveying only patience. Then suddenly a rampant gray wolf with an equally rampant cock stood in his place, holding his erect pose for a heartbeat before dropping to all fours.

The transformation was completely silent and almost anticlimactic. There'd been no crack of thunder, no lightshow, no painful-looking, grotesque contortion from man to animal.

She stared at Graeme in his new shape. Clearly, he believed actions spoke louder than words. Her heart in her throat, she approached him cautiously. Now that her mind wasn't fogged with lust, a gibbering voice wondered if she was insane.

He remained in wolf form, his dark tail wagging slowly, allowing her to look her fill. He was enormous—twice as large as normal wolves, his shoulder coming up to her waist. His head was easily chest height—which was brought home to her when he rubbed his narrow muzzle against her hard-tipped breasts. His blue eyes closed on a wolfish sigh, a warm gust of breath that brushed across her taut belly.

Swallowing with difficulty, Deanna touched him, her fingers sinking into his rough grizzled pelt. "Oh, my God." He was real. Not a hallucination brought on by some unsuspected perversion. The knowledge was strangely reassuring; she hadn't wanted to think she hankered for bestiality.

This was Graeme, not some savage animal. Which made it safe. Not that sex with a werewolf was safe, but at least she wasn't seeing things.

But he also thought she was a werewolf.

Which now seemed entirely possible.

She stilled, her mind racing through the logic of it and finding no holes in his reasoning. Why would he lie? By his own logic, if she wanted to avoid the Change, she should stop now. Tell him to leave her alone. That wasn't an argument of a man who just wanted to get laid; it was guaranteed to send any right-thinking woman fleeing.

A wet lick up her leg recalled Deanna to her predicament. Graeme had his nose under her sleep shirt and was sniffing her crotch, his agile tongue lapping the cream seeping down her thigh. His wagging tail made his approval of her condition clear in no uncertain terms.

"Graeme!" Protesting, she sprang away from the temptation he presented.

He lowered his head, his dark ears flattened in a sheepish gesture; yet, as he retired to the sofa, his tongue snaked out surreptitiously to lick his muzzle.

She turned her back on him. But still his werewolf scent called to her, promising wild sex and passion and freedom. Beguiling her with the unknown and the fantastic. Inviting her to abandon her resistance and give in to his seduction.

Needing to know her own mind, she struggled against the sense of rightness that urged her to simply accept matters as they stood.

Was it loss of control when it was her choice?

Deanna breathed Graeme's male scent in, filling her lungs with its lure. Continuing to be his lover could answer some of the questions he'd raised as to her heritage, but was it really curiosity about her background that drew her or this unusual attraction? What if it was weakness, wanting only to rely on his strength? In his embrace, she'd felt . . . safe.

And why wouldn't she?

He'd risked his life to save her. If the tree had given way sooner, while he'd been working to free her, he could have been dragged along when the car slid.

Time and again, he'd helped her. From offering to drive her around to bringing her to Miss Ginnie to carrying her bags, he'd lent a hand, but never really took over.

She blushed. Except during sex—and *that*, she'd invited.

Yet he'd never once hinted that she couldn't manage without him. He'd just offered his assistance.

Deanna gripped her sleep shirt, digging her fingers into the thin fabric. If she were back in Boston, she wouldn't have any qualms about pursuing a relationship with him. Were her doubts merely born of insecurity? She couldn't deny she wanted his big body, but she also enjoyed his company even when they weren't having sex.

Giving in to her fears would mean giving up all that.

If she turned away now, she could return to her nice, normal world, and maybe pretend she'd never met a werewolf. Perhaps even convince herself it had all been a hallucination. But if she did, she also might never know the truth about herself or her parents.

And if she Changed?

Ignoring the queasiness in her stomach, Deanna gave a mental shrug. She'd face that if and when it happened. Risks were what life was about. Remaining the same—not growing, not learning—was a kind of death, wasn't it? She seemed to recall something in her college courses about equilibrium and the heat death of the universe. She banished the stray thought from her head; now wasn't the time for digressions.

But she had to smile at her rationalization. The bottom line was she still wanted Graeme—wanted all of him—and didn't want to deny herself. Or maybe she just couldn't stand to lose such prime male flesh solely because of her own cowardice.

If she could have him, for however long she'd be in town, then the risk was worth it.

After all, it wasn't as if she was abandoning her plan to go to Hillsboro. She still intended to leave, once she had her possessions. This werewolf thing didn't answer most of her questions about her parents. They weren't even sure she was a werewolf; they only had his speculations.

When Deanna turned back to Graeme, he was once again a man lounging on the settee; he must have Changed while she'd been debating her options. Despite that, his cock was just as crimson and ready for action.

Just the sight of his arousal had cream trickling down her thighs. Yes, this was what she wanted. Regardless of the insatiable craving in her belly, the bone-deep hunger she felt for this intimacy, this was her choice.

Straddling his lap, she kissed him, a tentative brush of lips over somewhat salty lips that spread wildfire through her body. Salty from her juices. The realization only made her desire burn hotter.

Under her hands, his shoulders were tense; he was clearly restraining himself, leaving her to make up her mind without any pressure. Waiting for her decision.

She chose a foil pack from the box beside him and tore it open with deliberate care. Holding her breath, she placed the condom on the broad head of his cock. She slowly unrolled the thin latex over his thick shaft, feeling the resilient flesh jerk beneath her fingertips and giving herself time to absorb the significance of her actions.

Yes, this was right.

Deanna pulled her sleep shirt off, suddenly impatient with the soft fabric clinging to her skin. It would just get in the way; neither of them was going to sleep anytime soon.

He cupped her breasts, his thumbs finding the tight buds of her nipples. "You're sure about this?"

"Ummm, very sure." She closed her eyes briefly, savoring the sweet delight darting from her breasts to her core. The fleeting darkness only heightened her other senses, bringing to the forefront of her attention the scent of sex and virile male, the rough calluses on his palms, and the heat of him between her thighs. Her womb clenched, demanding satisfaction, now that she'd made her decision.

Rising to her knees, Deanna caught Graeme's cock and aimed it at her pussy. She eased her weight down, little by little taking him into her body, impaling herself on his hard shaft. The slow progress left her breathless, a singing tension that was centered in her core. It grew louder as she slid lower, until it roared in her ears, drowning out her gasps of excitement. Good God, he was so big!

He helped her along, raising his hips off the sofa and thrusting up—but gently, without the force she knew his powerful body was capable of. "Damn, you're so tight." A few hours of intense lovemaking hadn't been enough to limber her muscles.

Gradually, her channel stretched until he was tucked deep

inside her, nestled against her very core with only the thin condom between them. For a fleeting moment, she wished there was nothing separating them, nothing to dull the sensation of his hard ridges scraping against the delicate inner membranes of her channel.

But only for a moment.

Then Graeme started moving and all thought fled, save the need for *MORE!*

Pleasure danced over her nerves in a cascade of sweetness, rippling through her body in wave after blissful wave to finally tingle in her curling toes.

He rolled his hips, swirling his cock inside her in a marvel of incredible control, stoking the need in her belly to blistering heat.

Overwhelmed by the product of such gentle movement, Deanna choked on an indrawn breath, her hands locking behind his neck as her body clenched around him. Her back arched involuntarily, pressing her heavy breasts into his palms.

Then he did it again.

"Ooooooh!"

She rose on her knees, moving quicker, riding him harder. Her hunger built up rapidly and he let it, doing nothing to restrain her ascent. In fact, he urged her on, fondling her with possessive hands that fanned the flames of her desire.

Needing more, Deanna bent forward and took what she wanted. Spearing her fingers through his short hair, she claimed his mouth in a thorough kiss of conquest.

Her choice.

Graeme reciprocated equally, matching her thrust for thrust, his cock and tongue delving deep into her. His wild scent strengthened, surrounding her until she couldn't breathe without filling her lungs with his musk. Couldn't move without feeling his thickness stretching her pussy.

The wet slap of flesh on flesh mingled with gasps and grunts, low moans and lower growls. Rising in a crescendo of absolute need. A fever of desire burning her up.

It couldn't last.

Rapture blew through her like a dizzying whirlwind. It erupted in a glorious burst of scarlet, scattering her senses in all directions. The fire in her veins consumed her, leaving her to drift on the currents of bliss.

Sighing with repletion, Deanna collapsed on Graeme, her strength draining out of her with the last of her orgasm until she was a boneless heap of extremely sated female.

And through it all, the couch hadn't creaked. Thank God. She sent a prayer of gratitude heavenward for solidly built furniture as she settled deeper into sensual lassitude.

But her lover apparently wasn't done yet.

Still hard, he pulled his cock out in a smooth move that had her still-fluttering pussy quivering with wistful interest. He gathered her in his arms and laid her with her back on the rug, arranging her limbs around her.

Too euphoric to do anything more than wonder vaguely at his intentions, she lay there, waiting for him to enlighten her.

With a growl of satisfaction, Graeme knelt over her and gave her belly a nip that pierced the haze of sexual contentment enfolding her.

Just that easily, he rekindled the carnal hunger he'd tamed, prodding it to renewed enthusiasm.

Surprised by his action, Deanna hissed in a breath, her eyes popping wide.

Clearly determined to awaken a response from her, he caressed her all over, following up with lavish kisses and licks, interspersed with sudden nips that had her shuddering with need.

"Graeme!" Despite the memories of their afternoon lovemaking, she still couldn't believe he was ready to keep going.

Yet he was.

He built up the flames in her blood, teasing her with intimate touches that weren't enough. Chased away by his attentions, the languor blanketing her senses fled her body.

Deanna writhed as need flailed her. Sweet heavens, she didn't know how she could want him so much so soon after that dazzling orgasm.

Spike after sharp spike of delight shot up her spine, stirring her libido to greater desire. She arched her back, raising her breasts to Graeme's lips, wanting them on her throbbing nipples.

Moist heat engulfed one mound as he gave her what she wanted. The suction blasted her nerves with pleasure, like splashing gasoline on a raging bonfire. She begged for more with what little breath she had, her throat tight from her exertions, her voice breaking on a surge of excitement. The fever in her core spun out, spearing her loins with wicked hunger.

Then hard hands rolled her over onto her belly, raised her until she was on all fours.

Graeme mounted her from behind, worked his thick cock into her welcoming body with short, brutal thrusts that drove the breath from her lungs, little digs that forced her swollen channel to stretch and open for him.

Braced on her hands and knees, Deanna moaned, needing to voice her desperation. He felt huge from that angle! She could feel every inch of him filling her sheath through the thin condom, that thick head rasping over her tender membranes.

He teased her nipples, pulling and tweaking the hard points, rolling them between his fingers.

She met his thrusts desperately, the wet slap of skin on skin like primitive music in her roaring ears.

With a last powerful thrust, he came with a roar of triumph. As he took his release, his twitching cock swelled impossibly larger, stretching her nearly to the point of pain.

Torrid power flooded through Deanna, spilling to her curled

toes and the very tips of her fingers. It surged up her spine in a wave of scalding pleasure, a relentless pressure demanding release.

It exploded in an incredible starburst of pure ecstasy.

Deanna threw her head back, howling her delight to the night. Nothing less could express the violent pleasure erupting through her body, searing her to the bone.

6

Dazed by the surfeit of sensation still echoing through her body, Deanna blinked. Pale fur dominated her vision. Tawny fur that covered large paws stretched out along both sides of her head. She tried to flex her fingers and saw the paws move. Saw dark claws scratch the bare floor. *Felt* the claws biting into wood. And *didn't* quite feel the wood under her elbows—at least, it wasn't rough, not the way it had been before. Turning her head to investigate this anomaly, she discovered more fur padding said elbows.

Oh.

Graeme was right. She was a werewolf.

She laid her head back down on the floor, stunned by the development. Intellectually, she'd accepted the possibility of being a werewolf. But, in her heart, she hadn't expected to receive confirmation this quickly, though Graeme had implied it could happen.

Her father really had been a werewolf.

Feeling vulnerable lying flat on her belly, Deanna tried to scramble up. But Graeme was still inside her, still stretching her, still impossibly thick. She tried to move but couldn't budge him. He felt like he was wedged in tight.

He groaned above her, his weight pressing down on her. Large gray-furred paws were planted on either side of her; he'd apparently Changed when she had.

She braced her arms—forelegs—to pull away, but teeth closed around her shoulder, holding her in place. She quivered at that intimate threat, her legs going weak with carnal excitement. Her core gave another convulsive shudder, the latest in the violent aftermath of pleasure.

The delicious aftershocks from their mutual release continued to wash through her for several minutes, gradually fading to a sweet ache, along with Graeme's erection. Finally, he slipped out with a low grunt, taking his weight off her.

She rolled over to face him. He really was a handsome wolf, his premature gray translating to flecks of silver in his thick coat that gave him an air of distinction. The condom hanging off his cock was an incongruous note that made her grin.

Following her gaze, Graeme snorted in surprise. He clawed off the latex, then snuffled her belly fur, his warm breath tickling.

Startled by a shiver of joy that spread through her veins, Deanna snapped at him and scrambled to her feet. Claws clicked on the wood, reminding her of her condition.

Curiosity pricked, she scrambled for the bathroom. She dragged the door open and studied herself in the long mirror. The moonlight streaming down through the loft window was enough to raise golden highlights on pale fur.

Deanna stared at her reflection, once more taken aback. She twisted around, studying herself from other angles. She'd really transformed into a wolf—a rather sleek one, at that—complete with thick cream-tipped tail. She gave said tail an experimental wag. *Yup, it's mine, all right.*

A soft huff drew her attention back to Graeme, who seemed

to find her vanity amusing, if the laughter in his eyes and the tongue lolling from his grinning mouth were any indication.

Miffed, she walked out, holding her body stiffly, unable to mask her irritation. She was about to give him a cold shoulder when loud hollers rose from outside the door—catcalls and shouts of encouragement from several different throats.

Deanna spun around toward the source of the noise.

The sound of breaking glass punctuated the din. Then an acrid scent assaulted her nose, the stench overpowering all others. *Gasoline!*

Turning to Graeme, Deanna pawed her nose, trying to ask him if he smelled what she did. Telepathy would have been so useful at the moment. How in hell did werewolves communicate?

He tossed his head, apparently in agreement. He herded her away from the door, his fangs bared in a silent snarl as he kept his arctic gaze on the blank panel.

The whoops and hollers got even wilder, if that was possible. There was an unintelligible shout and Graeme's pricked ears went flat, his hackles bristling around his head . . . as though he recognized the muffled voice.

Was there more to it than a bunch of hooligans whooping it up? But why the gasoline?

Light flickered under the front door, an unsteady, reddish yellow glow that wasn't produced by a flashlight. *Fire!*

They had to get out of here!

But how? They couldn't Change to escape. Naked as they were, they'd be no match for the rabble outside.

Deanna stared at Graeme in horror. She didn't know how to Change back! If she died tonight, would her body return to human or remain a wolf? She shook herself, throwing off the macabre thought. That wasn't important.

She forced her mind back to the problem. The lone door opened to the porch—that was out of the question. The windows were too high; in her wolf form, she didn't think she could manage even the lowest one without breaking a leg.

Graeme scrambled for the bench. He clawed at the firewood under it, scattering the logs with a hollow clatter.

The hutch! Yes! Deanna joined him at clearing a way to the access doors. Being smaller, she was able to squeeze under the bench while Graeme continued digging.

There. Only a simple latch held the doors closed. A swipe of her paw was all she needed to release it. Cool air rushed in as the doors swung wide, bringing with it the smell of rain and forest—and nothing else.

Hopefully, that meant whoever had set fire to the cabin wasn't waiting for them on this side.

She scrambled through and dropped the short distance to the ground, the clicking of her claws loud to her straining ears.

No one. The rear clearing was empty, save for herself. No one lurked in the shadows; nothing moved except the rustling trees. But before she could sigh in relief a low growl sounded behind her, gruff with a note of frustration.

Graeme was stuck in the hutch, his dark forelegs stretched out, his head and shoulders lodged in the narrow aperture. The low bench probably meant his hindquarters were just as flat behind him. Unable to move his legs, he couldn't get through. Reverting to human form probably wouldn't help since his shoulders would be even wider.

Oh, no. Deanna pawed his forelegs, hoping to work him loose. Suddenly, the smell of smoke strengthened, mixed in with the gasoline stench. Spurred on by the reminder of their danger, she worried the hutch and his thick fur.

Nothing she did helped. Her wolf form had no grip to speak of and she didn't know how to Change back to human form to correct the situation.

Graeme barked at her, a low, soft *whuff* that tried to communicate something. When she scratched at the wood trapping him, thinking to widen the space, he pushed her away, his muzzle jerking up in a sharp imperative.

His meaning was unmistakable: Leave. Escape while she could.

She bared her fangs at him, her refusal emerging as a growl. The hell she was abandoning him!

He pushed at her again and she instinctively snapped at him, catching his leg between her jaws. She blinked at the unusual sensation of fur in her mouth, then realized the possibilities. Biting down, she braced her legs and pulled.

Damn, he was heavy. He tried to help her, but his free foreleg couldn't reach the ground. It was all up to her.

Pulling for all she was worth, Deanna inched away from the wall. The strain was enormous. Digging her claws into the ground, she threw all her energy into saving Graeme, her focus narrowing down until he was the only thing she saw.

The fire didn't matter. Their attackers didn't matter. Only Graeme.

Inch by slow, painful inch.

Then Graeme managed to get his other leg under him and push off.

Her legs slid out from under her.

Yipping, Deanna found herself rolling on her side and down an incline. *Oof.* The short drop barely registered. Shaking her fur into order, she stuck her head up to check on Graeme, who was clawing his way forward and out. She sprang back to the hutch and, ignoring his grumbling growls, took his leg between her jaws once more to speed his progress. This time, knowing what to expect, she was able to keep her grip on him and stay on her feet.

A few more tugs and he was free!

Panting at the exertion, Deanna lowered her head and got a noseful of smoke. She snorted. With the hutch unblocked, the smell seemed to pour out of the hole. Through the opening, she could just make out the edge of the front door, now limned by flames.

A nudge in her ribs recalled her to their danger.

Graeme turned away from the cabin to face the forest. After a last look, Deanna allowed him to lead her through the trees and along a stream to his Jeep.

Once there, he Changed back, making it look as easy as rolling over in bed. Again, there was none of the pain or elaborate special effects of Hollywood movies. One moment, a huge gray wolf stood by the car, and the next, a brawny, naked man.

Ignoring the eye candy and his dangling bits, she barked at him in frustration.

"Relax." He rubbed her ears, setting off an unexpected shiver of preposterously decadent delight through her unfamiliar body. "Think of your human form and let it happen. That's all there is to it."

The surge of pleasure reminded her of her response to his lovemaking. Then she discovered he was right. Just like that, she was on her knees in front of him, her cheek pressed to his warm, callused palm . . . without fur to protect her from pebbles and the hard stems of dry leaves. She stood up, her lover rising with her.

Fishing his car keys from inside his shoes, Graeme unlocked the Jeep for Deanna. "Stay here. I have to make sure they don't get away with this." He mentally counted up the number of rowdies who had been at the Hogg Wylde earlier and tried to estimate how long it would take the volunteer fire crew to respond. With the cabin's perch high on the mountainside, the fire would be like a beacon in the darkness, visible everywhere in town.

About to get in, she paused with her hand on the door, a frown knitting her brows. "They're drunk. You can't handle that many all by yourself. Shouldn't you call for backup?"

"The fire brigade's coming. There's no way they could miss

the fire. But I can't wait for them. I've got to stop those yahoos here, catch them red-handed. If they drive away . . ." Graeme shook his head in frustration, silently cursing them for this latest idiocy and himself for forgetting the danger they posed. After this, there was no way Deanna would want to stick around once her car was recovered. "The sheriff will let them off just as he has before." It was a shitty thing to do, in his opinion, but Henckel's bunch was a winning team and the local golden boys. Unless incontrovertible evidence was shoved in their faces, most of the townsfolk would look the other way and make excuses for them.

A stubborn expression settled on Deanna's face. "I'll help you." She planted her feet squarely on the ground, her shoulders straight, determination written in every line of her body. Her posture brought her breasts to distracting prominence, moonlight glowing on the high slopes.

His mouth dried. It was probably unintentional on her part, but it still made stringing together a coherent sentence something of an effort.

"All right. We'll have to do it as wolves. If they see you like this"—his eyes flicked over her nudity automatically, unable to resist a glance—"who knows what they might do."

She nodded assent.

"Try not to hurt them. We don't want to trigger a wolf hunt."

Deanna frowned, probably wishing she could do damage—Graeme couldn't fault her since he wanted the same himself—but she nodded again.

He Changed back into a wolf and for the second time watched Deanna's body shimmer and vanish into a similar form. It still took his breath away to know that he'd been right and she really was a werewolf.

On the way back to the cabin, Graeme kept a worried eye and ear on Deanna as he cut through a feathery stand of maidenhair ferns. He'd never really thought about it before, but movement in wolf form was probably instinctive. Certainly, despite her lack of experience, Deanna displayed very little awkwardness, her pale shape pure grace in motion as she loped at his side. But that didn't mean she knew how to use all the weapons at her disposal or had full control over her wolf.

The past couple of days had shown him just how powerful instinct was. If he, with more than a decade of lupine experience, had difficulty reining in that side of himself, when instinct spurred his wolf brain to action, what more of Deanna, who was the target of the attack?

A strengthening in the scents of the forest warned him they were near the creek even before the sound of tumbling waters reached his pricked ears. They'd run only a short distance when another scent drifted across their path.

Raising his muzzle, Graeme tested the air, snarling involuntarily at the sour odor. He'd smelled it earlier, while leading Deanna to his Jeep, but had been more concerned with getting her to safety. Now, he followed the trail across the stream and into the woods.

Deanna sneezed, then sneezed again, soft huffs that barely broke the silence of the night. She pawed her nose, snorted, then shook her lithe body as though ridding herself of an unpleasant sensation.

Letting his tongue hang between his jaws, Graeme grinned at her, unable to hide his amusement at the picture she made with her elegant muzzle all screwed up in disgust. He'd learned long ago to take the bad with the good when it came to the sharper olfactory senses of his wolf form, not that it made the stench borne on the rising wind in any way more agreeable.

They found the idiots' pickups parked in a nearby clearing strewn with empty beer cans and stinking of piss, alcohol, and other things that raised Graeme's hackles. The bone-headed bunch must have stopped there to work up their nerve before going on foot to the cabin.

Closer in, the smell of gun oil stood out—pure and clear compared to the other odors—which gave him something else to worry about. The racks in the pickups all had their full complement of rifles, which was somewhat reassuring. Those yahoos just intended to burn Deanna out, not shoot her . . . unless they had pistols.

But that was for later. First, he had to make sure Henckel's bunch wouldn't get away.

He Changed back to human form to disable the trucks, while Deanna kept a listening posture, clearly serious about watching his back. The kind of partner any wolf worth his pelt would want at his side.

To prevent escape, Graeme disconnected the high-tension wires from the ignition coils. It would have been simpler to slash the tires, especially with his claws, but it might not have been as effective. As drunk and woolly as those idiots seemed to be, they might have driven for miles before noticing a flat. Now, all that was left was to keep them occupied until Woodrose's volunteer fire brigade arrived.

Cold apprehension raising the fur along her back, Deanna followed Graeme through banks of spicy-smelling bushes, toward the ruckus. Sticking close, she kept her eyes on him since his large form seemed to vanish into the shadows. If she wasn't careful, he might decide to lose her in the forest—for her own good, of course—while he dealt with the arsonists.

No matter how much she wanted to return to his Jeep and just avoid the hooligans, she had to support him. She'd never forgive herself if something happened to him and she hadn't been there to help.

When they broke through the trees surrounding her cabin,

she realized he'd taken her at her word about backing him up. If he'd been tempted to go it alone, he hadn't acted on it.

Embarrassed by her suspicions, she directed her attention at the crowd whooping it up around the burning structure. To her surprise, the arsonists turned out to be around a dozen clean-cut young men who didn't seem old enough to buy the beer in their hands.

But when they egged one of their number to toss a make-shift torch at the cabin, she knew their age didn't matter. And when Graeme bared his fangs and stalked out of the tree line to face them down, she knew she couldn't let him face them alone, despite the giant butterflies in her stomach.

He struck from the shadows, bowling over a hooligan to snap at someone else, then retreated to the shadows. He did so again and again, sowing confusion among the bunch.

Staying among the trees, she watched closely, studying his technique and noting the care he took not to scratch them. It seemed simple enough. By keeping to the shadows, Graeme made it look like there were more wolves than just the two of them.

Then one of the arsonists grabbed a broken bottle by its neck and advanced on Graeme.

Growling, Deanna scrambled into the clearing to lunge at the staggering man. A swipe of her paw disarmed him. Yelling, he kicked out wildly. She dodged the blow, ducking under the arc of his foot, then used her body to knock him off balance.

Anger and outrage flowed through her, cleansing her of her earlier fear. These worthless thugs dared attack her? She bared her fangs, snapping at a nearby rump. Only luck and a sudden panicked jerk on her target's part kept her from doing damage. The jarring clash of her teeth shocked her back to herself—and the risk of a wolf hunt to Graeme.

Whoops! Dashing to the shadows, Deanna checked her lover

and found him busy with a pair of hooligans. She hoped he hadn't noticed her lapse.

Working side by side with him, she herded the arsonists against the burning cabin.

A wailing fire truck sped down the dirt track, trailed by patrol cars. At last!

At its approach, Graeme nudged her flank and flicked his head to the woods.

Knowing he wouldn't leave if she stayed, Deanna ran to the trees, then waited for him to lead the way back to his Jeep. While she normally had a good sense of direction, she wasn't that confident about her lupine senses. Besides, all the new scents and sensations, the different sights, distracted her from the trail.

From the protection of the shadows, they watched the firefighters arrive on the scene to discover the cowering group. Then, exchanging a look of satisfaction, they withdrew into the forest.

Back at the Jeep, Graeme Changed to human form and started dressing. "Hurry. I want to make sure they don't get away." He handed her his uniform top as soon as she was steady on her two legs.

Deanna pulled it on around her otherwise naked body. It fit her like a tent and hung to her knees, the large neck providing her with a daring décolletage. Raising the lapels, she buried her nose in them and sniffed, catching Graeme's male scent, reassuring beyond belief to something primitive inside her. She didn't have time for more since he was soon ready.

It was a short drive to the cabin. They had to park behind the fire truck and two patrol cars.

One of the deputies standing over the arsonists huddled to one side started at their appearance. "Gray? What're you doing here?" His quick appraisal took in Deanna's dishabille with a glint of speculation.

Graeme stepped in front of her, placing himself between her and the hooligans regaining their bravado. "We were out back when they torched the cabin."

"You don't say?" A hard grin flashed across the other man's face. "You take care of her. We'll handle them." A look of understanding passed between the two deputies; apparently, it was enough to satisfy Graeme, since he stepped back, drawing Deanna with him to sit in the Jeep.

The rain started gently, fat drops falling sporadically, then with greater fervor as the wind strengthened, bringing with it the scent of renewed life and obliterating the traces of paw prints on the hard ground.

Aided by the rain, the firefighters managed to subdue the blaze. Most of the cabin looked to have survived intact, if somewhat charred, in the silvery moonlight.

Through the downpour, she watched Graeme's fellow deputies hustle the cursing, staggering drunks into the backseats of their patrol cars. They ignored the arsonists babbling about wolves, since everyone knew there hadn't been wolves in the area in more than a century. Hopefully, no one would ever give their story any credence.

Low in the west, the full moon hung below the gathered clouds, nearly brushing the treetops, ghostly in the twilight of the approaching dawn. All of a sudden, the events of the night seemed to catch up with Deanna, exhaustion dragging on her limbs like lead weights. It now seemed unreal.

Was she really a werewolf?

Deanna sat back and let herself drift. The next thing she knew Graeme was handing her a bag. "Here."

"Thanks." She opened it to inspect its contents, wrinkling her nose at the smoky stench. Her new clothes. She made a glum face. There was no way she could wear them without laundering them first, not with the sharpening of her senses since her Change. She couldn't imagine mixing her scent with that.

"Hey, it's not so bad." He tilted her chin up to smile down at her, the carnal invitation in his eyes obvious in the brightening dawn. "I've got a washer and dryer at home. You're welcome to use it."

His male scent called to her, reminding her of a multitude of pleasures she'd shared with this gallant man. Her body heated, melting with eager delight, but something held her back. She knew she could trust him to respect her independence, but there was the even-greater question of her werewolf heritage.

She caught his wrist, steeling herself against his reaction to her warning. "I'm still leaving for Hillsboro, once my things are recovered." Now, more than ever, she had to find out where her parents came from.

A bushy brow rose. "It's in the same state, not the ends of the earth. What's a few hours' drive?"

Relieved by his reply, Deanna smiled back, more than willing to take him up on his implicit offer. "Then I'd like that. Very much."

Here's a sneak peek at A TASTE OF HONEY,
on sale now from Aphrodisia!

1

The other day my friend—let's call her Sue—came crying to me about the latest disaster in her already-pockmarked love life. He was perfect, she sobbed. Smart. Cute. Employed. (Trust me, that's a new one for her.) On their first date they met for brunch and talked for hours. On their second date he showed up with flowers and took her to the hot new restaurant she mentioned wanting to try.

And afterward he took her back to his ultramodern loft and banged the hell out of her.

You know what happened next, don't you, girls?

He said he'd call. Of course, he didn't.

The dog.

But don't be so quick to put this doggie down.

The way I see it, it's not his fault. It's hers.

Of course, loving and supportive friend that I am, I didn't tell her so.

But really, when are the Sues of the world going to grow up and stop taking it so hard when the boys they bang merely act as expected?

The flowers, the restaurant? Unoriginal moves to get us in the sack. And once they do, they're off, sniffing another ass like any good dog would.

You know me, I'm not saying don't give them what they want—assuming you get what you want too.

But if you're going to be like Sue and spend the morning after crying over your used condom, save yourself the heartache (and your friends the earache) and stay home with your pocket rocket.

> —Excerpt from "Stripping It Down: A Modern Girl's Adventures in Dating" by C. Teaser, from online magazine *Bustout.com*

"Come on, Kit, it's your turn."

Kit Loughlin winced and took another sip of her chardonnay as eleven pairs of eyes gave her their undivided attention. Why did these types of gatherings always degenerate into this?

"Really, there's not much to tell," she protested.

Not that she had any qualms about discussing her sex life, given that she mined it (and embellished it) regularly on a twice-weekly basis for "Stripping It Down."

But telling all under a pseudonym was one thing. Baring all at her best friend Elizabeth's coed bachelorette party was another.

"Come on," Nicole, another bridesmaid, urged. "Everyone else has revealed the sordid details of their first time. You have to go."

Once again she fought the urge to smack Sabrina, the bridesmaid whose stupid idea this game had been in the first place. Why would anyone in her right mind think it was a good idea for a soon-to-be-wed bride and groom to reveal the details of their past sexual encounters? In front of a crowd, no less.

Yet both the bride, Elizabeth, and the groom, Michael, had

jumped in with gusto, eagerly regaling their friends with stories of backseat groping and awkward penetration.

Kit had been hoping to skip her turn, purposely removing herself from the giant sectional that dominated the living room of the Mexican villa to take up a post by one of the windows overlooking the beach.

Everyone else had told their story. Now she was trapped.

She ignored a particularly piercing pair of green eyes that seemed intent on boring a hole straight through her.

"C'mon, Kit, don't be such a prude," Elizabeth prodded with a tipsy giggle.

Easy for her to say. When Elizabeth described her first time, she didn't have the distinct pleasure of having the other party in the room staring at her.

Jake Donovan watched her, one dark eyebrow arched, smirking in a way that made her want to smack it off his face. God, if she had known Jake would be joining them on their hedonistic weekend to Cabo, Kit never would have come.

"Yeah," Jake rumbled in a voice that after twelve years still had the power to send waves of heat down her spine, "we all want to know."

She glared at him, six foot four of gorgeous sprawled on the couch in casual arrogance, the perfect genetic blend of his Italian mother and Irish father, with strong, masculine features and green eyes that stood out against his naturally dark skin.

He wasn't even her type—not anymore, anyway—in his yuppie uniform of golf shirt and khaki shorts.

She went for artsy, rocker types. Guys who wore Gucci and Prada and product in their hair. Not stuffy venture capitalists with their dark hair cut conservatively short and their all-American ex-football-player brawn draped in the latest corporate logo wear. She met enough of those through her day job as a business reporter for the *San Francisco Tribune*.

But she couldn't discount the way his eyes glowed against his tan or that his abdomen had none of the softness she'd come to associate with men of his ilk. Unlike his three younger brothers, Jake had left their little town of Donner Lake and never returned, eschewing his father's construction business for an MBA. But even though he didn't do anything close to manual labor, his biceps strained the sleeves of his golf shirt, veins visible along the swell as he took a sip of Pacifico and grinned.

So he went to the gym in between making millions as a venture capitalist. He still had no right to look so smug. Especially given what she knew about his prowess in the sack.

Or lack thereof.

"Really, there's not much to tell," she repeated, casually taking a seat on the arm of the overstuffed armchair occupied by Michael's brother, Dave. "It was over so quickly I barely remember it myself."

Jake sat up straighter.

Got your attention, eh, big boy? Suddenly she relished the chance to let Jake know exactly what she thought of his stick-it-in-and-come technique. "It was all very typical, really," she continued. "I was seventeen, and the guy was a friend of my brother's—a few years older, of course, so I'd had lots of time to build up a big, hard crush on him."

All the women in the room affected sympathetic smiles.

"So one night, he shows up at our house looking for my brother. It was summer vacation, and he and my parents had already gone to the city for the weekend." Everyone ooohed. Except for Jake. He was staring at her quizzically, as though he himself didn't know exactly where this was going.

"And this guy, who was totally drunk—although I was too stupid to realize it at the time—tells me some sob story about having a big fight with his girlfriend." She rolled her eyes and took another drink of wine, relishing the way Jake was shifting uncomfortably.

"The next thing I know, he's kissing me, and of course, having the giant crush on him that I do, I don't stop to think that perhaps this is not the best idea." Pausing for maximum impact, she said, "Five rather painful and awkward minutes later, and I was watching his bare ass disappear out the front door."

Even the guys winced at that one.

"What happened after that?"

Kit snorted. "Like you have to ask? He got back together with his girlfriend and never talked to me again."

Jake was glaring at her now, his acre-wide shoulders so tight she could see the outline of his muscles straining against the soft cotton of his shirt. She met his glare head-on, daring him to dispute any part of her story.

She reached for the bottle of chardonnay and tipped the last of it into her glass. "I'll go get more wine," she said, eager for an excuse to escape the room and Jake's frosty green stare.

She ran down to the wine cellar on shaky legs, praying she wouldn't do a header down the stone staircase. Her pink strappy stiletto sandals certainly didn't help matters. Warning herself to calm down before she broke something, she took the last three steps with extra care and leaned against the cool stone wall of the corridor.

She'd managed to keep it together ever since Jake showed up yesterday morning. After the stunned shock wore off, she'd retreated behind her usual brash friendliness, never hinting that she and Jake were more than casual acquaintances who had gone to high school a few years apart in the same tiny California mountain town.

Leave it to some stupid party game to dredge up twelve-year-old memories best left dead and buried.

What was the fascination with the first time, anyway? For Kit, it had been nothing more than an uncomfortable tearing of a flap of skin and a necessary death of any romantic illusions she might have fallen victim to.

She should be grateful to Jake for that at least. Who knew what kind of asinine things she might have done by now in the name of love?

Taking a deep breath, she shoved uncomfortable thoughts of Jake out of her head and admired the veritable treasure trove of vino that surrounded her. She had to give her best friend's fiancé credit. When Michael took his friends on vacation, he did it in style. The villa he'd rented had eight bedrooms, a full staff, and an infinity pool overlooking Land's End.

Kit was contemplating a bottle of ninety-one pinot noir when she sensed the warmth of another body behind her.

A big, tan hand wrapped around her hip, and hot breath grazed her neck. "Interesting story you told up there, Kit. Funny, I don't remember it going exactly the way you described."

Her whole body stiffened and she struggled not to melt back into his chest. Reaching casually for the bottle, she said, "I think I included all the pertinent details."

"And made up a few. I did put my pants on before I left. Not that you'd know, since you ran upstairs crying and locked yourself in your bedroom."

She turned around, stepping back in an attempt to put more space between them. Her bare back met the cool foil of dozens of bottles. He was so tall she had to tip her head back to see his face. "Considering your performance, can you blame a girl for crying?"

His full, firm lips compressed in a tight line, and he braced his arms on either side of her shoulders. "I never apologized for that night, Kit. It didn't go the way I wanted—"

Kit ducked under his arm and darted over to the refrigerator that housed the whites. "Don't get yourself all worked up over an awkward hump on my parents' couch." Ugh, the last thing she wanted to do was rehash their one brief, clumsy encounter. She'd spent twelve years burying the stupid, idealistic seventeen-year-old she'd been, and she had no interest in resurrecting her tonight.

"Now come on, Kitty Kat," he said, and she winced at the use of her childhood nickname, "the least you can do is let me make it up to you."

Jake's serious, apologetic expression melted away, replaced with a crooked—damn her hormones for noticing—sexy smile and a hot, lustful gleam in his gaze.

Kit's jaw nearly dropped at his arrogance. She may have gotten over the trauma of that night twelve years ago, but she certainly hadn't forgiven him. And she definitely wasn't interested in having him "make it up to her."

"Trust me, I'm over it."

He moved in until she had no choice but to rest her hips against the top of the minifridge. "You're not just a little bit interested in finding out what tricks I may have learned in the last decade?" He glanced meaningfully down at the deeply plunging front of her silk halter top. She didn't need to look down to know that her nipples were two hard points outlined against the flimsy peach fabric.

Reaching out with one finger, he traced the neckline of her top to where it ended almost at her navel. "Cold?"

She would have said yes, but even she wasn't that much of a liar.

He stepped closer, his hair-roughened knee brushing the inside of her thigh. The ragged hem of her denim micro-mini slid up another two inches.

A thick, dark lock fell across his forehead as he bent close enough for her to feel the heat of his breath on her cheek. Her heart rate picked up, and she wondered vaguely if he could see it beating against the bare sun-kissed skin of her chest. How was it, after all this time, he still had the power to transform her into a weak-kneed adolescent?

"You had your shot," she whispered, her lips so close to his she could almost taste him, "and you failed miserably. I'm not big on second chances."

He leaned forward, and the moist heat of his mouth against her collarbone sent a pulse of heat straight to her groin. "I think," he murmured as his tongue flicked along the sensitive cords of her neck, "in this case," his lips closed over her right earlobe and Kit told herself she would get up and move in two seconds but God she loved her ears sucked, "you should make an exception."

Before she could breathe, his mouth closed over hers, lips molding and shaping as his tongue flicked against the seam.

Hot damn, he had learned some new tricks.

She kept her fists clenched firmly at her sides but couldn't stop herself from parting her lips, just a little, for one tiny bit of a taste. He pressed his advantage, plunging his tongue inside, licking and sucking until she had no choice but to fist her hands in his hair and wrap her legs around his hips.

"God, I've been dying to touch you," he groaned into her mouth. "From the second I saw you, acting so cool. Burning so hot underneath."

As though to prove himself right, he shoved his hand between her thighs and pulled aside the now-drenched strip of lace covering her mound. He uttered a low grumble of satisfaction as his fingers met smooth flesh, already slippery wet from just one kiss.

Some sane, rational corner of her brain sent out frantic signals, warning her to stop this before it went too far—as though it hadn't already.

Which were promptly drowned out as he nosed aside the gathered neckline of her top and sucked one hard, rosy nipple deep into his mouth.

She tossed her head back and moaned as a thick, blunt finger stroked against her clit. She clenched her fingers in the fabric of his shirt, wanting to tear it off but not having the presence of mind to do so. Spreading her legs wide to give him better access, she rocked her pelvis against his hand, shuddering when he sank two fingers in to the last knuckle.

"Mmm," she moaned as he twisted his fingers inside her, his thumb jumping into the mix to give her clit some much-needed attention. One, two strokes against the slippery bud and she was gone, the walls of her vagina clamping down in an orgasm so intense her screams echoed off the stone-lined ceiling.

He kissed her softly, quieting her, pressing his palm against her sex until the last tremors of her climax faded away.

Like a slap in the face, Kit suddenly became aware of her position. Legs sprawled wide on top of a minifridge, one boob hanging out of her halter, and Jake Donovan's hand once again in her pants.

Hopping off the fridge before he could catch her, she hitched her top back over her shoulder and smoothed her skirt back down her hips. She glanced at her watch. "Wow. You made me come inside of five minutes. You *have* improved."

He grinned and made a move to grab her. "I could make you come with both hands tied behind my back."

She had to get the hell out of that cellar before she begged for a live demonstration. "You've proven your point well enough." She haphazardly grabbed a few bottles of wine from the shelves. Arms full, she flashed him what she hoped passed for a sly, sophisticated smile and said, "Thanks. I needed that." She half ran back up the stairs, ignoring his shout of protest. *See how you like being left high and dry, cowboy.*